Countess Cosel

By Józef Ignacy Kraszewski

Translated by Guy Jean Raoul Eugène Charles Emmanuel de Savoie-Carignan, Comte de Soissons

Skomlin
House of Memory and Imagination

First Skomlin International Edition - October 2017

Skomlin
House of Memory and Imagination
For more information visit *www.skomlin.com*

A Skomlin Book
Melbourne, Australia

First published in Warsaw 1873
First English version, New York 1901
© Skomlin, 2017

ISBN: 978-0-9874014-1-0 *(paperback)*
ISBN: 978-0-6481826-0-3 *(eBook)*

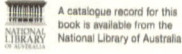

A catalogue record for this book is available from the National Library of Australia

The paper used in this publication meets the minimum requirements of ANSI/NISO Z39.48-1992 (R1997) (Permanence of Paper). The paper used in this book is from responsibly managed forests. Printed in the United States of America, the United Kingdom and Australia by Lightning Source, Inc.

Countess Cosel

All was silent, dark, and sad in the King's castle, in the capital of Saxony. It was an autumn night, but at the end of September, the leaves are only beginning to turn yellow, cold winds are very rarely felt, the days are usually bright, and the nights warm.

But on this evening the wind was blowing from the north; long black clouds followed each other in quick succession, and if a star made its appearance for a moment in the lead-coloured sky, it was quickly covered by the thick clouds. Before the gates of the castle of Georgenthor, and in the court-yards, silent sentries were pacing to and fro. The windows of the King's apartments, usually so brilliantly lighted, were dark. This was a most unusual event during the reign of Augustus, surnamed the Strong, because he was wont to break horse-shoes, men, sadness, and ill-fortune—but nothing could break him. Throughout the whole of Germany, indeed, throughout the whole of Europe, he was famed for the brilliancy of his court. There were none who could surpass him in magnificence, refinement of taste, and lordly prodigality.

This year, however, Augustus had been defeated. The Swedes had taken from him the electoral crown of Poland, and the almost dethroned King, chased from the kingdom, had returned to the Kurfürsten-neste, to weep over the millions he had spent in vain, and the fearful ingratitude of the Poles. The Saxons could not understand how anyone could fail to admire such a good and noble lord, or how anyone could be unwilling to die for his sake.

Augustus understood this still less than they did. The word "ingratitude" now accompanied every mention he made of Poland, and at length his courtiers avoided talking about it, about the King of Sweden, and about those things that Augustus the Strong had promised himself to set right.

When Augustus returned to Dresden, that city made every possible effort to distract its lord, and it was only on this evening that everything was quiet within the castle. But why? The King had not gone to any of his other castles; the Leipsic fair had not yet begun; and besides, it had even been rumoured in the court, and throughout the city, that Augustus intended to order a series of balls, and carousals, to spite the Swedish monarch, and to prove to that august personage that he cared nothing for the temporary defeat he had sustained.

The few passers-by who wended their way along the streets surrounding the castle, gazed at the windows in astonishment, wondering why, at this early hour, everything should be so quiet in the King's apartments. But anyone who penetrated further, and passing through the first large gate, crossed the courtyard, would have discovered that it was only on one side of the castle that silence reigned supreme, and that the interior of the building was seething with life and animation.

Despite the keen north wind that was blowing, the windows on the first floor were wide open, and through the curtains poured forth streams of light, reflected from many mirrors; whilst from time to time there issued from the depths of the hall, peals of boisterous laughter, which, ringing through the spacious courtyard, startled the watchful sentries, and echoing against the grey walls, gradually died away in the distance.

This laughter was accompanied by more or less noise, which alternately increased, subsided into murmurs, or died away into silence. At times there was loud clapping of hands as though after a speech, and then again was heard deep, sonorous, full-toned, king-like laughter, the laughter of a person not afraid of being heard, or of being answered in shouts of derision. At each fresh outburst of merriment, the guard pacing, halberd in hand, beneath the castle windows, paused in his walk, raised his eyes, and then with a deep sigh looked down on the ground.

There was something awful in this midnight feast, held while the wind was blowing fiercely, and the capital lay wrapt in sleep.

Here the King was making merry.

Since his return from Poland, such evening debauches, with a few intimate courtiers, had been more frequent. Augustus the Strong, defeated by Charles XII., was ashamed to appear at great feasts; but as he needed some distraction from the sad thoughts that oppressed him, he gathered round him a few courtiers to whom he was attached. For these he ordered his servants to bring out the golden wine that was yearly imported from Hungary for the King's private use, and of this they drank until daybreak, by which time every one had fallen from their seats. Then Hoffman came, and conducted the King, still laughing heartily, to bed.

To these select assemblies of the priests of Bacchus only a few persons were admitted, only those, in fact, in whom Augustus had entire confidence; for it was said that after drinking a few bumpers the King was dangerous. His strength was the strength of Hercules, and his anger the anger of Jove. If he were made angry in the morning, he said nothing, but his face grew crimson, his eyes glittered, and his lips trembled. He would turn away, and would not look at the person who had offended him. But after a few draughts of wine it was a different matter; at such times he had thrown many a one through the window, who had fallen on the pavement to rise no more.

His anger was rare, but it was terrible as a thunderbolt. In ordinary life there could not be found a more affable or benevolent lord. It has even been remarked that the more he disliked a man, the more sweetly he smiled on him; and the day before they were imprisoned in Königstein, where his favourites had sometimes had to remain for several years, Augustus would embrace them as though they were his dearest friends; so noble was his nature, so wishful was he to soften the hard lot of his people.

As it was necessary for the lord to have some amusement, it was nothing remarkable that two bears should sometimes be brought to the castle, or two enemies made drunk, and then induced to fight. This was a sport in which the King especially delighted, and when two drunken Vitzthums, Friesens or Hoyms, began to quarrel, he used to split his sides with laughing. This was such an innocent recreation.

The King could make them quarrel very easily, for he knew everything— he knew who was in love, and with whom; which man hated the other; how much money they had taken from his treasury without his permission; he even knew what each of his courtiers was thinking, and if he did not know, he guessed. Who the spies were who betrayed them, the courtiers could by no means discover; and the result of this was that each one suspected his neighbour; brother was afraid of brother; the husband distrusted the wife; the father had no confidence in his son; and King Augustus the Strong looked on, and laughed at the mob!

Yes, from his exalted position he looked down on the comedy of life, not disdaining to play in it the rôle of Jove, Hercules, and Apollo—and in the evening the rôle of Bacchus.

On the evening in question, being very sad and weary, the King determined to make all his ministers and favourites drunk, and then make them confess for his amusement.

The select companions of the King's feast were seated in a brilliantly lighted room, one side of which was occupied by an enormous sideboard, bright with silver and cut glass. Amongst those present were: Count Taparel Lagnasco, who had just arrived from Rome; Count Wackerbarth, from Vienna, Watzdorf, called the peasant of Mansfeld; Fürstenberg, Imhoff, Friesen, Vitzthum, and Hoym; and last, but not least, Friedrich Wilhelm, Baron Kyan, famous for his wit, who made every one else laugh, whilst he remained perfectly serious.

The King, with dress and vest unfastened, sat leaning on one elbow—he was very sad. His handsome face, usually so bright, was veiled in a mist of sorrow. Several empty bottles bore witness to the fact that drinking had already continued for some time, yet on the King's face no results of the goodly wine were visible. The golden liquid had not been able to make his gloomy thoughts more bright.

The courtiers jested with each other, endeavouring to make their lord laugh, but without avail. Augustus sat silent and thoughtful, as though he heard not a word that was spoken. This was most unusual; the King was so seldom sad, indeed he was ever eager for mirth and distraction. His companions grew uneasy and looked at him askance.

At the opposite end of the table sat Kyan, gloomy, and unassuming. As though to mock the King, he also leaned on one elbow, stretched out his legs, and looked up at the ceiling with a deep sigh.

His melancholy air gave him an absurd appearance.

"Hark you," whispered Fürstenberg, nudging Wackerbarth with his elbow—they were both tipsy by this time—"do you see our lord? Nothing makes him smile—and it is already eleven o'clock—he ought to be in a good humour by now. This is our fault."

"I am here as a guest," replied Wackerbarth, shrugging his shoulders. "It is none of my business; as you know him better than I do, you should find the proper way to amuse him."

"He is tired of Lubomirska—that is clear," added Taparel.

"And then it is difficult to digest those Swedes," whispered Wackerbarth. "I do not wonder at him."

"Eh! Eh! We have forgotten all about the Swedes; some one else will defeat them for us, we can be sure of that, and then we will go and gather the fruits," said Fürstenberg. "He is not bothered about the Swedes, but he has had enough of Lubomirska—we must find him some other woman."

"Is that such a difficult matter?" whispered Wackerbarth.

Then they began to whisper together, but so low that they could not be overheard, for, as though suddenly awakened from slumber, the King was looking round on his companions. His glance wandered from one to another, until it rested at length on the tragic pose of Baron Kyan, and on seeing this the monarch burst into a hearty laugh.

This was quite sufficient to make every one else laugh.

"Kyan," cried the King, "what is the matter with you? Has your sweetheart betrayed you? Have you no money? You look just like Prometheus, with an invisible eagle devouring your liver."

Kyan turned slowly round, much after the fashion of a wooden doll, and drew a deep sigh; so deep was it that it extinguished a six-light candelabra that was standing near him.

"Kyan, what is the matter with you?" repeated the King.

"Your Majesty," replied the Baron, "personally, there is nothing the matter with me. I am neither hungry, nor in love, nor in debt, nor jealous; but I am in despair."

"Why? What has happened? Speak!"

"I am grieving over our beloved monarch!" answered Kyan. "Born to be happy; endowed with a godlike face, with Herculean strength, with a generous heart; created to have the world lie at your feet—and yet your Majesty is sad!"

"Yes, that is true!" said Augustus, frowning. "I am sad!"

"Fifteen of us are sitting here, and none of us know how to make you merry; the women betray you, and grow old; the wine turns sour; your money is stolen; and when in the evening you wish to enjoy yourself in merry company, your faithful subjects meet you with death's-head faces. What wonder, then, that I, who love my King, am in despair?"

Augustus smiled; then, seizing a goblet, he knocked with it on the table. Immediately two dwarfs stepped forth from behind the sideboard, and stood before the King.

"Iramm," said the King, "order a big-bellied bottle of Ambrosia to be brought here! Kyan, I make you cup-bearer."

Ambrosia was the name given to the Hungarian wine furnished to the King, and pressed out for him specially by Count Zichy. It was the wine of wines, thick like syrup, treacherously smooth, but strong enough to make a giant dead drunk.

Iramm and his companion disappeared, and shortly afterwards a negro entered, bearing a silver tray, on which was an enormous bottle. All the guests rose at once and greeted it with low bows.

"Kyan, do your duty!" cried the King.

Kyan rose. The dwarfs brought another tray with glasses; but on the cup-bearer whispering something to them, they withdrew behind the sideboard, from whence they emerged a few moments later, bringing glasses of various sizes.

With the dignity of an official who is fully conscious of the importance of his position, Kyan began carefully arranging the glasses.

In the centre he placed a large and beautiful glass for the King, this he surrounded by smaller glasses destined for the favourites, and outside these was another row of glasses, much smaller than the last, so small indeed that they looked like thimbles.

All watched him with curiosity.

Then, taking the large bottle, Kyan began to pour out the wine, being careful not to shake it. First he filled all the smallest glasses. It is true that these did not hold much wine, but there were so many of them that before they were all filled, the bottle was half empty. The cup-bearer next filled the larger glasses. The wine in that large bottle grew speedily less, and by the time he came to the King's glass there was no wine left. Then Kyan poured into it the lees that remained at the bottom of the bottle, and looked at Augustus.

"What a splendid cup-bearer you are," said the King, laughing. "I am the last. What does that mean?"

The courtiers also laughed.

"Your Majesty," said Kyan, placing the empty bottle on the table, "this is nothing new. What I have done today with the wine is only what your officials do every day with the income of the state. In the first place, every small employé fills his own pockets, then the superiors, of course, do not forget themselves, and after that there remains nothing for the King."

The King clapped his hands, and looked round on those present.

"Kyan, your health! The parable is worthy of Æsop. But order another bottle for me."

The negro brought a second bottle of Ambrosia.

All laughed because the King laughed, but they looked askance at Kyan, who, having taken the smallest glass, was drinking to the health of the Hercules of Saxony.

Then they all fell on their knees, and, raising their glasses, shouted acclamation.

The King emptied his glass, and said,—

"Let us talk of something else."

Fürstenberg was the first to rise.

"Your Majesty," said he, "at this hour one should only speak of that which rules over both the night and the day; and that is Woman."

"Good!" exclaimed the King. "Let every one describe his favourite. Fürstenberg shall begin."

The King smiled maliciously as he said this, and Fürstenberg made a grimace.

"The precedence has been given to me," said the young favourite, "but this is only a proof that his Majesty sees everything. The King knows that I cannot lie, and this is why he exposes me to such a humiliation. But I entreat your Majesty to excuse me from drawing a picture of my favourite."

"No, no!" exclaimed several voices. "It is not necessary to give the portrait a name, but the King's commands must be obeyed."

All knew, more or less, why the young Prince was reluctant to speak. This was a critical moment of his life, for he was playing a love comedy with a widow over forty years of age, and famous for the fact that, owing to the thickness of the paint she put on her face, it was impossible for any one to see the colour of her skin. The widow was rich, and Fürstenberg was in need of money.

When they became too noisy, the King commanded silence, and said,—

"You must depict this painted love of yours."

To gain courage to perform the task imposed on him, the giddy young courtier emptied his glass.

"My love," said he, "is the prettiest lady in the world. Who can deny it? Who can tell what is hidden beneath the mask which she puts on in order to prevent common mortals from looking at her?"

A loud burst of laughter here interrupted him.

Beside him sat Adolf Hoym. He was a well-made man, but his expression was disagreeable and his small eyes had a timid look. Hoym was famous for his love adventures, but for several years he had kept them so secret that it was thought they no longer had an attraction for him. It was said that he had married, but no one had seen his wife. She was hidden away at his country house.

Hoym was already tipsy, that could easily be told by the strange movements of his head, and by the efforts he made to raise his arms by dropping his eyelids.

It was the best fun possible for the King and his companions to catch the Secretary of the Treasury in a state when his mind could no longer control his tongue.

"Hoym's turn now," said the King. "You, Hoym, can have no excuse. We all know that you are a connoisseur of female beauty, and that you cannot live without love; nothing ever goes beyond these walls. Come, now, confess!"

Hoym turned his head, and played with his glass.

"He! he! he!" he laughed.

Baron Kyan filled up his glass.

Hoym seized and emptied it with the stupid avidity of a drunken man consumed with a burning thirst.

His face grew crimson.

"He! he! he! You wish to know what my love looks like," he began. "But you must know that I have no need of a mistress, for I have a wife beautiful as a goddess!"

All burst out laughing, but the King looked at him inquisitively.

"You may laugh," continued Hoym, "but the man who has not seen her, has not seen Venus, and I think even Venus herself would look rather like a country washerwoman, if placed beside her. Can I describe her? In her eyes alone there is so much power that no mortal could resist her. Praxiteles could not have shaped a more perfect form. It is impossible to describe the charm of her smile, and yet the stern goddess does not smile every day."

They nodded, but without believing what he said. Hoym would have stopped here, but the King said,—

"Describe her better, Hoym."

"Who can describe perfection?" said Hoym, raising his eyes. "She possesses every good quality, and has not one single drawback."

"I am quite ready to believe that she is beautiful," exclaimed Lagnasco, "for fickle Hoym has been constant to her for three years."

"He exaggerates! He is drunk!" interrupted Fürstenberg. "Would you dare to say that she is more beautiful than the Princess Teschen?"

Hoym shrugged his shoulders, and glanced timidly at the King, who said quietly,—

"There must be no consideration, except for the truth. Is she more beautiful than Lubomirska?"

"Your Majesty," exclaimed Hoym enthusiastically, "the Princess is a beautiful woman, but my wife is a goddess. There is not another woman anywhere, at the court, in the city, in the whole of Saxony, or indeed in the whole of Europe, who is as beautiful as my wife!"

The hall re-echoed with a gigantic peal of wild laughter.

"Hoym is very amusing when he is drunk!"

"How funny the Secretary to the Treasury is!"

"What a very droll man!"

The King did not laugh. Hoym, under the influence of the Ambrosia, had evidently forgotten where he was, and to whom he was talking.

"Yes, laugh!" he exclaimed. "You all know me! You call me Don Juan; you acknowledge that I am a judge of female beauty. Why should I lie?"

Here he looked at the King and was terrified at the expression of his features. So terrified was he that he almost became sober. He would have liked to withdraw, but, being unable, he stood there pale and trembling.

In vain the others tried to make him talk further; Hoym only looked down at the floor and became thoughtful.

The King nodded to Kyan, who filled Hoym's glass with Ambrosia.

"We have drunk the health of our divine Hercules," cried Fürstenberg, "now let us drink to the health of our godly Apollo!"

Some drank kneeling, others standing; Hoym, who had risen tottering, was obliged to lean on the table. The effects of the wine, that fear had checked for a time, returned. His head swam—he emptied his glass at one draught.

Behind the King's chair stood Fürstenberg, whom that monarch caressingly called Fürstchen. To him Apollo now turned,—

"Fürstchen," said he quietly, "Hoym has not lied; he has been hiding his treasure from us for several years, we must force him to show it to us. Do what you please, no matter what the cost, but we must see her."

Fürstenberg smiled; he and the others were much pleased at this. The King's present mistress, Princess Teschen, had against her all the friends of Chancellor Beichlingen, whom she had succeeded in overthrowing, and after whose downfall she had inherited the palace situated in Pirna Street, and although Fürstenberg had served her against the other ladies who had laid siege to the King's heart, yet he was ready to serve Augustus against the whole world. Lubomirska's beauty was not very great; to tell the truth, she was somewhat passée, and her manners of a fine lady had begun to weary the King, who liked his mistresses to be of a more daring and more lively temperament. Fürstenberg had guessed all this from the King's conversation. Rushing across to Hoym, he leant over his chair, and said aloud,—

"My dear Count, I am ashamed of you! You have lied most impudently, and in the presence of the King too. You have been practising a joke on him and on us. I admit that the wife of such a connoisseur as you are may, perhaps, not be a scarecrow, but to compare her to Venus, or even to the Princess Teschen, that is a wretched joke."

Again the wine began to act on Hoym's head.

"What I have said," exclaimed he angrily, "is nothing but the truth! *Tausend Donnerwetter Potz und Blitz!*"

All laughed at the rough exclamation, but at such friendly reunions the King forgave all such liberties; and, while he was drinking, even common mortals were allowed to throw their arms round his neck, and kiss him, and were not afraid that their Hercules would turn and strangle them.

"I bet a thousand ducats," shouted Fürstenberg, "that your wife is not more beautiful than any of the other ladies of the court."

They poured more wine into Hoym's glass, who now drank from despair.

"I accept!" said he, speaking through his clenched teeth.

"I will be the judge," said Augustus. "And we cannot postpone sentence; Hoym must bring his wife here immediately, and introduce her at the Queen's first ball."

"Write at once, Hoym! The King's courier will carry the letter to Laubegast," said Fürstenberg.

"Yes, write; write!" resounded from all sides.

Paper was laid before him in a moment, and Fürstenberg put a pen into his hand. The unfortunate Hoym, in whom the fear of the husband was aroused, as often as he remembered the gallantry of the King, could not tell how he ever wrote to his wife, commanding her to come to Dresden.

But in the twinkling of an eye, the paper was snatched from his hand, and some one had rushed with it into the courtyard, and ordered the King's courier to ride with it at once to Laubegast.

"Fürstenberg," whispered Augustus, "I can see by Hoym's face that, should he become sober today, he will send a counter order. We must make him dead drunk."

"He is so drunk already, that I fear for his life!" returned the Prince.

"I do not," replied Augustus quietly, "I hope I should be able to find some one to fill the office that would become vacant by his death."

The smile with which the King accompanied this speech had such an effect on those present, that they all crowded round Hoym, pouring wine into his glass, and suggesting toasts, with the result, that within half-an-hour Hoym fell asleep on the table, his face, pale as a corpse, his head hanging, and his mouth open. For the sake of security, they did not convey him home, but placed him instead in one of the King's rooms, where he was watched over by the giant Cojanus, who received orders not to let him return home, should he unexpectedly come to his senses.

Having got rid of him, they continued their carouse.

The King was now in an excellent humour, and the radiance of his countenance was reflected in the faces of his courtiers. Day was already dawning when two lackeys carried Augustus the Strong to bed. He had succumbed last of all, except Fürstenberg, who, taking off his wig to cool his head, grew thoughtful, and muttered to himself,—

"So we shall have a new ruler, then. Lubomirska meddled too much with politics. She wished to subdue the king, but he does not require a mistress with brains! She has to love him, and amuse him; that is all her business. Now we shall see the Countess Hoym!"

Laubegast is situated on the banks of the river Elbe, two hours' ride from Dresden. It is a small village, containing only a few better-class dwellings, and these are hidden from view among old linden trees, and tall, black pines.

Count Hoym's villa was built in the French style, and ornamented as well as its modest size permitted. It was evident that its owner bestowed great care on the beauty of his house. The small courtyard was surrounded by an iron railing. Seen through the sheltering trees, the house looked like some lordly residence, but it was as quiet as a monastery.

There were no signs of gaiety about it. Two old lackeys and a few servants might be seen from time to time, walking near the house, and occasionally, towards evening, a lady would come forth, on whom the population of Laubegast would gaze with admiration, but always from behind the shelter of the bushes.

In truth, no one in the neighbourhood had ever before seen such a beautiful woman.

She was young, and tall, and a pair of bright, dark eyes gave animation to her pale face. There was something majestic in her movement as she walked. But she was sad, like a figure taken from a sarcophagus—she never smiled. She had dwelt here for several years, visited by no one save Hoym's sister, the Countess Vitzthum. It was thus that Count Hoym guarded his wife from the intrigues of the court, and he did not even like to see his sister too frequently visiting his wife's retreat. The Countess Vitzthum, however, only shrugged her shoulders contemptuously.

The Countess Hoym's only distractions were the pious books of Protestant dreamers, which she read with great avidity. Occasionally she took a walk under the surveillance of the old butler.

Life here was monotonous, and quiet as the grave, but at the same time passions never entered to cause disturbances. It was only when the King and court were absent, that the Countess Hoym was permitted to visit the capital for a short time. This long seclusion had made her proud, sad, and bitter; she despised the world, and was full of strange asceticisms. She thought that her life was ended, and that she was awaiting death, although she was very beautiful, and not more than twenty years of age; but all who saw her could scarcely believe she was older than eighteen, so remarkably youthful was her appearance.

The Countess Vitzthum, who in the turbulent life of the court had lost all her freshness and half her beauty, was provoked at the unfading charms of her sister-in-law. She was also irritated by her other good qualities; her noble pride of virtue; her indignation at corruption; her contempt for intrigue and lying; and last, but not least, by the majestic manner in which the Countess Hoym looked upon her lively, laughing, and fickle sister-in-law.

Countess Hoym, on her side, did not like the Countess Vitzthum; she felt an instinctive repulsion towards her. For her husband she had a cold contempt, having learned through her sister-in-law that he had been unfaithful to her. By one tender look, she could bring him to her feet; she knew her power, but she had no wish to use it. He seemed to her too villainous to care for. She received him coldly, and parted from him with indifference. Hoym was furious, but he felt feeble in the presence of his wife, and all quarrels were stopped by his taking his departure.

Thus the sad monotonous life at Laubegast went on. Sometimes Anna thought of returning to Holstein, and taking up her abode with her family who dwelt at Brockdorf; but she was not on good terms with them. Her father and mother were both dead, and her sister, the Countess of Brunswick, née Holstein Plön, would not have cared to see her at court. She remembered only too well the behaviour of the sixteen-years old Anna, who had slapped the face of Prince Ludwig Rudolf, when, attracted by her marvellous beauty, he had tried to kiss her.

Thus it was that the beautiful but unfortunate Anna had no place to which she could turn for comfort.

Notwithstanding the corruption of the court, and the nearness of Dresden, in which it is difficult to hide such a beautiful being from the gaze of the people, Anna had been so carefully concealed in her retreat on the shores of the Elbe, that despite the continual movement of the lazy gang surrounding the Sovereign, no one had noticed her.

Except one.

That one was a young Pole, who lived at the court, which he had been forced to enter quite against his inclination.

The first time Augustus the Strong visited Poland after having been elected King of that country, he wished to show his strength to the Polish nobles. With this intent, he began one evening, after dinner, to break horse-shoes and silver plates. The Poles regarded this as a bad omen for their country, and one of them, wishing to break the spell, said he knew a lad who could do the same. The King felt the sting conveyed in the remark, still he expressed a wish to see his rival. Thereupon the Bishop of Kujawy promised to produce the noble referred to, who dwelt at Cracow. His name was Zaklika, and he came of a powerful family, though at present he was very poor. Then the incident was forgotten, and the Bishop would never have mentioned it, being conscious that he had committed an indiscretion, had not the King reminded him of it, and asked to see Raymond Zaklika.

The youth had just ended his studies at a Jesuit convent, and was uncertain what he should do. His wish was to enter the army, but he had no money with which to purchase a commission, and, being a noble, he could not enter otherwise. After long searching, Zaklika was found. The Bishop was obliged to purchase him a decent suit of clothes, before he could present him to the King. Then he was kept ready to be brought forward at the first favourable moment, for the King usually rose to display his strength after he had feasted, and was in a good humour.

At length one day, when the King was breaking silver cups and horse-shoes, which his courtiers always kept in readiness for him, he turned to the Bishop, who was quietly looking on, and said,—

"Father, where is your Hercules?"

Zaklika was summoned.

The youth was straight as an oak, good-looking, and modest as a girl. Augustus smiled on seeing him. He could only converse with him in Latin, for as yet the youth knew neither French nor German. Still there was no need for many words. Two new silver goblets stood before the King;

Augustus took one of them, and, pressing it between his fingers, bent it as though it had been a leaf.

Smiling ironically, he pushed the other towards Zaklika, saying,—

"Now you try. If you can bend it, it is yours."

Timidly the youth approached the table, and, taking the bumper, he pressed it so hard that the blood rushed to his head; but the cup was broken in pieces.

The King's face was expressive of great astonishment, and still greater discontent. The lords who sat round, tried to persuade him that the cup was thin.

The King then turned to the horse-shoes—they broke beneath his fingers like dry branches—but Zaklika could do the same with perfect ease. Augustus took out a new thaler and broke it. A thicker piece of Spanish money was handed Zaklika. For a while the youth remained thoughtful, then he grew eager on the matter, and eagerness lending him fresh strength he broke the coin.

A cloud rested on the King's forehead, and his court grew sorry that such a trial had been permitted. To reward Zaklika, the King ordered the two cups to be given him, then, after a moment's reflection, he told the youth to remain at the court. A small post was assigned to him, but the next morning he was told quietly never to dare to show his strength in that way again, or some evil thing might befall him.

Thus he remained hanging about the court; a splendid livery was provided for him; he was allowed a few hundred thalers by way of salary, and plenty of liberty, his only duty being to follow the King wherever he went. Augustus did not forget him, and gave orders that he should be provided with every comfort, but he never spoke a word to him. Having plenty of time at his command, Zaklika began to study French and German, and within two years spoke both languages fluently. Being unable to spend all his time in study, he used to wander about Dresden, visiting all the adjoining villages and forests on foot. He was also of a very inquisitive turn of mind, and climbed all over the rocky shores of the Elbe, yet he never met with any accident.

During one of his rambles he visited Laubegast, and finding the shade of the linden-trees very pleasant, lay down on the ground to rest. Unfortunately for him, it was about the time when the Countess Hoym used to take her walk. On seeing her the youth was petrified with admiration—he could not breathe. He rubbed his eyes, thinking he must be dreaming; that so lovely a being existed in the flesh, he could not imagine. Poor fellow! Thus he sat until nightfall, gazing continually, yet being unable to satisfy his eyes. He thought one look at the lovely woman would have satisfied him, but the longer he looked, the more he desired to gaze on her. In short, such passion and longing arose within his breast, that every day he rushed to Laubegast like a madman; his head was completely turned.

As he did not confide in any one, he could obtain no advice, nor learn that the best cure for such an illness is to avoid the danger.

Soon the youth was so much in love that he grew pale and thin. The Countess's servants having noticed him, and guessed what was the matter, told their lady about him in jest. She also laughed, but afterwards she looked on him in secret. It may be that she took pity on the youth, for she ordered him to be brought before her, and having scolded him severely for tramping round about her house, she forbade him ever to show himself there again.

There being no one present at their interview, the youth grew bold, and replied that he committed no sin in looking at her, that he did not come for anything else, and that even should they stone him, he must still continue to come, so great was his longing to see her.

Then the Countess grew angry, and threatened to complain to her husband, but this threat likewise was without effect. For several weeks she avoided the paths on which she was accustomed to see him, and, changing the direction of her walks, wandered along the banks of the Elbe, until one day she noticed Zaklika, standing up to his neck in the river, so that he might be able to see her. In great wrath she summoned the servants, but with one plunge Raymond had disappeared. For some time after this she saw nothing of Zaklika, for he had found a new hiding-place; thus all question about him ceased; and no one noticing him at court, he acted just as he pleased.

Only once was he summoned before the King. In an access of rage, Augustus the Strong had cut off a horse's head, and now that powerful monarch desired to show that Zaklika was incapable of performing this feat. An old, strong-boned horse was brought, but at the same time the youth was given to understand that if he valued the King's favour, he had better let the animal alone. But Raymond was so carried away by the desire to show his strength that he cut off the horse's head as with a razor. The King shrugged his shoulders, and drowned the memory of his defeat in wine. No one looked at Zaklika, but those who were kindly disposed towards the youth found opportunity to whisper to him that he had better go away somewhere quietly, because on the slightest excuse he would be sent to Königstein.

But Raymond was not in the least alarmed at their words, and continued his excursions to Laubegast. His love had made quite a different man of him. It is needless to say that Countess Anna Hoym never said anything to any one about this young man.

At Laubegast the gates were always shut at dusk, and the dogs released from their chains; the servants retired early, but the lady of the house would sit reading until late into the night.

That same night, when they were all drinking at the castle, and the wind was blowing keen and cold across the open fields, the beauteous Anna, having undressed, sat reading the Bible, of which she was very fond.

It was already far on into the night, when the tramping of horses' feet was heard, and the dogs began to bark so terribly that the usually fearless lady grew alarmed.

Robbers did not often attack houses in those times, especially near the capital, still such things did happen occasionally. The Countess, therefore, rang the bell, and aroused all the servants. Some one was shaking the gate violently, and the barking of the dogs grew fiercer and fiercer. The armed servants went to the gate, where they found the King's messenger waiting impatiently, with a carriage drawn by six horses. The dogs were chained up, the door opened, and the messenger delivered the letter.

At first Anna thought some misfortune had occurred—she grew pale— but recognizing her husband's handwriting, her calmness returned. At that moment there recurred to her mind the sad fate of the Chancellor Be-ichlingen, who one night fell into disgrace, and was sent to Königstein. Count Hoym had frequently told her that he did not believe in the King, and that he should never feel safe until he had crossed the borders of his own principality.

When she had read her husband's letter, ordering her to come to Dresden immediately, she was greatly surprised. She could not refuse to go, for she did not wish to expose herself to the comments of the servants, and besides she was drawn thither by curiosity. She therefore ordered the necessary preparations to be made, and in less than an hour she had left quiet Laubegast behind for ever.

But strange thoughts took possession of her during her journey. She was afraid of something, and this made her so sad that she nearly wept. She could form no idea of the danger which she felt was threatening her, but she was afraid nevertheless. She knew that the King had returned, after an absence of several years, and that with his return to Dresden, the court was full of intrigues and races for favour, in which every possible means, good or bad, were employed. Many of the things that happened there, though apparently light and trivial, were, in reality, tragic.

At the very moment when those who were sacrificed were thrown into dark and terrible prisons, lively music was being played at the ball given in honour of those who were victorious. Often and often Anna had gazed on the mountain of Königstein, so full of mysteries and of victims.

The night was dark, but the carriage, which was preceded by two men on horseback, carrying torches, rolled swiftly on its way. She scarcely noticed when it stopped before her husband's mansion, which was situated in Pirna Street. Although the Count was expected, the servants were all asleep, and it was impossible to awake them immediately. No apartment had been prepared for the Countess, and she shuddered at the thought of being obliged to enter her husband's room.

The office of the Secretary to the Treasury adjoined the large hall, which, although richly furnished, looked gloomy and sad. On finding that her husband was from home, the Countess's astonishment increased still more, but the servants explained that this was the King's night, and that the entertainment was usually continued until daybreak. Being obliged to remain and rest, the Countess chose a room situated at the opposite side of the office, and separated from all the other apartments. In this she ordered a camp-bed to be placed, and having shut herself in with a servant as companion, she tried to sleep. But the beautiful Countess sought sleep in vain; she only dozed, waking up at the slightest sound.

The day was already bright, when, having fallen asleep for a few moments, she was aroused by hearing footsteps in the office. Thinking it was her husband, she rose and dressed.

The morning toilet she put on only made her appear the more beautiful, while fatigue, uneasiness, and fever increased her charms. She entered the office, but instead of meeting her husband as she expected, she perceived a stranger, whose bearing, combined with the expression of his features, made a deep impression on her.

The man was attired in the long, black dress of a Protestant minister. He was no longer young; he had a massive head, and deeply sunk, dark grey eyes. His mouth wore a bitter smile, in which quiet contempt for the world was curiously blended with serenity and gravity, and this gave to his face an expression so striking that it was impossible to help gazing at him attentively.

The Countess looked on him in astonishment, but he, as though alarmed at the apparition of a woman, stood silent and motionless, with widely-opened eyes, in which could be clearly seen involuntary admiration for this marvellous masterpiece of God.

Thus he stood, his lips trembling, and his arms raised in silent surprise.

The two strangers looked at each other, examining one another attentively. The man retreated slowly. The Countess looked round for her husband. She had just made up her mind to retire, when the stranger inquired,—

"Who are you?"

"It is rather I who should ask who you are, and what you are doing in my house?"

"In your house?" repeated the man in surprise. "Then are you the Count's wife?"

Anna bowed. The old man gazed on her with eyes full of pity, and two large tears rolled slowly down his dried and yellow cheeks.

On her side Anna regarded him with extreme curiosity. This unassuming man, broken by the cares and hardships of life, seemed to be animated by some unknown sentiment; he became grave and majestic. In his presence that proud lady felt almost humble. The features of the silent old man glowed with a secret inspiration. Suddenly coming to his senses, he glanced round timidly, and then advanced a step.

"Oh, you!" he exclaimed, "whom God has created for His glory, you beautiful vase of virtue, a being full of light, and like unto an angel in purity, why do you not shake from off your shoes the dust that now clings to them from their contact with this unclean Babylon? Why, oh why, do you not flee from this place of corruption? Who was so perverse as to cast such a beautiful child into this sordid world? Why are you not afraid? Are you not aware of your peril?"

Anna listened to the old man, whose voice intimidated her for the first time in her life. She was indignant at such daring on the part of the minister, but she could not feel angry with him.

Without giving her time to reply, he continued:

"Do you know where you are? Are you aware that the ground on which you stand shakes beneath your feet? Do you realize that these walls open; that people disappear if they prove an obstruction; and that here human life is a thing of nought, when it interferes with a single drop of pleasure?"

"What fearful things you are telling me," exclaimed the Countess at length, "why do you wish to terrify me?"

"Because I see that you are innocent and pure, and that you know not what you may expect here. You cannot have been here long."

"Only a few hours," replied the Countess.

"And you did not spend your childhood here, or you could not look as you do now," continued the old man.

"My childhood was spent at Holstein; I have been Count Hoym's wife for several years, but I have lived in the country."

"Then I suppose you do not know much about your husband?" said the old man, shivering. "I pity you, for you are beautiful and innocent as a lily, and now a herd of savage beasts are going to trample on you. 'Twere better had you bloomed and shed forth your perfume in God's desert."

He became silent and thoughtful. Anna moved a few steps nearer to him.

"Who are you?" she inquired.

The old man appeared not to hear her, so she repeated her question.

"Who am I?" he repeated. "I am a sinner; a wretched being, the laughing-stock of all. I am the voice crying in the wilderness. I am he who predicts downfall, annihilation, and days of misery. Who am I? I am God's messenger, sent to point out to His people the path of virtue, but to whom none will hearken. I am an outcast to the rich—I am despised—but I am true and pure in the sight of the Lord."

The last words were spoken quietly, then he became silent.

"How strange it all is!" said the Countess. "After years of tranquillity, passed in the country, I am summoned here by my husband, and here I meet you, who are to me as a voice of warning. Surely in this there must be the finger of God!"

"Yes, verily!" rejoined the old man, "and woe to those who heed not God's warning. You ask who I am. I am a poor preacher, I have spoken against powerful lords, and therefore their vengeance pursues me. My name is Schramm. Count Hoym knew me when I was a mere lad, and I have come here to ask his protection, for my life is threatened. This is the reason I am here; but who brought you hither?"

"My husband," replied Anna briefly.

"Ask him to let you go away," he whispered, looking timidly round as he spoke. "I have seen all the beauties of the court, and, taken all together, they cannot compare with you in beauty. Woe be to you if you remain here. They will entangle you in a net of intrigues; they will intoxicate you with songs; they will still your conscience with fairy-tales; they will accustom you to shame. Then one day, intoxicated, weary, feeble, you will fall over the precipice."

Anna Hoym frowned.

"Never!" she exclaimed. "I am not so feeble as you think. I am aware that

I am surrounded by peril, but I have no desire for a life of luxury. No, the life of the court has no attractions for me. I despise it!"

"You must not trust in your own strength; flee, flee from this hell!"

As he spoke, he stretched out his arms, as though he would have liked to drive her away. But Anna stood motionless, and smiled scornfully.

"But where could I go?" she inquired. "My fate is bound up with that of my husband. I cannot break the ties that unite me to him. I am a fatalist. I believe what will happen will happen—only never will they be able to conquer me. It is rather I who shall rule over them."

Schramm looked frightened; Anna stood before him full of strength and pride, the smile still on her lips.

At that moment the door opened, and there entered, confused and hesitating, Count Adolf Magnus Hoym.

He never looked very attractive amid the elegant company of the King's favourites, but after a night spent in revelry, his appearance was still worse. There was nothing noble in his features, and his face, which was commonplace, was only remarkable for the quick, convulsive changes it underwent. His grey eyes were either hidden beneath his bushy eyebrows, or glowing with fire and animation; his lips were now smiling, now contorted; now his forehead frowned, but the next moment it was clear and unruffled. It seemed as though some secret power were continually struggling within him, and changing the expression of his features.

Even at the moment when he perceived his wife, it seemed as though some hidden influence were at work within him, giving rise to the most contradictory feelings. First he smiled at her, but the next moment his anger seemed about to break forth. With a violent effort, however, he controlled himself, and entered the room. But on perceiving Schramm, his eyebrows contracted, anger was clearly visible on his face.

"You madman, you fanatic, you clown!" he shouted, without waiting to speak a word to his wife. "You have been doing some fresh mischief, and again you come to me to help you out of your difficulty. But I cannot help you. You act as you please. You think that a minister may do anything; and that you can declare what you call God's message to every one. You fancy you can play the part of an apostle. But I tell you again, as I have told you a hundred times already, that I cannot help you."

The minister stood motionless, gazing into the Count's eyes.

"But I am God's servant," he rejoined. "I have sworn to bear witness to the truth, and if they desire to make a martyr of me, I am ready."

"A martyr!" laughed Hoym, "that would be too great a favour, they will kick you out, that is all!"

"Then I shall go," said Schramm, "but so long as I am in Dresden I shall speak the truth."

"And you will preach to deaf people," retorted the Count sarcastically, shrugging his shoulders as he spoke. "But enough of this, do what you please, I should be glad if I could protect myself. I told you to keep quiet. In these times you must flatter or you will be trampled on, and perish. Sodom and Gomorrah indeed! Goodbye, I have no more time."

Schramm bowed without a word, cast a pitying glance on Hoym's wife, and then, after gazing on the Count for a moment in silent surprise, he turned to leave the room.

Hoym pitied him.

"I am sorry for you; go! I will do my best to help you; but read your Bible and say nothing. This is the last time I shall advise you."

Schramm went, and husband and wife were left alone.

Even now Hoym did not greet his wife, evidently he was at a loss what to say, and was in consequence embarrassed and angry. Seizing his wig, he began to pull at it.

"Why did you summon me so hastily?" said the Countess proudly, with reproach in her tones.

"Why?" exclaimed Hoym, raising his eyes, and rushing to and fro across the room like a madman. "Why? Because I was crazy! Because those scoundrels made me drunk! Because I did not know what I was doing! Because I am an idiot and an ass!"

"Then I can return?" asked Anna.

"You cannot return from hell!" shouted Hoym. "And thanks to me you are now in hell!"

He tore open his waistcoat as he spoke, and sank into a chair.

"Yes," he continued, "I shall go mad! but I cannot make war against the King!"

"What do you mean?"

"The King, Fürstenberg, Vitzthum, all of them, my own sister too, for aught I know to the contrary, all have conspired against me. They have learned that you are beautiful; that I am an idiot; and the King has ordered me to show you to him."

"Who told them about me?" inquired the Countess quietly.

Hoym was silent, he could not say that he himself had done it; he gnashed his teeth, and sprang from the chair. Suddenly his anger changed to cool and biting irony.

"Let us talk reasonably," said he, lowering his voice. "I cannot undo what is done. I asked you to come here because it was the King's wish, and you know that Jupiter launches his thunderbolts at anyone who thwarts his will. Everything and everybody must contribute to his amusement—he tramples other persons' treasures beneath his feet, and then casts them on the dung-hill!"

Again he began his walk up and down the room.

"I have laid a wager with the Count von Fürstenberg that you are more beautiful than all the ladies at the court. Was I not an idiot? I allow you to answer me that. The King is to be the judge, and I shall win the thousand ducats."

Anna frowned, and turned from him in the greatest contempt.

"You villain!" she exclaimed angrily. "First you keep me shut up like a slave, and now you bring me forward like an actress on the stage, to help you to win your wager, by the brightness of my eyes and the smiles of my lips. Could any one conceive deeper infamy?"

"Do not spare me; you may say what you please," said Hoym, full of grief and remorse. "I deserve everything you can say. I possessed the most beautiful woman in the whole land; she smiled only for me. I was proud and happy. Then the devil made me drown my common sense in a few cups of wine."

He wrung his hands.

"I am going home," said the Countess. "I shall not remain here; I should be ashamed. Order my carriage!"

She moved towards the door; Hoym smiled bitterly.

"Your carriage!" he repeated. "You do not realize where you are. You are almost a prisoner, you cannot leave this house. I should not be surprised to find that guards had been placed before the door. Even should you succeed in escaping, the dragoons would pursue and bring you back. No one would dare to help you."

The Countess wrung her hands in despair. Hoym looked at her with mingled feelings of jealousy, grief, meanness, and sorrow.

"Listen to me," said he, touching her hand, "perhaps it is not so bad as I think. Those who wish to perish, can easily perish here. But you, if you like, need not look beautiful; you might look severe, forbidding; you might even look repulsive, and thus save yourself and me."

Here he lowered his voice.

"You know our King," continued he, with a strange smile; "he is a most munificent lord, he scatters broadcast the gold I am compelled to extort from his poor subjects. There is not a monarch more munificent than he, but at the same time there is not a monarch who requires such continual pleasures. He breaks horse-shoes, and he breaks women; then he casts them both away. The friend he embraces today, he imprisons tomorrow in Königstein. He is a good King! He smiles until the last moment on the victims he is sending to the scaffold. He has a compassionate heart, but no one must oppose him."

He dropped his voice still lower, looking round the room suspiciously.

"He likes new mistresses: like the dragon in the fairy tale, he lives on the maidens brought him by the frightened population; he destroys them. Who can count the number of his victims? You may perhaps have heard the names of some of them, but the number of those who are unknown is three times greater than the number of those whose names are recorded. The King is a man of strange taste; for two days he is in love with the lady dressed in silks; then tiring of her he is ready to love the woman in rags. Königsmark is still beautiful; Spiegel is by no means plain; Princess Teschen still enjoys his favours; but he is tired of them all. Again he is seeking whom he may devour! Ah! he is a great lord! He is beautiful as Apollo, strong as Hercules, lecherous as a Satyr, and terrible as Jupiter."

"Why are you telling me all this?" exclaimed Anna angrily. "Do you think I am so wicked, that at the King's desire I should forsake the path of honour? It is plain you do not yet know me! You insult me!"

Hoym looked on her with compassion.

"I know my Anna," replied he, "but I also know the court, the King, and the people who surround him."

"I have sworn to be faithful to you, and that is sufficient," she retorted proudly. "You do not possess my heart, it is true, but you have my word. Women such as I do not break their vows."

"The Princess Teschen is proud!"

Anna shrugged her shoulders contemptuously.

"I can be a wife," exclaimed she, "but I could never be a mistress. I could not endure that such shame should rest upon my brow."

"Shame!" repeated Hoym. "It only burns for a time; the wound soon heals, although the scar remains for ever."

"You are disgusting!" interrupted the Countess angrily. "You have brought me here, and now you insult me with your vile insinuations."

Emotion checked her utterance; and Hoym said humbly,—

"Forgive me, I have lost my reason. I know not what I am saying. To-morrow has been appointed for the court ball. The King has commanded me to attend with you; you will be presented to him. It seems to me," added he softly, "that you can do anything you wish—you can even not look beautiful. I am willing to lose my wager."

Anna turned away contemptuously.

"You ask me to act a comedy to save your honour!" said she, with a sarcastic smile, "but I hate falsehood. Your honour is not at stake. Anna Countess von Brockdorf does not belong to the class of women who can be purchased for a handful of diamonds. Not a word more. I despise you all. I shall not be present at the ball!"

Hoym grew pale.

"You must be present," said he, in an agitated voice. "This is not a question of a childish fancy; my head and wealth are at stake. The King has issued his commands."

"I do not care!" retorted Anna.

"You intend to disobey the King?" inquired Hoym.

"Why not? He rules over everything, I know, but he does not rule over family life. What can he do to me?"

"Nothing to you," replied Hoym, uneasily. "He is only too polite to beautiful women, but he will send me to Königstein, and confiscate our estates. Misery and death threaten us!"

He covered his face with his hands.

"You do not know him," he whispered. "He beams and smiles like Apollo, but all the time he is terrible as the god of thunderbolts. He has never yet forgiven any one who doubted that he was all-powerful. You must be present at the ball, or I shall perish!"

"Do you think, then, that the threat of your peril is so terrible to me?"

She shrugged her shoulders and walked towards the window.

Hoym followed her, pale as a ghost.

"For God's sake listen to reason!" he exclaimed, "You cannot intend disobeying the King's commands."

He had scarcely finished speaking, when there was a tap at the door, and a lackey entered. Hoym frowned.

"The Countesses Reuss and Vitzthum," announced the servant.

Hoym rushed towards the door, and was just about to send the lackey with a message that he could not receive any one, when he beheld the beautiful Countess Reuss, and, behind her, his own sister.

He had thought that as yet no one knew of his wife's arrival, but the visit of these two ladies convinced him that the folly he had committed when drunk had already made him the laughing-stock of the town.

Much confused, he ordered the servant to leave the room.

Countess Reuss, fresh and pretty, although a little too plump, and with a charming smile lighting up her features, had nothing terrible in her appearance, yet, looking at her, Count Hoym grew still more confused, as though some fresh misfortune threatened him through her.

Countess Vitzthum easily read her brother's feelings in his eyes, yet despite the Count's evident embarrassment, the two ladies continued smiling pleasantly.

"Hoym!" said Countess Reuss, in her sweet, melodious voice, "I really ought to be angry with you. Here is your wife come to Dresden, and you never told me a word about it. I learned it from Hulchen by a pure accident."

"What?" exclaimed the Count impatiently. "Even Hulchen knows of it already?"

"Oh, yes! She and every one are talking of it. They say that at length you have shown some common sense, and that your wife will no longer be condemned to wither away in the desert."

She approached the Countess as she spoke, looking at her inquisitively.

"How are you, my dear Countess?" said she, shaking hands with her. "How delighted I am to welcome you here in your proper place. I am

COUNTESS COSEL

your first visitor, but, believe me, it is not curiosity that has prompted this
visit, but an earnest desire to serve you. Tomorrow you will appear at the
Queen's ball, my beautiful hermit. You do not know Dresden; I entreat
you command my service. Your sister-in-law and I have been uneasy about
you. Poor frightened birdie."

During this speech, the lady whom the Countess Reuss had called a
frightened bird had stood proud and erect, looking just as though she had
ruled in this mansion for years past.

"I thank you!" she replied coldly. "My husband has just told me of the
ball. But is my presence necessary? Can I not be taken ill from emotion
that so great a favour has been shown me?"

"I should not advise you to make any such pretext," replied Countess
Reuss, whom Hoym was leading to the gloomy reception room. "No one
would believe that you were ill, for you look exactly like Juno, full of
health and strength; and no one would believe that you were frightened
either, for you are perfectly fearless."

Countess Vitzthum took her sister's arm, and taking advantage of the
moment when her brother could not hear what she said, whispered,—

"Dear Anna! there is no reason for you to fear, or to excuse yourself; now
at last your captivity is at an end. You shall see the court, the King, and
all our splendour, which is unrivalled throughout the whole of Europe. I
congratulate you. I am convinced that a most splendid future awaits you."

"I had become so accustomed to my life of tranquillity," replied the
Countess, "that I desired nothing different."

"Hoym," continued Countess Vitzthum, "will be consumed with jealousy." Then she laughed.

The three ladies and the confused Secretary to the Treasury were still
standing in the reception room, when the lackey summoned Count Hoym
from the apartment. As soon as he had gone, Countess Reuss seated herself, and addressing her beautiful hostess, said,—

"My dear, it is such a pleasure to me to be the first to welcome you at
the commencement of your new life. Believe me, I can be useful to you.
Hoym most unwillingly gave you this opportunity, which if rightly used,

30

will carry you very high indeed. You are beautiful as an angel."

Countess Hoym was silent for a moment, then she replied coldly,—

"You are mistaken, dear Countess, in thinking I am ambitious. The foolish years of my life are long past. Whilst living in my quiet country home, I was obliged to think much both about myself and the world, and now my only wish is to return to the country, and continue my study of the Bible."

Countess Reuss laughed.

"Everything will be changed now," said she. "At present let us talk about your gown for tomorrow's ball. Vitzthum, you and I must advise her what to wear; she will not do her beauty justice if left to herself. You must take care of the honour of your brother's house."

"She will be the prettiest person there, no matter how she dresses," replied Countess Vitzthum. "Teschen cannot be compared to her—she is withered. There is not another woman at court that can be compared to Anna. In my opinion, the more modest the gown is, the more becoming it will be to her; let others have recourse to artifices."

The conversation about silk and stuff that followed became both animated and polemical. At first Countess Hoym took no part in it, but sat listening to the two friends, who, however, were very careful not to arouse her suspicions. But little by little, she was drawn by that magnetic attraction that dress always exercises over the mind of every woman. She said a word or two, and soon their conversation, mingled with laughter, flowed on smoothly and swiftly.

Countess Reuss listened attentively to every word her hostess uttered, regarding her all the time with a strange uneasiness; from time to time she questioned her, hoping to discover some hidden meaning in her replies. Countess Hoym soon forgot her irritation, and becoming animated, laughed, uttered witticisms suited to her age, and kept up an easy flow of conversation that sparkled with intelligence. Countess Reuss laughed.

"Anna!" she exclaimed, "you are charming! Enchanting! Incomparable! Tomorrow evening you will have the whole court at your feet. Hoym will have to see that his pistols are in readiness. Teschen will be taken ill; she will faint—she has a penchant for fainting, it is such an opportunity for displaying her charms!"

Countess Vitzthum laughed. Then Countess Reuss went on to relate how the Princess Lubomirska had captivated the King's heart by fainting when he fell from his horse. They both fainted, for the King, having been severely wounded, lost consciousness. Her awakening was charming, for when she opened her eyes, Augustus was kneeling at her feet.

"But alas!" added Countess Reuss, "today, even though she should faint, the King would no longer be pleased with her. His first rapture is over. At Leipzic fair, he amused himself with some French actresses. But worse than that, they say he fell madly in love with the Princess Anhalt-Dessau, but that he was disappointed by her coldness. He has told Fürstenberg that his heart is free, and that he is ready to offer it to some other beauty."

"I hope, my dear Countess," said Anna proudly, "that you do not compare me with French actresses. The King's heart is not a very attractive present, and mine is of more value than to be satisfied with the remnants of a heart formerly the property of the Princess Teschen."

Countess Reuss blushed.

"Be quiet, child," said she, looking round; "who has said anything of the kind? We prattle about everything, and it will do you no harm to be prepared for any emergency. We will send you our dressmaker, and if you have not brought your diamonds, or should you require others, Mayer will lend you, secretly, anything you want."

With this both ladies rose, and began to take leave of their hostess, who conducted them, in silence, to the door. Hoym was already busy in his office.

After entering the Countess Reuss's carriage, both ladies remained for a time silent and thoughtful. The Countess Vitzthum was the first to speak.

"What do you prophesy?" she asked.

"Hoym can consider himself a widower," replied her companion, in a whisper. "She is proud, and for a long while will resist the good fortune offered her, but there is nothing that makes the King more enthusiastic than resistance. She is beautiful, daring, witty, and quaint; and all these are qualities that not only attract, they also bind. We must manage to be on the best of terms with her now; later, when she has taken hold of the reins, it will be too late. I will help you, and you must help me. Through her we shall hold the King, the secretaries, everybody, and everything. Teschen is lost, and I am glad of it, for I could never get anything from that tedious, sentimental Princess. Besides she has got quite enough; her son is recognized, she has obtained a title; she is enormously rich; she has ruled us too long already. The King is tired of her, and now, more than ever, he requires consolation and distraction. Fürstenberg, you and I must overthrow that stranger. Only we must be wary, for Anna will not allow herself to be taken by storm—she is too proud."

"Poor Hoym!" laughed Countess Vitzthum. "But if only he had some sense—"

"He would profit by her," interposed Countess Reuss. "He did not love her any longer, the old libertine, and he himself prepared the drama of which he will be the victim."

"I distrust Fürstenberg."

Countess Reuss looked at her inquisitively, and a spark of irony glittered in her eyes; she shrugged her shoulders.

"There are some people who are predestined!" said she sneeringly.

Suddenly she began to laugh.

"Do you know," she continued, "she should wear an orange dress, and coral ornaments. She has black hair, and the fresh complexion of a child. Such a costume would be most becoming to her. Did you notice what fire she has in her eyes?"

"And how proud she unfortunately is!" said Countess Vitzthum.

"Let her once see the King," rejoined Countess Reuss; "let Augustus once wish to please her, and I warrant she will soon lose her pride."

In Pirna Street, which in times of yore was the most elegant street in the small walled city of Dresden, stood Beichling House, once the residence of the unfortunate Chancellor, who was now a prisoner at Königstein. Princess Lubomirska, née Bohun, divorced from her husband, the master of the pantry at Lithuania, and beloved by Augustus II., who, after the birth of her son, the famous Chevalier de Saxe, had created her Princess Teschen, had received Beichling House as a reward for the overthrow of the Chancellor, in which she had greatly assisted. And it was in this palace that she always resided, when not living on her estates at Hoyerswerd. But now a change had come. Those first years of passionate love and knightly gallantry, when the beautiful King could not live for a single day without his dear Ursula, and when the charming Princess, then but twenty years of age, galloped forth impatiently to meet her royal lover, were gone; those happy times passed in Warsaw, in travelling through Germany, in splendid balls at Dresden and Leipzic, seemed to have departed for ever.

Ever since that ball at Leipzic, when, to punish the gallantry of Augustus II., who was paying court to the Princess Anhalt-Dessau, the merciless Queen of Prussia, Sophia Caroline, had assembled that monarch's three ex-mistresses, Aurora Königsmark, the Countess Esterle, and Frau Haugwitz, in order to confuse him and Princess Teschen—ever since that ball, although it had ended in the most tender assurances of constancy on the part of the King, Princess Teschen had felt uneasy. She was always thinking that she too might be abandoned by the inconstant Augustin. It was true that, despite his secret love affairs, the King always showed great respect and affection for Princess Teschen. She had considerable influence over him, and was very skilful in leading him with golden reins, held by a slender white hand, but still she felt that the King might abandon her at any moment.

Her mirror told her that she still preserved that beauty and freshness of which she took such care; but that beauty and freshness no longer possessed the charm of novelty for the King, and he easily grew weary, and always required something new and fresh to distract him. He enjoyed the conversation of the beautiful Princess; he liked her cleverness in court intrigues, her policy covered by a veil of womanly frivolity, her perfumed perversity, and the skilful manner in which she used the entangled intrigues of others for her own benefit. Augustus used still to visit her for a couple of hours, or more, but had the Queen asked her today, as she had on a former occasion, when she intended to leave Dresden, she could not, as she had done then, reply boldly, that as she had come with the King, so would she leave with him. Thus her beautiful blue eyes were veiled by a cloud of sadness, but the softness in those eyes, so full of melancholy, was misleading, for the Princess possessed an iron perseverance when endeavouring to attain a desired object. From day to day her uneasiness increased, she feared every moment to receive an order to leave Dresden, and such an order would separate her from the King for ever.

Outwardly all was still unchanged, she was still respected at court, but she read her approaching downfall in the eyes of the courtiers, and from time to time she noticed ironical smiles, and malicious glances cast in her direction.

The Princess loved Augustus, she loved him passionately, and she had even thought that the volatile King would settle down, and that she would one day become Queen, but these illusions had vanished. She felt now that she was bound to meet the same fate as her lord's former favourites. Disenchanted and disappointed, she occasionally recovered her former gaiety and coquettishness when she desired to please the King, but when in her palace she wept secretly, and promised herself revenge. Letters were now despatched to Radziejowski, Primate of Poland, more frequently than ever. The King, however, was aware of the peril of incurring the Princess's wrath, as she was niece to the first dignitary of the Republic, and he made every effort to persuade her of his continued attachment. But in the meantime she was surrounded by spies, for the King feared her vengeance, even before he had deserved it.

The love of Augustus II. had changed to pure gallantry, its chill could be felt. Princess Teschen still occupied the first place at court, after the Queen; but in the King's heart she was placed on the same level as Her Majesty. The King was indifferent to her.

Her dreams of eternal love had passed like spring clouds—nothing now remained to her but offended pride.

When Princess Lubomirska left her family, visions of the crown had floated before her eyes—but these visions had disappeared, and there remained only the shame of unrealized calculation; the disgraceful situation of a woman without husband or home; a woman paid for momentary transports of love with titles, estates, and gold. The hour of her triumph had been short and fleeting, but the shame would endure for ever.

The Princess Lubomirska could not thus return to Poland.

Poor woman, she was afraid of being abandoned, and hurled headlong from that height on which she now stood hesitating, and wondering what course she should pursue. She was very weary, and she was right in calling herself unhappy, even before she was so in reality.

The palace in Pirna Street was, as usual, full of courtiers, beautiful ladies, and gallant cavaliers. The King especially favoured the latter, for he hoped that one among them might take off his hands that heart which now oppressed him by its too lachrymose affection.

The Princess's tears made Augustus the Strong very impatient, he never wept himself, and greatly disliked to see her weep. Moreover, it annoyed him that where he came seeking for distraction, he met with nothing but endless reproaches.

The Princess also employed her spies. She knew the King's every movement, and every word he uttered was reported to her. She spied on him jealously. She knew all the details of that orgie at which Hoym had first been made drunk, and then compelled to send to Laubegast for his beautiful wife. And now, uneasy and feverish, she was wondering whether she should accept the challenge, and go to the Queen's ball, or whether she should contemptuously ignore the gauntlet that had been thrown to her.

Towards eleven o'clock in the morning she was informed that the Countess Hoym had arrived. No one had seen her as yet; none knew her; none could describe her. All agreed, however, that she was beautiful, that she was born in 1680, and that she was therefore the same age as Princess Lubomirska; but none could predict the amount of danger to be expected from her beauty.

All kinds of stories were repeated. Pitiless Kyan was reported to have said, "It is no matter whether she is beautiful; it will be sufficient if she is unlike the Princess."

And Princess Teschen was only too well aware that the Countess's beauty would not be the principal consideration with the King; it would be the pleasure of a new sensation.

She had fewer visitors than usual this morning, for all were busy rushing hither and thither through the city, carrying and gathering the news.

Some said that the King, according to his usual custom when he cared about the splendour of a ball, was carefully preparing the programme himself, and that he was already very impatient for the result of the wager between Fürstenberg and Hoym. Others said that Fraulein Hulchen and Countess Reuss were intriguing together, their object being to entangle Countess Hoym in their nets, and thus assure themselves of her favour.

Countess Vitzthum assured every one that her sister-in-law's beauty would eclipse that of all the court beauties.

The Princess sent out for tidings, received the reports of those who still remained faithful to her, wept, and gave herself up to despair. Thrice had she succeeded in retaining her hold over the King when he had wished to break with her, but now it seemed as though her last hour had really come. She wrung her hands—suddenly a strange thought took possession of her mind—she glanced at the clock. Hoym's house was not far distant. She whispered something to her attendant, then, muffling her face in a thick veil, she quietly descended the stairs, and entered the vestibule. A litter was in readiness, she entered it, then, instead of carrying her through the street, the two bearers, to whom the servant had given whispered instructions, went along in the rear of the gardens. A door in Hoym's garden was opened by some one, the Princess alighted from her litter, and, after a hasty glance around her, hurried up the stairs, and entered the Count's house. A young man in the antechamber opened the door to her, Lubomirska hastened down a dark corridor, and rapped at a door that had been pointed out to her.

She had to wait some time before it was opened, and even then it seemed as though the servant who opened only wished to see who was outside, for she would not have allowed the Princess to enter, had not that lady placed a few ducats in her hand. Then Princess Teschen pushed open the door, and entered.

Anna Hoym was walking across the room, at the moment the veiled lady appeared on the threshold. Surprised at the sight of an unexpected visitor, she drew back with an angry frown.

Pulling off her veil, Lubomirska gazed inquisitively at the Countess; then her lips trembled, she grew deadly pale, staggered and fainted.

Anna and the servant hastened to her assistance, and between them they raised the unconscious lady.

Her swoon, however, did not last long. Suddenly she sprang up like a madwoman, and gazed on her rival with dilated eyes; then she silently made a sign that she desired the servant to leave the room.

The two ladies were accordingly left alone.

This strange occurrence filled Countess Hoym with uneasiness. After long years spent in the quiet of the country, the new and feverish life that had now begun for her startled and surprised her.

Lubomirska extended her white, cold, trembling hand towards the Countess.

"Forgive me," she said, in feeble tones, "I wanted to see and warn you. The voice of duty compelled me to come hither."

Anna remained silent, gazing curiously at her extraordinary visitor.

"Yes, look at me!" continued the Princess. "You are beginning the life which for me is ended. Once I was as you are, innocent, happy, quiet, and respected, living at peace with my conscience and my God. I had my husband's princely title, and, better than all, I had an unsullied name. Then there came a crowned monarch, and he took all this from me with his smile. His sceptre and crown he laid at my feet; he gave me his heart. I followed him. Look at me. Today I have nothing. The name I have is borrowed, my heart is broken, my happiness is gone for ever; instead, the mark of shame is on my forehead; my soul is full of bitterness, the future is dark and threatening, and I am tormented with cares for my child. I have no one in this world to whom I can turn. My relations would disown me;

those who yesterday crawled at my feet, will forget me tomorrow. He will push me aside like a stranger."

Anna blushed.

"Madam!" she exclaimed. "Why do you foresee a danger for me that I cannot see myself? I do not understand your words. Who are you?"

"Yesterday, I was almost a Queen, but I know not what I am today," replied the Princess.

"But I do not wish for any crown," said Anna, "there is not one that does not burn the forehead. Why do you apply these threats to me?"

"Warnings, not threats," interrupted Lubomirska. "Forgive me, a crown is approaching your brow, the people have given it you in advance. I desire to show you its thorns."

"You are mistaken," replied the Countess calmly. "I shall not stretch forth my hands for any crown. I am too proud. Be calm."

Teschen sank on the sofa, her head drooped, and she began to weep. Her heart-breaking sobs aroused Countess Hoym's pity, and she approached her sympathetically.

"Everything that has happened to me today is so mysterious," said she. "Who are you?"

"Teschen," murmured the Princess softly, raising her eyes as she spoke. "You have heard of me, and you can guess why they have brought you here. A fresh face is necessary for their weary lord."

Anna uttered an indignant cry.

"Villains!" exclaimed she. "Then they would traffic with us, as though we were slaves—and we—"

"We are their victims."

"No! I will never be their victim," interrupted the Countess; "I am so proud that I would endure any misery, rather than surfer such humiliation."

Teschen looked at her, and sighed.

"If it is not you, it will be another," she replied. "My hour has come. But if you are strong enough, I beseech you, avenge us all. Spurn him. Show him the contempt you feel for him. His actions cry to God for vengeance."

She replaced her veil, shook hands silently, then with the hasty exclamation, "You are warned, defend yourself!" she hurried from the room, leaving the Countess speechless.

Before she had recovered herself, the Princess had disappeared.

The same man who admitted her was waiting on the stairs. She re-entered her litter, and, whilst drawing the curtains, noticed a young officer with a pale face looking anxiously into her eyes.

The young man's features were noble, aristocratic, and expressive of courage and energy, but at that moment they were distorted by grief and indignation. He seemed unable to believe his eyes. He approached the litter.

"Princess Ursula!" said he, in a voice broken by emotion, "can I believe my eyes? I beseech you, tell me the whole truth, then I will mount my steed, ride away, and never return. Princess! I am mad with love, while you—"

"It is quite true that you are mad," said the Princess brusquely, "and you are blind as well, or you would see that I am coming from Hoym's house, and with him I could not possibly be in love."

She grasped his hand.

"Come with me, I will not release you until I have explained everything. I do not wish you to accuse me unjustly—that would be too much! I could not survive that!"

The Princess, her beautiful eyes full of tears, looked so eloquently at the young man, as she uttered these words, that all traces of sorrow disappeared from his face.

Obedient to her commands, he followed the litter; when it stopped, he helped her to alight, and together they entered the palace. Tired and broken in spirit, the Princess sank on the sofa, and motioned to the young man to seat himself by her side.

"Prince, you behold me angry and indignant. I have just returned from visiting her whom my horrible enemies have brought here, that the King may have the distraction of a new face; whom they have brought here to drive me away, and to overthrow my influence with the King. Have you heard about Countess Hoym?"

"No," replied the young man, who was Prince Ludwig von Würtemberg. "I have only heard them laughing at poor Hoym, whom they made drunk, so that they might compel him to show his wife."

"Yes," exclaimed the Princess, "they well knew how to arouse Augustus's curiosity. But I have seen her; she is beautiful, and she is dangerous."

"So much the better!" cried the Prince, springing from his seat. "Then you will be free!"

Teschen blushed, and looked inquiringly at the young man—there was a moment's silence, then she stretched out her hands towards him. He seized them, kissed them with fervour, and was still holding them, when a little woman, who bore some likeness to the Princess, rushed into the room, laughing maliciously.

It was difficult to guess how old she was, for she had one of those faces which, never being fresh, do not grow old for a long time. Her sharp, grey, malicious eyes were full of animation, her lips wore an ironical smile, whilst her features bespoke her a feverish gossip and an unbearable intriguante. She was dressed with the greatest care; had a dainty figure, and small feet. She clapped her hands in delight when Prince von Würtemberg withdrew his lips from the Princess's hand.

"Bravo! Bravissimo!" she screeched. "I see that my sister has secured military protection for her retreat; for it seems to me that the moment has arrived when we shall have to retreat from the King's heart and court."

The speaker was the Princess's own sister, and married to the Baron von Glassenapp.

"My dear sister, I have not seen you for a long time," prattled on the little lady, "but at the moment of peril, I always appear. Teschen, do you know that Hoym's wife has arrived? I saw her when she was at Dresden during the King's absence, and I then foretold that, like the beautiful Helen of Troy, she would bring misfortune to some one. She is beautiful as an angel, and dark, which for a blonde like Teschen, is always dangerous. She is animated, witty, malicious, and proud as a Queen. Your power is ended."

She laughed.

"Well, you still have a chance of princely titles," she continued, not allowing any one an opportunity to put in a word. "I was only able to catch a poor Pomeranian Baron—but you got Lubomirska, you have Teschen, and for provision you are trying to get Von Würtemberg."

The Prince stood blushing and angry. Teschen lowered her eyes, and murmured through her set teeth,—

"I could have a fourth, if I wished."

"I will tell you his name, if you like," interrupted the Baroness, and, running up to her sister, she put her mouth to her ear, saying,—

"The Prince Alexander Sobieski, is it not? But he will not marry, while Ludwig will. Try and hold him."

The Princess turned from her sister in disgust, and the Baroness looked in the mirrors, flitted about the room, all the while keeping an eye on the couple, at whom she laughed dreadfully.

"If you are clever, Teschen, you may still come out of this crisis triumphant. Hoym's wife is a simpleton; she will disgust the King; she will attract him at first by her beauty, but she will repulse him with her pride; after her, Teschen will appear dear and sweet. Well, one must forgive the King's fancy. Such men have great sorrows, and great privileges. Only I am sorry," she continued, "that every one is tearing you to pieces already. The Countesses Reuss and Hulchen are offering sacrifices to the new goddess, while Fürstenberg and even brother-in-law Vitzthum are ready to supplant Hoym. Poor Hoym, when his wife leaves him, I would marry him, if it were not for my duties. But the old libertine never cared for me."

Here Prince Ludwig rose to take his leave, and the way in which Princess Ursula shook hands with him did not escape the notice of the Baroness, who bowed to him distantly.

There was silence for a few moments after the sisters were left alone.

"You must not take it so tragically," began the Baroness, "any one could have foreseen that this would happen sooner or later. The King is tired of a blonde, you have a principality, you have estates in Hoyerswerd; you have millions, diamonds, a palace; you are still young, still beautiful; and there is Prince Ludwig, who is ready to marry you. I tell you frankly, I would gladly exchange my lot for yours, and I would give you Schulemberg in addition."

"But I loved him," interrupted the Princess, weeping bitterly.

"But that is all over," rejoined the Baroness, "I know that you were both in love with each other, for a whole year at the least, during which time the King betrayed you secretly, at least, ten times, and you repaid him in the same coin."

"Sister!" exclaimed the Princess indignantly.

"Well, then, you did not. But during that time you were able to obtain for yourself the love of the Prince von Würtemberg. I am called malicious and wicked, but I should not have been able to do it. I only found Schulemberg after I had been bitten by Glassenapp."

She laughed a little, and then continued,—

"Listen, Kings have a custom, when taking leave of their favourites, to ask for the return of the diamonds they have given. I warn you, therefore, to put yours in a safe place."

She looked at her sister, who apparently did not hear what she was saying.

"Are you going to the ball?" she inquired.

"The ball?" repeated the Princess, thoughtfully. "Yes; I must go to the ball. I shall go dressed in mourning, and without any jewels; but tell me, will a black robe be becoming to me?"

The Baroness laughed.

"Undoubtedly!" she replied. "Mourning is becoming to every one. But if you think that by doing this you will soften the hearts of Augustus and his courtiers, you are mistaken; they will all laugh at you; they do not like tragedies."

"What will be, will be!" replied the Princess. "I shall go in mourning. I will appear before him like a silent ghost."

"And as Countess Hoym will be merry and fresh, you will also disappear like a ghost. Believe me, the past can never be recalled."

She looked at the clock.

"It is late already! I shall see you again at the ball—I shall be there, but I shall be in the background, like a spectator who applauds the actors. Goodbye!"

Most of the guests had arrived. The magnificence of the dresses with which the ball-room was crowded, hid from view the calamities caused by the war that had lately visited Saxony. The King's dress was covered with diamonds, large diamonds formed the buttons of his tunic, whilst a profusion of the same precious stones glittered on the hilt of his sword and the buckles of his shoes. His majestic figure looked quite youthful, and the expression of his features was more suited to a victor than to one who had been obliged to fight for his throne against a most determined adversary.

The dresses of the ladies also glittered with precious stones, although many of the court beauties had no need of these adornments. The Queen alone was modestly dressed; Augustus gallantly hastened forward to meet her; the musicians played a fanfare. The principal actresses, however, had not yet arrived.

The King had already begun to frown in true Olympic fashion, and was looking at Fürstenberg in a way that that nobleman understood perfectly, when, despite the respect due to the presence of the sovereign, murmurs arose at the entrance to the ball-room. The eyes of all the guests were eagerly turned towards the doorway.

"They come!" whispered Fürstenberg.

He was right; and the next moment, Hoym, his face pale and sad, entered the room, accompanied by his wife.

Perhaps never before had there been seen beauty so dazzling, even at that court so famed for beautiful women.

Countess Hoym walked amongst the ladies with the dignity of a queen; she was fearless, calm, dignified, and so lovely, that there was a general murmur of admiration. The King looked at her intently, but failed to catch her eyes. As she was to be presented to the Queen, she allowed herself to be conducted to Her Majesty, but she did not appear to be dazzled by the splendour of the court, or by the Apollo-like beauty of the King, who, it was evident, had placed himself so as to appear before her to the best advantage. A quiver of impatience passed over his features.

Hoym led his wife forward, looking like a man condemned to death. His enemies were delighted at the sight of his agony, which he made no attempt to conceal. The Queen looked kindly on the Countess, and smiled on her graciously, but she was full of pity for the fate that awaited that beautiful woman. She even sighed slightly.

As soon as the formalities of the presentation were concluded, the musicians played a polonaise, and the King opened the ball with the Queen.

Princess Teschen had not yet arrived. All the other ladies were present, however, even Fraulein Hulchen, who, although ill, had overcome her sufferings in order to satisfy her curiosity.

The first dance was just ended, when the sounds of renewed murmuring announced that something unusual had occurred. All the guests, and even the King, looked in the direction whence the sound proceeded—there on the threshold, as though hesitating whether or no she should enter, stood Princess Teschen. She was clad in deep mourning. On seeing who it was, Augustus went forward to meet her, looking very much annoyed.

"Whom have you lost," he inquired ironically, "that you appear here in a dress so little suited to a ball?"

"I have lost your Majesty," murmured Teschen softly.

The inquisitive eyes that had been regarding the Princess were now turned towards Countess Hoym, and even the ladies acknowledged that the latter was by far the more beautiful.

Augustus was intoxicated at the sight of her beauty, and the moment Countess Vitzthum had separated her from her husband, he approached Hoym, and clapping him on the shoulder, said confidentially,—

"My dear Count, you have won that thousand ducats off Fürstenberg. I congratulate you on your good fortune, and also on your wife's beauty. There is no doubt that she is the most beautiful lady at our court. Oh, Hoym, what a happy man you must be!"

But seeing Hoym, as he stood with drooping head, listening to the King's congratulations, no one would have supposed him to be happy. On the contrary, he looked like one humiliated and crushed; like a man repenting his evil deeds; like one who, did he but dare, would groan aloud in his anguish. Fürstenberg bowed, looking ironically at the King.

"I see, your Majesty," said he in a whisper, "that I must pay the costs of the King's decision, and that I must also pay the piper."

Augustus turned towards him, and, extending his hand to be kissed, said,—

"Do not complain, Fürstenberg; pay the thousand ducats, and take ten thousand from my treasury as a reward for the opportunity you have given me of beholding such a masterpiece of beauty."

Meanwhile, Princess Teschen sat alone—every one had deserted her. Having observed this, Augustus, following his usual custom of sweetening, as far as possible, his subjects' downfall, went over to her. Those unacquainted with the King's mode of procedure were much surprised at seeing him walk in that direction. But Countess Reuss and Fraulein Hulchen, who observed his movements, were well aware of its meaning.

"Teschen is overthrown!" said the Countess, addressing her friend. "The King has gone over to her!"

The old courtiers also, who had seen the King embracing Chancellor Beichling the day before he was sent to Königstein, knew how to interpret His Majesty's tenderness towards the Princess Teschen.

"Do you know," said the King, seating himself by her side, "that looking at you in that black dress, you are so beautiful that you remind me of that tournament at Warsaw, when you fainted through anxiety for my safety?"

"But Countess Hoym is more beautiful than I am, than the tournament, or the remembrance of my fainting," replied the Princess sarcastically.

"Countess Hoym may be beautiful, even most beautiful," said Augustus, "but there are things more beautiful than beauty itself—and one is a tender and loving heart. Dear Princess, do not make such a spectacle of yourself; return home, put on your blue dress, that is so becoming to you, and wait for me for supper."

A deep blush overspread the pale face of the Princess Ursula.

"My King! my Lord!" she exclaimed, forgetful of all that had gone before. "Is this true? Is it possible that Augustus is still mine?"

"Pray do not doubt me," replied the King gravely. "Why should I lie?"

It was true. At that moment the King did not lie; Countess Hoym's beauty had made a great impression on him, but at the same time it had filled him with a sort of fear. The energy of her character betrayed itself in her every movement and glance, and he felt that he should be obliged to lay half of his power at her feet. Anna's face said, "I must rule;" the face of Ursula said, "I love you, and I am dying for your love!" Countess Hoym even appeared to him too sad and serious. That, therefore, was the reason he went over to console the Princess; he had no wish to lose her, and place his neck beneath the yoke of a woman who seemed not in the least anxious to conquer him.

Countess Hoym was very tastefully dressed; she wore no jewels, but her coiffure and the colour and cut of her dress lent an added charm to her beauty. The portraits of her taken at that time, represent her as having a face of an exquisite oval, a small nose, lovely lips, and very expressive, large black eyes, whilst her features were very delicate, and her long black hair very abundant. Her hands, bust, and waist were of a corresponding beauty; and her fair face blushed and paled with every succeeding emotion.

Although exposed to the gaze of several hundred persons, Anna Hoym was not in the least confused; at first she was silent and dignified, but she speedily became accustomed to the dazzling splendour, which appeared to her to be an ordinary thing here, for although the court in which she had passed her young days was not so splendid as that of Dresden, the forms, she found, were the same.

Princess Teschen at once prepared to obey the King's command, and having cast on him one languishing glance, she left the ball-room almost triumphant. A few moments later Augustus stood beside Countess Hoym's chair. He gazed at her in silence, and, having noticed his approach, Anna rose. The King requested her to be seated, and she obeyed, but without any exaggerated respect.

At that time it was the custom that when the King desired to talk with any one, those standing near immediately retreated. This custom was observed in the present instance.

"Countess, you are the most beautiful lady at my court," said the King

47

gallantly, bending towards her as he spoke. "I am delighted with the new and splendid star that has now risen on my horizon."

Anna raised her head proudly.

"Your Majesty!" replied she, "at night, any small light looks like a star, but with the daylight it expires. I know how to appreciate your Majesty's favour, and it is to this favour that I attribute these flattering words."

"I only repeat what I hear," said Augustus.

"People who see me for the first time," rejoined Anna, laughing, "usually see badly. A new object amuses; that alone is truly beautiful which, after many years, still appears beautiful."

The King was silent, for he understood that the beautiful lady beside him was referring to his gallantry towards Princess Teschen. But after a few moments, he said,—

"You are too modest."

"Oh, no!" replied Anna with animation. "I do not attach any value to beauty."

"But beauty of face indicates beauty of soul," rejoined the King.

Anna lowered her eyes. The King did not leave her.

"After the long solitude imposed on you by your husband," continued Augustus, "the court must appear very strange to you."

"Not at all," replied Anna. "I spent my youth at a court which, although more modest than your Majesty's, gave me just the same idea as to what all courts are."

"And what are they?" inquired the King.

"A well-played comedy," answered the Countess.

"And what rôle do I play in it?"

"Perhaps that of a manager, who is deceived and robbed by every one."

Augustus, slightly surprised, inquired,—

"Do you find everything here deceitful?"

"How could it be otherwise?" asked Anna. "Kings never hear the truth."

"It may be so," said Augustus, "and that is the reason they so frequently search for lips from which they may hear it."

"But perhaps," rejoined Anna, "they only find lips that know how to administer poison more skilfully than the others."

"Your speech," said the King politely, "proves to me that you do not like splendid courts. I greatly regret this, for I thought that the light from your eyes would brighten our gloomy skies."

"Your Majesty," replied Anna with animation, "I should sound here with a false note. I know not how to sing like the others."

To turn the current of their conversation, Augustus now began to make humorous remarks about the ladies and gentlemen surrounding them. And from this Anna discovered that he knew far more about the characters, inclinations, and even of the secrets in the lives of his courtiers, than she would have expected.

"You see," added Augustus, "that this comedy holds no secrets for me; and what renders it very amusing is that these people imagine that they deceive and blind me."

"Thus the gods look on the earth," concluded the Countess.

The King was much pleased at being called a god. As she spoke those words, her eyes, for the first time, met those of the King, which were fixed on her full of enthusiasm and admiration. In Anna's eyes there was only an expression of cold curiosity, not unmixed with fear.

After this, the King left her slowly. His courtiers all tried to divine his thoughts. Fürstenberg was the first to encounter him.

"Your Majesty," said he, "may I dare to ask if the most beautiful is also—"

"The most witty," said the King, finishing his sentence for him. "We must tell Hoym that he must not on any account venture to take her from Dresden. She is very interesting indeed—a little bit cold, but that will pass with time."

Hoym, who had been watching from a distance, was unable to guess his wife's thoughts; but the moment Anna was left alone Countess Reuss, Fraulein Hulchen, and Countess Vitzthum hastened forward and surrounded her.

The King noticed it, and shrugged his shoulders.

"They already bow before the rising sun," whispered he to Fürstenberg.

"But I very much fear that they will be disappointed."

Fürstenberg looked surprised.

"You also are mistaken," said Augustus, bending down and speaking in his ear. "Hoym's wife is beautiful, I have examined her carefully: she is an animated Greek statue, but she is too energetic, too intelligent; and besides, she would wish to rule. A few days' pleasure with her is all that I desire. Her beauty attracts me, but her character repels me."

Fürstenberg now looked very much astonished, and the King went away.

During all this time, no one had noticed the pale face of a young man, whose head towered above all the others in the crowd around the door. His glance rested continually on Anna, and when the King approached her, his eyes gleamed with anger. At first Countess Hoym did not observe him, but when the King had left her, and she had more leisure to look around her, she perceived and recognized Zaklika.

As her eyes rested on his pale face, she grew a trifle confused. Then, uncertain whether she was mistaken or not, she looked again, and this time she met his eyes gazing towards her. Now there was no longer room for doubt: her silent admirer from Laubegast stood before her. In the expression of his face, she seemed to read pity, sorrow, and uneasiness.

His looks made her uneasy, and every moment she glanced in his direction, hoping he might have disappeared. But no, he was still there, and with the same expression on his features. Why should that poor, unknown vagabond of a man interest her more than the shining majesty of the King, or than the courtiers, who were all bent on petting her? That was a question she was quite unable to answer. She only felt that a mysterious chain of some strange destiny united her to that stranger.

Was he an executioner awaiting the hour of her torture, or was he a victim awaiting the execution? Anna knew not, but a mysterious, tormenting voice seemed to whisper to her, prophesying the unfolding of some future destiny between herself and that stranger. Every time she met his glance, she shivered.

She laughed at her foolish fancies, and the echo in her soul replied with plaintive moaning.

It was in such a mood that Hoym found her, and he looked very yellow and sour as he offered her his arm to escort her home. Fate decreed that they went towards the door near which the stranger youth was standing. The crowd stepped aside to let them pass. As she crossed the threshold, the Countess glanced fearfully around, and perceived the stranger from Laubegast leaning against the wall. Having met her glance, the youth knelt on one knee, and she felt him seize the hem of her dress and press it to his lips. When, however, she turned, he had disappeared.

There before her stood the Countess Reuss, who invited them to supper so cordially that the Secretary could not refuse.

Fürstenberg was behind her. They proceeded immediately to the house of Countess Reuss, where, in company with a select circle, they spent about an hour. The famous Egeria Hulchen was the leader there. She was an old maid, but the King gave heed to her words, and frequently asked her advice. Around her gathered all those who wished to rule, or to keep up their influence. The King laughed at this clique, but, by its unseen springs, it ruled both him and the court.

Countess Reuss was one of the principal acting figures at the court of Augustus II. In her house were held the most important councils. Here plans were laid for the overthrow or rise of one or other of the lord's favourites; here also was predicted the favours that awaited the various ladies; and here, too, they foretold with great exactness the moment when the King's variable affection would require to change the object of its devotion.

Hoym was aware that Countess Reuss, foreseeing a new favourite, was trying to win her to her side; he was shocked by her obsequiousness, which allowed all to guess that she foresaw in Anna a substitute for Princess Teschen, but he could not be angry, or rather, he could not show that he was angry. Through Fraulein Hulchen and her relations, Countess Reuss had a very great influence at court, and it would be dangerous to make an enemy of her. Consequently he appeared not to notice anything amiss, and accepted the invitation.

The party assembled in the drawing-room was very animated, while in the boudoir adjoining, where persons were moving in and out, the hostess, her friend, Fürstenberg, and other members of the clique were talking business. The largest circle of guests talked of silk and stuff, and gossiped of matters familiar to every one.

According to the prevailing opinion, the King's tenderness towards Teschen was a sure sign of her downfall. But Augustus II. was obliged to spare her, for many reasons. Her relation to Sobieskis, and Radziejowskis, and her influence in Poland, obliged the King to reckon with her.

In the boudoir, Countess Reuss was asking Fürstenberg what the King had told him concerning Countess Hoym.

"I know the King," replied the Prince, "especially as regards his disposition towards women. Countess Hoym was sharp and proud—that repelled him for a time, but her beauty appeals to his senses, and his senses always subdue him. He is afraid of her, and therefore he will desire her all the more—and you know that he must always have that for which he longs. It appears that Countess Hoym is not inclined to play the part of an easy favourite, and the King will exhaust all his strength before he conquers her, but there is no doubt that he pleases her."

"Then you think that her time will come?"

"Yes. Speaking from my knowledge of him, the King would like to gratify his fancy, but he has no desire for more solid relations; it depends entirely on her, and how she conducts this affair."

"Do you know anything about her, Chancellor?"

"I can only guess," replied Fürstenberg. "I believe that neither her husband, nor any one else, perhaps not even she herself, knows how she will act when she is extolled. Today she is a proud and noble woman; she has a strong character, she is witty, she is clever."

"But she would let herself be guided?" inquired Countess Reuss.

The Prince became thoughtful.

"I only know this," he replied at length, "I prefer to deal with intelligent persons, rather than with those who do not know what they are doing."

Silence followed this remark, and presently the Countess signed to him to leave her alone. When he had departed, she walked up and down her boudoir several times, then she entered the drawing-room. Here she man[oe]uvred so cleverly, that she was able to approach Anna, take her away from the circle of guests, and lead her into the boudoir, where, after making her take a seat by her side, she spoke as follows:—

"Dear Countess, if you have any patience and indulgence for an old friend, permit me to speak with you frankly. No one can hear us in this room. I wish to advise and help you. You know sufficient of the court, the times in which we live, and of yourself, to be certain that you have not been brought to Dresden in vain. The King is weary of Teschen, and he must be in love with some one, it is his nature, and we must be indulgent to such a great and good lord, in whom the whole world will forgive such weakness. For us who surround the King, it only remains to derive as much good from this as we can. You can occupy the most brilliant position by the King's side, only you must be quick, and you must also be well aware of what you are going to do."

"Dear Countess," replied Anna, "I have no ambition, I do not care for riches. I have a husband, and I desire to remain an honest woman."

"I would not raise any objection to your doing so," rejoined Countess Reuss, smiling, "but permit me to say that I can see no reason why you should become a martyr. Hoym is awful; he is worn out, he is a libertine, he betrays you; it is impossible for you to love him; sooner or later, the heart must speak."

"I shall silence it!"

"Once, or twice, but afterwards there will come the years of weariness and longing, when, in your despair, you will throw yourself on some one's breast, and even then you will not be happy. I know the world well; such is our lot. The King, however, is fascinating and beautiful, and life with him may become a paradise."

"But he is inconstant, and I do not understand capricious love. It disgusts me! Such love is not for me!"

"It is the women who are at fault," responded Countess Reuss, "if they do not know how to make such relations permanent. It would be useless to bind him with an oath, for the first priest would release him from it. Your best guarantee of stability will lie in your common sense, tact, and beauty. Every woman must know how to keep a husband, or a lover—it is our business."

Countess Hoym shrugged her shoulders.

"It is a very poor love that one has to keep tied by a string!" exclaimed she. "I do not care for such love! But frankness for frankness, dear Countess," she continued, in a whisper. "I do not pledge myself. At present, I wish to remain faithful to Hoym, and it is only love that would ever make me unfaithful to him. The moment I love, I shall leave Hoym and go openly to the one I love; and the man who loves me shall be my husband."

"But the King! the King!"

"Whether he be a king or no, matters not to me," said Countess Hoym.

"Do you know that the King is married, although he does not live with his wife?"

"He will be obliged to obtain a divorce and marry me," rejoined Anna. "I have no wish to play the rôle of either Esterle, or Königsmark, or of Teschen."

Having said this, she rose and walked majestically across the room; Countess Reuss was silent, there was nothing more to be said.

"You will do as you please," said she, after a while. "As a good friend, it was my duty to warn you and give you good advice. Let us remain friends, but allow me to tell you this: the position you disdain is not so base and secondary as you imagine. The King will bow to your wishes; you may rule the country, and do much good; you may succour the unfortunate, make the people happy—all this is worth something."

"My honour is dearer to me than all that," replied Countess Hoym. "Let us speak no more on this subject."

They left the room. The ladies in the drawing-room looked at them curiously, trying to guess the subject of their conversation. Anna's face was crimson, the Countess Reuss was pale, yet both were smiling.

Suddenly the light of torches shone out beneath the window, and, looking out, Fürstenberg perceived the King on his way to visit Teschen, but he looked as sad as a man who had been sentenced to suffer some severe penalty.

Adolf Magnus, Count Hoym, who occupied a position corresponding to that of Secretary to the Treasury, had no friends, either at court or in the country. All hated him, because he imposed taxes on beer. The Saxons resisted the King as much as they could; and the King, who never had sufficient money to meet his enormous expenses, was enraged at their resistance. It was the nobles who made the strongest resistance, and the King was advised to despoil them of all their privileges, and surround himself with foreigners, who would not have any relations either with the nobility or with the masses of the people.

Augustus had partially followed this advice, and the majority of his secretaries and favourites were taken from foreign lands. Italians, Frenchmen, and Germans from other provinces occupied all the most important positions in the state. Hoym, being a very able man in finding new sources of income for the King, enjoyed great favour with His Majesty; for Augustus required millions, for Poland, for the army, for entertainments, and for his favourites. Hoym, however, had no great confidence in the King's favour; the fate of Beichling and several others had rendered him distrustful, and he intended, as soon as he had grown rich, to seize the first opportunity to escape from Saxony with his head and his money.

Except Beichling, who was at that time imprisoned at Königstein, Hoym did not possess a single friend. Marshal Plug hated him; Fürstenberg could not bear him; the others disliked him.

When, after the wager had been laid, Hoym was commanded to bring his wife and present her at court, no one pitied him; on the contrary, all laughed at his distress.

The day following the ball, Hoym was obliged to bring the King his report. The new tax levied on liquors had met with resistance. In the province of Luzyce, in particular, the nobles openly rebelled against it. The King could not bear the slightest resistance to his will. When the report was ended, Augustus the Strong turned to Hoym, and, frowning angrily, said,—

"Go today; go immediately, arrest those who are at the head of this opposition, and compel the others to obey my will!"

His presence in Luzyce not being in the least necessary, Hoym tried to persuade the King to send some one else, and allow him to remain in Dresden, where he had affairs of greater importance to attend to.

"There is nothing more important," replied Augustus, "than breaking the power and quelling the resistance of those arrogant nobles. Take a squadron of Dragoons with you, and depart instantly. Should they dare to assemble, scatter them. Tell them not to follow the example of the Polish nobles, for I will not suffer anything of that kind from my own subjects. In two hours you should be on the road to Budzisyn."

His subjects might discuss matters with the King when he was drunk, but when sober Augustus had his will, and only one word.

This expedition, following, as it did, closely on the ball, seemed to Hoym very suspicious. He knew the King, the court, and all that was passing there, and he was convinced that he was being sent away so that he might not prove an obstacle to the monarch's wishes, and that Augustus might be left at liberty to court his wife. Still he could do nothing to prevent it. He had no friends; he could not even trust his own sister. He felt that all the court was against him.

On returning home, he threw the papers on the table, tore his dress, then, throwing open the door with a great noise, rushed like a madman into his wife's apartment.

She was alone. He looked at her inquisitively, and at even the smallest objects surrounding her. Anger was depicted on his pale features. Anna looked up at him calmly. She was accustomed to such scenes.

"You can rejoice, madam," he exclaimed. "I was fool enough to bring you here, and now they will do with me as they please. I am an obstacle in the King's path, therefore His Majesty sends me away. I leave here in an hour, then you will be left alone."

"And what do you mean by all this, if you please?" inquired the Countess contemptuously. "Do you require a troop of guards to defend my honour?"

"No. But I think that my presence would at least restrain their effrontery," shouted Hoym. "They would not send me away were I not an obstacle to them. In all this I see the finger of dear Fürstenberg, who laughed ironically as he paid me that thousand ducats. I know that he has received ten thousand from the King for his brilliant idea of bringing you here."

"Hoym!" exclaimed Anna, rising, "enough of these insults. Go! Go! Do what you please, only leave me in peace. I can protect myself."

Hoym was silent; his face grew gloomy, for the hands of the clock announced the hour of his departure.

"I do not need to warn you," he said. "You know all that may happen to you here. But one thing I must tell you, I will not endure any shame. Others may be indulgent—I cannot be!"

"I have not sunk so low as those ladies," said Anna, interrupting him. "I shall not betray you, because in so doing I should humiliate myself. Should you make my life yet more unendurable, I shall leave you openly."

Hoym said nothing further. He hesitated for a moment, but a rap was heard at the door. It was the King's messenger come to remind him of the hour of departure.

In the castle the occupants were watching for Hoym to cross the bridge. According to a pre-arranged plan, Countess Reuss was to invite Anna to her palace, there the King could journey incognito. Countess Vitzthum was immediately despatched to accomplish this mission secretly, but Anna refused. It was in vain that the Countess strove to prove to her that none would know of her visit; her sister-in-law guessed their plans, and told her so.

"You are too intelligent," laughed Countess Vitzthum, "for me to try to conceal the truth from you. It is possible that the King may wish to become better acquainted with you, and that knowing everything, he might call at Countess Reuss's castle. But what would you do should he, in order to satisfy his curiosity, call on you here? You could not shut the door on the King. Would it be more seemly for him to spend a few hours alone with you in your own home?"

"But the King would not do such a thing. He would not cast a shadow on my reputation!"

"Everything is possible for him to do. He is wearied and curious, and he cannot endure any resistance to his will. The women have taught him despotism by their submission. If you do not accept the Countess Reuss's invitation, the King will certainly come here."

"How do you know this?"

"I do not know anything," said the Countess Vitzthum, laughing, "but I know our lord perfectly. I remember a certain evening in my own life," she added, sighing.

Anna wrung her hands.

"Then it is necessary to be armed here, as on the road, against highway robbers! I will find a pistol and dagger!"

Countess Vitzthum endeavoured to soothe the irritated woman, and to turn everything into a laugh.

"You must know," said she, "that never in all his life has Augustus used force with any woman. That is not his nature. He is far too good-looking and too fascinating to have recourse to rough treatment."

After much conversation Anna finally decided to visit Countess Reuss that evening in company with her sister-in-law. With this joyful news Countess Vitzthum hastened to her friend, and Fürstenberg carried the tidings to the castle.

The King said that he would pay a short visit to Princess Teschen, and then on his way back he would send his carriage to the castle, and proceed in a litter, and incognito, to call on Countess Reuss.

Any other woman, who was unhappy with her husband, would have been only too glad to seize this opportunity of a splendid, although unstable career, with the certainty of acquiring riches, and the hope that perhaps a marriage would eventually cover the fault of a moment. But Anna, Countess Hoym, had been educated in strict principles; she felt indignant at the light-hearted conduct of those women, who consented to serve as playthings for their wearied lord. She realized the possibility of a divorce from Hoym, for she was disgusted with him, but she would not give up her husband save for love of the King, and for a marriage with him.

Such an idea would have excited the mirth of any one to whom she mentioned it. To wish to chain so frivolous a man as Augustus seemed an utter absurdity.

The King was handsome; he strove to please; the glamour of power and of the crown increased his charm; what wonder that Anna's heart yearned for him! Although she felt that she could be happy with him, she could not, even for a moment, admit the possibility of such happiness being realized in any way other than by marriage.

During the time that elapsed after the ball, amidst the pressure of the intrigues that were being carried on around her with the object of enabling Augustus to approach her, Anna was continually thinking and pondering. At length she said to herself,—

"I may be his, but I must be the Queen."

And she determined to resign everything rather than be the creature of intrigues. She felt that she was strong; the mirror assured her of her beauty and charm; she read in the King's eyes the impression she had made on him—she resolved to take advantage of it.

"I shall never degenerate," said she to herself. "I would rather be Hoym's unfortunate wife than Augustus's mistress. I must be his wife or nothing."

She had already resigned herself to her fate, the only question was as to the conditions. Yet none suspected that Countess Hoym had resolved to break with her husband, although they had calculated that circumstances might arise that would induce her to do so.

Anna had been indulging in dreams, and dreams are dangerous companions in solitude. Pride and the desire to rule had slowly risen within her soul, and made her ready to capitulate.

When the hour fixed for the visit arrived, Anna was ready. She had dressed herself with the greatest care, and her robe was both tasteful and modest. Her complexion did not require the aid of paint, it was snow-white by nature, and her luxuriant black curls did but the more increase the transparency of her skin. But these attractions were as nothing when compared with her eyes, so full of fire, and possessed of such a bewitching charm. A glance from those eyes could drive a man mad, and they said more than their owner would have cared to express with her lips.

Looking in the mirror, she found she was so beautiful that she smiled with satisfaction. Her dress was black enlivened with crimson ribbons, which made a most picturesque costume. The Countess Vitzthum, who came to fetch her, screamed with admiration on beholding her, so beautiful did she appear, and she for one would have felt no surprise had a crown been thrown at her feet.

"You say you wish to live with my brother," said she, "and yet you dress so beautifully to receive the King?"

"No woman would willingly make herself appear homely," replied Anna coldly.

"But you are quite a master in the art of dress, and need no advice. Well, let us be going."

The same kind of admiring exclamations greeted her on her arrival at Countess Reuss's house. At the ball, her beauty had surpassed all expectation, here it was dazzling. Even those ladies who had not given up being beautiful felt old and withered beside her. Although they knew that she was twenty-four, Anna did not appear to them to be more than eighteen.

No one felt more pleasure in her appearance than Countess Reuss, for she was now sure of the success of her plans. All crowded around Anna, rendering her homage as to a queen, and trying to gain her favour. Fürstenberg, who arrived a few moments before the King, was lost in amazement.

"I know the King," said he, "she will be able to do anything she likes with him if only she knows how to stand firm."

Anna was guided by instinct, and needed none to teach her.

After a few moments the door opened cautiously, and the King entered the room. While yet on the threshold his eyes were eagerly searching for Anna. Perceiving her, he blushed, then he turned pale, grew confused, and, forgetful of his hostess, he rushed forward to greet Countess Hoym. On his brow there was now no trace of regret for lost millions, anger at Polish ingratitude, shame at his defeat by the Swedes, or any sign of disappointment.

Anna welcomed him coolly, but her dress alone was sufficiently eloquent. That she wished to please him was evident, and this gave him hope.

Although Anna had made a great impression on him, the King was, nevertheless, very careful to observe all those forms of civility due to the fair sex, and although he hated the Countess Reuss, he sat beside her for a few moments, chatting courteously, yet all the while looking towards Countess Hoym. He whispered to Fraulein Hulchen, smiled at Countess Vitzthum, and gratified all the ladies by his glances. During this ceremony, Countess Vitzthum had time to lead her sister-in-law into an adjoining room under the pretence of having an interesting conversation with her. It was a strategical man[oe]uvre to enable the King to have a sweet tête-à-tête, for the moment Augustus appeared in the doorway, Countess Vitzthum retreated towards the drawing-room, and soon disappeared.

It is true that the door remained open, and the portière that was raised allowed the chattering ladies to gaze on His Majesty, but no one could hear a word of what the two were saying.

"Madame, today you are quite different to yesterday, and even more beautiful! You are bewitching!" he exclaimed, without any restraint.

"Your Majesty's indulgence is so well known, that it is difficult to believe these most flattering compliments," replied Anna.

"Do you wish me to swear it? I am ready to take an oath by all the gods of Olympus, that I have never seen such a beautiful woman. I am amazed at the cruelty of that destiny which has given such an angel into Hoym's hands."

In spite of herself, Anna laughed, and for the first time a row of pearl-like teeth appeared behind her coral lips. Her laughter made her yet more beautiful.

The King looked at her hands, they were so beautiful, that he was seized with a passionate desire to kiss them, and it was with difficulty that he abstained from pressing one of them to his lips. They were perfection. His head was beginning to be turned.

"Were I a tyrant," said he, "I should forbid Hoym ever to return hither, I am jealous of that Vulcan."

"Vulcan is likewise jealous," responded Anna.

"But Venus cannot love him!" said the King.

"Should love be wanting, there are other chains that bind yet stronger than those of love—the chains formed by oath and by duty."

The King smiled.

"An oath in love!"

"No, your Majesty, in marriage."

"But there are sacrilegious marriages," observed Augustus, "and I regard as such, those marriages in which beauty is united to ugliness. In such cases the gods give absolution for the broken oath."

"But pride will not suffer one to accept it."

"You are too severe, madame."

"More so than your Majesty supposes."

"Countess, you terrify me."

"Your Majesty?" Anna smiled. "Why should my lord care aught about severity?"

"More than you suppose," replied the King, repeating her own words.

"That I cannot understand," whispered Anna.

"What? Then you do not wish to see that I was conquered by your first glance."

"That will not last until day-break, I fancy. Your Majesty has this in common with the gods, that you love and forget easily."

"No," exclaimed the King, "believe me, those are calumnies. Is it my fault that I have never yet met with a heart, a mind, a beauty to which I was able to attach myself for ever? It is not I who am unfaithful, I am betrayed. Each day these goddesses lose some charm, miracles become ordinary phenomena, the angels lose their wings, and, instead of finding love in the heart, I discover only coquettishness and coldness. Am I the guilty one? Believe me, madame," he continued, with enthusiasm, "I am busy searching for a woman to whom I could belong all my life long. To such a woman I would give myself entirely."

"It is difficult to believe that," whispered Anna, "and it is still more difficult to imagine a perfection that would be worthy of your Majesty."

"I find it in you," interrupted the King. "You are bewitching," he added, stretching forth his hands to seize hers.

Anna wished to withdraw them, but etiquette did not allow of this, and, seizing her white hand, the King began to kiss it, and this he continued to do for so long, that at length Anna grew afraid that those in the drawing-room would see this familiar behaviour, and, with all due respect for His Majesty, slowly withdrew her hand.

Augustus rose full of emotion.

"I cannot separate myself from you," said he, "I see that I shall be obliged to summon the power of the King to aid my ardour, which does not appear to move you in the least. You cannot leave the city. I arrest you. As for Hoym, only your intercession—"

He did not finish his speech. Anna had no idea of interceding.

Their conversation would have lasted much longer, for Augustus was very excited, only Countess Reuss entered, to beg the King to partake of a collation of sweetmeats, fruits, and wine. The King consented, and drank the first glass of wine to Anna's health.

Fürstenberg watched him attentively.

"Teschen is lost!" whispered he to Countess Vitzthum.

"And my brother likewise!" replied she, also in a whisper. "Provided only that my sister-in-law has sense!"

"I wish she had not so much," rejoined Fürstenberg. "Look what self-possession she has preserved, the King did not succeed in turning her head, but it seems to me that he has lost his own."

The collation ended, the ladies again withdrew, and Augustus endeavoured to detain Anna by entering into a clever conversation. She remained, was animated and witty, but both the King and Fürstenberg remarked that she still retained her self-possession, and was not in the least intoxicated by her splendid triumph. It was the first time in his life that Augustus had met such a woman. She did not immediately succumb to his love as the others had done, neither did she appear to take any advantage of it.

It stung him to the quick.

This woman's calmness began to irritate him, but at the same time it increased his passion.

At first he had only intended to carry on a short intrigue with Countess Hoym, but he now saw that this would be more difficult than he had thought or calculated.

Anna laughed, jested, and was very amusing; she was evidently trying to entangle the King, but she herself remained calm and inaccessible. Instead of approaching his object, with the good fortune of Jupiter, Augustus perceived that he was drifting away from it.

At the close of the conversation, when the King became more pressing, and no longer concealed his ardour, he begged for a small place in the heart of the beautiful lady. Anna, who had already grown familiar with him, replied with precision,—

"Your Majesty forces me to make an unpleasant avowal. I am one of those unfortunate, feeble creatures, whose pride is their only strength. If your Majesty imagines that, dazzled by the allurements held out to me, I shall forget the respect due to myself, or that, carried away by a momentary madness, I shall forget the future, your Majesty is mistaken. Anna Hoym will never become the King's temporary favourite. She will give her whole heart, and for ever, or nothing."

Having said this, she rose and passed into the drawing-room.

Immediately after this, the King, accompanied by Fürstenberg, quietly left Countess Reuss's house. The Countess followed him to the hall, Augustus's face was gloomy and sad. From this, his hostess guessed how Anna had treated the King, but she was glad of it, for their relations promised to be the more lasting in proportion to the difficulty of the commencement. A short love intrigue, that did not overthrow the Princess Teschen, would not accord with her plans, for through Anna she expected that her own influence would be more firmly established.

"Dear Countess," whispered the King, as he bade her farewell, "try to animate that beautiful statue."

Before Countess Reuss could reply, the King had descended the stairs. The conversation that ensued between him and such an intimate friend as Fürstenberg was different.

"The woman is enchanting," said the King, "but at the same time she repels, and is cold as an icicle."

"Your Majesty, women are of different temperaments; it is no wonder that she protects herself."

"But she speaks frankly about marriage."

"Every woman thinks that love for her must be everlasting, and one can promise that to every one."

"It will not be done very easily with this one," added Augustus, "Teschen was much easier."

"But there is no comparison between them."

"Alas! that is only too true. She is far superior to Teschen. Send Hoym an order that he is not to dare to return."

"But what is he to do there?" laughed the Prince.

"Let him do what he pleases," said the King. "Before all things, he must collect as much money as possible, for it seems to me that my new love will be very costly."

"Your Majesty, then, is already talking of love?"

"And of fear, too! Fürstchen, you can do what you please, but she must be mine."

"And Ursula?"

"Marry her!"

"Thanks."

"Then marry her to any one else you please; all is over between us."

"Already?" inquired the Prince, with scarcely concealed joy.

"Yes! I shall gild Hoym, her, and you."

"But from whence shall we obtain so much gold?"

"That concerns Hoym," replied the King.

They entered the palace as he spoke, and Augustus went directly to his chamber. He was sad and thoughtful. The last campaign, disastrous as it was, had not caused him so much sorrow as the ill-success of this evening.

Thus began the reign of one woman at the Court of Augustus II., and it lasted longer than any other of the same kind.

The Court, and indeed the whole city, watched with great interest the course of this intrigue, the end of which could be easily guessed.

Hoym was forbidden to return. Every day the Countesses Reuss and Vitzthum, assisted by the Prince, invented some new pretext for bringing the King and the beautiful Anna together; every day she was bolder and more familiar with him, but since the evening spent at Countess Reuss's house, Augustus had made no further advances, neither had he heard from her anything different from what she had then said. The beautiful Anna showed no signs of yielding, and at length her coolness and self-possession began to alarm every one. They feared the King would be discouraged, and retire, and that then some one else would be suggested to him. Every time they attempted to question Countess Hoym, she replied that she would become a wife, but never a mistress. She demanded, if not an immediate marriage, to which there was an obstacle in the person of Queen Christine Eberhardyne, at least a solemn promise from the King that he would marry her, in the event of his becoming a widower.

The condition was most strange and unusual; in other times, or in other courts, or amongst a less light-headed people, it would have been impossible. The first time Fürstenberg mentioned it to the King, Augustus did not reply. A few hours later, he said,—

"I am already weary of this long courtship, we must end it once and for ever."

"Break it?" inquired the Prince.

"We shall see," replied the King briefly.

His confidant could learn nothing farther.

One day the King ordered a hundred thousand gold thalers to be brought him from the treasury. The bag was enormous, and two strong men could scarcely carry it. When they had deposited their heavy burden, the King seized it, and lifted it without the slightest difficulty. Fürstenberg, who was present, did not dare ask for what purpose such an amount was destined, the King's face was far too gloomy. It was clear that events of considerable importance were at hand. The King was silent. He visited Princess Teschen almost daily. That Princess almost drowned herself in tears when the name of Countess Hoym was mentioned in her presence, but she quickly dried them when she perceived the King. In this state of uncertainty several weeks passed away—a time that seemed to the courtiers all too long. They knew not to whom they should bow, nor to whom they should go with gossip. At length Hoym was not only permitted, but even commanded to return, for the treasury was empty, and he alone could fill it.

The day the Secretary to the Treasury was expected to return, Augustus, having placed the bag containing the hundred thousand thalers in his carriage, gave orders that he should be driven to Hoym's palace.

It was towards evening, and foggy. Countess Hoym was sitting solitary and thoughtful in her boudoir. Being unaccustomed to receive visitors, she was greatly surprised at hearing the voices of men conversing on the stairs, and her astonishment increased when, without any warning, the door opened and the King entered the room.

The door was immediately closed behind him. Anna was terrified, and seized the pistol which, ever since her arrival in Dresden, she had kept lying on the table. She had frequently been joked with about this precaution. Although she concealed the weapon in the folds of her dress, the King had noticed her action.

"You do not need to defend yourself," said he.

Anna stared at him, but was incapable of uttering a word.

"Listen," continued Augustus, throwing the bag of gold on the floor with such violence that the ducats were scattered. "I can give you gold, honours, and titles in abundance."

Then, taking a horse-shoe he had brought with him, he broke it, and cast the fragments on the piles of gold.

"But," he added, "I can also break resistance as I have just broken that iron. You have to choose between iron and gold, peace and war, love and hatred."

Anna stood looking with indifference on the gold and the broken horse-shoe.

"Your Majesty," said she, after a moment's silence, "I do not fear death, I do not wish for gold. You can break me as you broke that horse-shoe, but you cannot do anything against my will. Why do you not bring me the thing that can conquer me? Why do you not offer me your heart?"

Augustus rushed towards her.

"That has been yours for a long time," he exclaimed.

"I neither see it, nor feel it," said the Countess slowly. "The heart is shown in deeds. A heart that loves truly would never wish to dishonour the object of its love. My Lord, I cannot conceal from you that I love you. I could not resist your love, but I cannot stain it!"

The King knelt before her, but Anna retreated.

"Your Majesty, listen to me, I pray you."

"Command me!"

"Anna Hoym could never be yours except she felt she were worthy of you."

"What are your conditions?"

"A written promise that you will marry me."

Hearing this, Augustus frowned, and drooped his head.

"Believe me, Anna, such a condition is full of danger for yourself."

"I will not give it up. I would give my life for it. My honour requires it. Then I should be your Majesty's wife, in thought and in hope. Else you shall not touch me; I will kill myself if you do!"

The King retreated.

"Very well, then," said he, "if that is your wish, shall have it."

Anna gave a cry of joy.

"All the rest is as nothing in comparison with that!" she exclaimed in a voice full of happiness. "But first I must be divorced from Hoym."

"That shall be done tomorrow. I will have it signed in the consistory," said the King hastily. "Now, what further?"

"Nothing more on my side," she replied in a broken voice, as she knelt before the King. "That is sufficient for me."

"But it is not sufficient for the King, for me," said Augustus, seizing her in his arms, from which, however, Anna escaped by slipping down on the floor.

"I believe your Majesty's word," she exclaimed; "but before I permit myself to be touched, the chains that bind me must be broken, the divorce must be pronounced, your promise signed. I am Hoym's wife, I have sworn to be faithful to him—I must keep my oath."

Augustus kissed her hand.

"I am your slave, you are my lady! Hoym returns today, leave him; tomorrow I will have a palace ready for you. You shall have a hundred thousand thalers a year, I will lay my whole kingdom at your feet, and with it, myself."

Seeing him kneeling at her feet, Anna kissed his forehead, then she sprang backwards.

"Until tomorrow!" she said.

"Am I to leave you?" inquired Augustus.

"Until tomorrow," she repeated.

Then the King rose and left her. The heaps of gold remained lying on the floor.

That same night Count Hoym returned home. He hastened to his wife's apartment, but found the door locked, and, on inquiring of the servants, was informed that their lady was unwell and had retired to rest, after giving orders that no one should disturb her.

During his absence, which was of an unnecessary length, the Count had grown seriously uneasy about his wife. It was true that his spies wrote to him daily, informing him of her every movement, but as she was always accompanied by his sister, he could not foresee any danger. He felt, however, that the intrigue was growing ever stronger and stronger, and that it threatened his matrimonial life. Still he was powerless to prevent it, for at its head was the King, and him Hoym feared, for he knew him better than any one else did. Besides, he could not forget the fate that had overtaken Beichling. The best guarantee of safety that he had, lay in his wife's character, her pride, and her love for her good reputation.

When he returned to Dresden, he knew nothing but what his spies had informed him; in the city, and from the people of the court, he could not expect to learn anything.

The hour was late, but although at the King's castle a feast was in progress, Hoym had no wish to go thither; instead, he went straight to his own home, and having found his wife's door locked, he also retired to rest.

The following day the King sent for him, and he was obliged to obey the summons, and go to the castle without having seen his wife.

The King received him very kindly, he even embraced him, and this Hoym regarded as the worst possible sign. Next Augustus reproached him with having remained away so long, and although he himself had commanded that the Count should not return, he acted as though he knew nothing of the order.

Hoym gazed into the King's eyes in astonishment.

"It is evident that you have some enemies at court," said the King. "They wished to keep you away from me, but fear nothing, I am your friend, I will not allow you to be wronged."

Hoym thanked the King for his favour. Then, during their further conversation, His Majesty complained that he had not sufficient money.

"Dear Hoym," said he, "you must procure it, I need it so very badly."

It was towards noon when Hoym at length returned to his home. He had scarcely crossed the threshold of his room, than Anna, dressed in black, appeared before him. Never before had she looked more beautiful, calm, and dignified.

Hoym sprang towards her, but she received him coldly, and kept him at a distance.

"I have been waiting for you," she said. "I have come to thank you for every good thing you have done for me, and to assure you that I shall never forget it. But at the same time, I have to tell you that our marriage, which is not based on mutual sympathy, and therefore cannot give us any guarantee of happiness, must come to an end. We must be separated. You know I always speak frankly. The King has been good enough to assure me of his favour—I cannot refuse it. Moreover, I love him, and am determined to obey him. But I cannot be false to you. I am come, therefore, to ask you for a divorce; this will save the honour of your name. We cannot act otherwise. Should you consent to a divorce, you may rest assured of my gratitude; I will also endeavour to assist you in everything. Should you, on the contrary, prefer to resist my wish, it will not in anywise alter my determination, but it will cause me to forget my gratitude towards you, and to remember you only as a hindrance to my happiness."

From the first words of his wife's artful and formal speech, Hoym had guessed everything. He drew back as though struck by a thunderbolt. He had not suspected that matters had gone so far as that. His pale face became crimson. Several times he would have interrupted her, but the magnetic gaze that Anna fixed upon him kept him silent until her speech was ended. The indifference and self-possession with which she spoke filled Hoym with indignation.

By the time she had finished speaking, his anger was so great that he was unable to utter a word.

"Madam," shouted he at length, "you reward me nicely for having drawn you from your obscure corner. You will leave home and husband to depend on the favour of a most frivolous man."

But Anna did not allow him to proceed with his speech.

"Enough of this!" she exclaimed. "I know all that you are going to say; I know also what I intend doing. The care for my future fate you can leave to me. Nothing will alter my determination. I only ask you to choose and tell me whether, or no, you will consent to the divorce. Are we to be friends or enemies? Yes or no?"

Hoym was one of the most licentious of the courtiers; his relations with his wife were of the worst, but the moment he realized that he was to lose her for ever, grief, jealousy, and anger overwhelmed him to such a degree that he was unable to speak.

As was his custom when enraged, he began to tear his wig, and rush to and fro across the room, overthrowing the chairs as he went. He clenched his hands, stood for a few moments at a window, gazing into the street beneath, then he rushed threateningly towards his wife, and vainly endeavoured to speak. Then again he hurried from her. In short, he looked just like a madman who does not know what he is doing.

But all this outburst of fury made not the least impression on Anna. She only waited quietly, looking at him ironically. At length, being unable to obtain an answer, she said, coldly,—

"I see you cannot decide between peace and war. I would only remind you that war with me and the King would be a trifle dangerous."

She left the room as she spoke.

Hoym still continued his mad rushes to and fro.

He tore his clothes, he sat down, rose again, and gave way to every possible action of despair. And in this he continued until he was interrupted by the entrance of Vitzthum.

"Hoym!" exclaimed his visitor, "what is the matter?"

"You know that better than I do. It is you, my dearest friends, who have prepared this surprise for me. Anna leaves me! The King requires her! Why did she ever marry me? Why does she wish to make me the laughing-stock of the people?"

Vitzthum let him have his storm out, then he spoke.

"Listen, Hoym," said he. "I can understand that you would regret parting with the beautiful Anna, but you know well that she never loved you, and you led her such a life, that I doubt if you really loved her. Thus, then, there can be no question of love in the matter. Let us now talk calmly; I have come here by the King's command."

"And what, pray, does His Majesty command?" inquired Hoym sarcastically.

"He wishes your consent to the divorce, in return for which he promises you his favour," replied Vitzthum. "If you do not consent, I pity you, my dear fellow, but I must warn you that you expose yourself to great danger. You cannot fight against the King. The slightest wrong done to the Countess will be regarded as lèse majestatis."

"But why do you wish for my consent?" exclaimed Hoym. "The King can do anything he chooses without that. The Consistory will obey him. Let him take from me my most precious possession, but he must not ask me to thank him for so doing."

Vitzthum smiled.

"It is a proof of his favour, that he asks your permission to do a thing which he can as easily do without it. From this you should see that he desires to retain you in your present position."

"Only because he has need of me," muttered Hoym.

Vitzthum sat down on the sofa.

"Dear Count, think it well over; when I leave the room it will be too late."

Again Hoym rushed wildly about the room, overthrowing everything that came in his way. At length, throwing himself down on a chair, he began to laugh; but it was a laugh full of bitterness.

"Hoym, the King is awaiting your decision," said Vitzthum.

"It is mere irony to ask a man whom you have stripped of his clothes, for permission to keep them, and threaten him with a club should he refuse. Therefore, my dear brother-in-law, you will tell His Majesty that I am very grateful to him for taking the burden of that woman from me. Tell him I consent, that I am glad, happy, merry, that I kiss His Majesty's hand. It is a great honour to be able to offer the King a half-eaten fruit—ha! ha! ha!"

"You had better drink a glass of iced-water," said Vitzthum, taking his hat.

He shook hands with Hoym.

"Believe me," said he, in a whisper, "you have come out of this better than any of the others. I will tell the King you consent. You will cool off after a time."

The King was eagerly awaiting the answer, but, being impatient, he had ordered that he should be carried to Hoym's palace, where he entered Anna's apartments. Just as Vitzthum was preparing to go to the castle, he was informed that the King was waiting for him, only a few paces away. From his countenance, and the smile with which he entered His Majesty's presence, Augustus guessed immediately that Hoym would not oppose his wishes. But the beautiful Anna, addressing the ambassador, said,—

"You were more fortunate than I was."

"No one could be more fortunate than you are," replied Vitzthum, bowing, "but I was more patient. I allowed Hoym to work off his excitement, after that he consented."

The light of joy shone in Anna's black eyes.

"You bring me freedom and happiness!" she cried. "How can I ever repay you?"

A box lay on the table; this she seized and handed it to Vitzthum.

The King at once approached to see what it contained. In it was Anna's miniature.

"Ah!" exclaimed he, "that is too great a reward for you, Vitzthum. I confiscate it in the name of the King, and in exchange I will give you twenty thousand thalers."

Anna threw herself on the King's breast.

The day following, the Consistory granted the divorce, and on the third day this was, by Anna's wish, placarded on all the public buildings.

The same day, Anna left her husband's house and took up her abode in a mansion situated close to the palace, to which it was joined by means of a covered gallery, which had been constructed in a few hours.

The news spread like wild-fire throughout the city.

Countess Hoym had abandoned her husband's name, and had taken the title of Cosel, from an estate that Augustus had presented to her. He also intended to obtain the title of Countess for her from the Emperor Joseph, and, instead of the house she now occupied, she was to have a palace built for her similar to that described in the Arabian Nights.

Never for a long time had any of his favourites taken such a hold on the King's mind, heart, and passion. He passed whole days in her company, and was invisible to every one—indeed the whole world was forgotten by him.

Princess Teschen, towards whom, up to the last moment, the King had shown great tenderness, was the first to learn what had occurred. The divorce, the lodging near the castle, were sure proofs that her reign was ended. The King ceased visiting her, yet she still retained her liberty, and did not fall into disgrace.

Augustus was obliged to treat her kindly through fear of the Cardinal Radziejewski, over whom the Princess had considerable influence, for that prelate could cause the King considerable annoyance. The spies employed by Vitzthum could gain no information as to how the Princess intended to act. They tried to discover her secrets through her sister, Baroness Glasenapp, but the Princess was silent, and spent her time weeping. No one knew whether she was going to remain in Dresden, to retire to her estates of Hoyerswerde, or to return to Poland. In her palace no preparations for departure were visible, all remained the same as it had ever been, except that the visitors were less numerous. Those servants who still remained faithful to the Princess were suspected of spying, therefore every one was silent, and evenings were sad.

Prince Ludwig of Würtemburg alone visited her more frequently and stayed longer.

The court intrigues that had been directed towards the overthrow of Princess Teschen and the instalment in her place of Lady Cosel were, after the latter's victory, turned in another direction.

Fürstenberg, who, at the commencement of the intrigue, had been employed by the King as his intermediary, was now compelled to yield his place to Vitzthum. The rivalry of these two parties began in the court of Augustus II., who always took the greatest possible care to prevent the persons surrounding him from living peaceably together. He excited one against another, favouring now this person, now that, and giving each to understand that the other was his enemy. The mere sight of angry faces gave him great pleasure. In consequence of his mischief-making, one of his courtiers accused the other, and thus the King was made aware of all abuses.

Vitzthum was Hoym's brother-in-law. His family came from Thuringia, but for a long time it had been employed in the service of the Kings of Saxony. Grand Falconer Count Frederyk Vitzthum von Eckstadt was now about thirty; he had been at court from the time he was a page, and had been Augustus' friend since childhood. He always travelled with him, and after the downfall of the great Chancellor, Beichling, in 1703, he had obtained for himself the rank of Grand Falconer.

The King was fonder of Vitzthum than of the others, perhaps because he was not afraid of him. Vitzthum was not a genius; and then, too, he was always affable, polite, serviceable, a perfect courtier, and a very good-looking man. He mingled in no intrigues, he had no ambition, and he served the King faithfully.

Besides and behind Vitzthum, stood his wife, Hoym's sister, one of the cleverest intriguantes of the court, at which the women played almost as important a part as the men. Countess Vitzthum was still very pretty. She was tall, as were the majority of the ladies of the Saxon aristocracy. She had a fresh complexion, sapphire-blue eyes, a nose slightly retroussé, and she was so merry that she could be recognized from afar by her laugh. She played with the affairs of the court as one plays some game; she spied for the sake of spying, she listened at doors, carried gossip, set snares, kindled passions, excited quarrels, reconciled enemies; and besides all this, she managed her house and her husband's affairs admirably; without her, money would often have been lacking. Like her husband, she had a passion for gambling, but she gambled carefully and had good luck. She acquired estates, and pushed her husband, for whom, as he had no ambition, she was forced to be ambitious.

The Vitzthums did not belong to the most powerful party among the King's favourites; apparently they stood aside and lower in the scale than Flemming, Fürstenberg, Plug, and others, yet notwithstanding this, they were acquainted with every secret, influenced the King as well as the courtiers, and could be very dangerous foes. At the commencement of Cosel's reign, they took up a position that led her to suppose that they would share her likes and dislikes.

A few days after Cosel had taken possession of the house near the castle, the whole court felt that the new Queen would not be so weak, so inclined to weep and faint, as Princess Teschen had been. New life animated every one. The proud and beauteous lady considered herself as the King's second wife, and acted accordingly.

Augustus himself was only her most obedient admirer.

The court of Augustus II was not lacking in droll and original figures, whose business it was to amuse the King.

Every morning from the Old City there came on horseback Joseph Frölich, the fool, known to every one, from the street urchins to the ministers of state. Once, when Augustus had been in a very good humour, he had even ordered a medal to be struck in his honour, bearing this inscription: *Semper Frölich, nunquam Traurig*. Frölich was so accustomed to laugh as a matter of duty that he made others laugh and laughed himself from morning till night.

Frölich was small, round, and pink, and always dressed in a swallow-tail coat, of which, thanks to the munificence of the King, he had ninety-nine. He wore a tall, pointed hat, ornamented with a feather. Instead of a chamberlain's key, he carried a large silver vase on his back similar in form to a key, but as this was hollow it served as a drinking-cup, and from it Frölich was obliged to drink whenever the King ordered him to be present at his drinking parties.

As a fool, he would perhaps have wearied the King by his monotonous gaiety had he not had such a contrast in the melancholy rôle played by Baron Schmeidel. Schmeidel and Frölich, as Heraclites and Democritus, continually quarrelling, amused both Augustus and his court. When these two were exhausted, there were secondary fools, Saumagen and Leppert, to replace them. If to these we add the giant, Cojanus; twelve dwarfs, with the famous Hante and Traum at their head; and a fair number of negroes and albinos, we shall have some idea of the crowd whose sole duty it was to amuse their sovereign.

Frölich, the fool, was an intelligent and not a bad man. He lived quietly and saved his money, and very likely laughed in his sleeve at those who laughed at him. Every morning Frölich, dressed in his curious coat and hat, rode to the castle, from whence he returned, frequently very late at night, to his own house, called Narrenhaus, which was situated close to the bridge. It was very seldom that any one called on him, therefore Fraulein Lote, his elderly housekeeper, was greatly astonished when, very early one morning, she heard a knock at the door.

The fool was not yet dressed, neither was his horse ready, and the knock frightened him, for he feared that some capricious fancy had seized the King and induced him to send after him. Fraulein Lote was of the same opinion when, on peeping through the window, she perceived a tall young man in the court livery standing on the threshold.

After having glanced at him, Lote inquired what he wanted.

"I should like to say a few words to Frölich," said the new-comer.

"Is it from the King?"

There was no answer; but as secret messengers were by no means un-common, Lote did not dare to refuse him admittance, so, opening the door, she ushered him into the room where the fool was dressing. Frölich turned towards the stranger as he entered, and, immediately assuming his rôle, saluted him with exaggerated politeness, and, bending half-double, inquired,—

"What can we do for your Excellency?"

"Mr. Frölich," said the stranger modestly, "do not joke at a poor man; you may rather be excellency than me."

"What?" said Frölich, "I before you? Was it the King that sent you with such a joke?"

"No; I am come on my own account, and I beg you for a moment's conversation."

"An audience, eh?" said the fool, looking important. "Donnerwetter! Have I become a minister? But at our Court everything is possible. The ministers like each other so well that soon none of them will remain. Then your turn and mine will come; only I must be the Secretary to the Treasury."

Heedless of this buffoonery, the new-comer remained sorrowful.

"Well, I will grant you a moment's conversation," continued the fool, seating himself in an arm-chair and taking the pose of a person of great importance. Yet still the stranger did not smile.

"Mr. Frölich," said he, "you will be surprised when you learn that I come to you on a very serious matter."

"Then you have not entered the proper door."

"You are mistaken. I see you every day at Court, and I know from your face that you are a very good-hearted man."

"My dear man, I am sure you wish to borrow some money," interrupted the fool, "but I must tell you at once that it is useless. I give everything—advice, smiles, bows, but not money! I haven't any; the King has no money, so how could I get any?"

"I did not dream of asking you for money."

"Ah!" breathed the fool, "then what the deuce do you want from me?"

"I want to ask your protection."

"The idea! The protection of a fool! I see you wear the Court livery, but you have a foreign accent. Who are you?"

"I am a Pole; my name is Raymond Zaklika."

"A Pole, then a nobleman, that's understood," said the fool; "be seated, I respect the nobility, and as I am a burgher, I shall stand."

"Don't joke, Mr. Frölich!"

"I should swallow my own tongue, if I didn't joke. But we have not much time, so tell me what you want."

For a few moments the youth was unable to speak; the good humour of the fool evidently disconcerted him.

"Permit me first to tell you a little about myself," said he at length.

"Only a little? willingly."

"I came to the Court by a mere chance. I am sure you must have heard of me. Unfortunately for me, I can break horseshoes and cups as well as the King does. For that I have been ordered to remain at the Court."

"I remember now," laughed the fool, "and I do not envy you in the least. Who was so simple as to advise you to rival the King?"

"Since I have been at the Court the life there has disgusted me; every one avoids me; I haven't a friend, a protector; I have no one!"

"But to wish to choose me as a friend and protector, is as good an idea as the breaking the horseshoes was. Man, if I could break anvils, I would not break a straw, for fear of exciting the jealousy of others; I should not like to be in your place."

"That is why I thought that at least Frölich would pity me."

The old fool's eyes dilated, then suddenly his face grew stern and sad, and he folded his arms across his breast: then, advancing towards Zaklika, he took hold of his hand, and began to feel his pulse, as though he had been a doctor.

"I am afraid you have lost your common sense," said he quietly.

"I shouldn't be surprised," said the youth, smiling.

The fool's face brightened again, as though from habit.

"What is the matter in question?" he inquired.

"I wish to get discharged from the King's service."

"That's very easily done," said the fool. "Do some stupid thing, then they will build a scaffold in the new market, and you will be hanged."

"There's plenty of time for that," replied Zaklika.

"What do you propose doing, should they discharge you? Are you going to return to your own country, and wrestle with the bear?"

"No, I shall remain at Dresden."

"Are you in love with a pretty girl?"

The youth blushed.

"No," replied he, "I shall give fencing and riding lessons, or I might enter the military service."

"Do they not give you enough to eat at the Court?"

"We have plenty."

"Do they not pay you?"

"They do."

"Then why don't you like your position?"

The youth looked confused.

"I have nothing to do," said he, "and it worries me.

"It's strange!" said the fool, "you have plenty of bread, and you are searching for misery. But I don't see how I could be useful to you."

"Very easily. I very frequently stand by the door; by some witty saying you could draw the King's attention towards me, and when he is in a good humour he has different fancies."

"Suppose he has a fancy to shoot you?"

"You would protect me."

"*Donnerwetter!*" exclaimed the fool, "for the first time in my life I see that I am a man of importance, for people come to ask me for protection. You have opened my eyes. Out of pure gratitude I should like to do something for you! Who knows! They say that Kyan is to be appointed commandant of Königstein, then I could at least become Court preacher! I grow ambitious!"

And having seated himself again in an arm-chair, he began to laugh, at the same time looking pityingly on the young man.

"The end of the world! *Donnerwetter!* A Polish noble asks a fool for protection, and the Swedes, who eat herrings, beat the Saxons."

The fool saluted, in the fashion of a minister closing an interview. Zaklika took the hint, and left the room.

It was a strange idea to seek help from a fool, but his strong love for Countess Hoym had put it into his head. He wished to enter the service of the woman, to look at whom was his greatest bliss. He desired nothing further than to look at his goddess. He never dreamt of anything else. He wished to be her guard, her unknown defender; he guessed that she must have many enemies, he feared for her safety, and he longed to lay down his life in her service. The youth had a strange disposition; although apparently slow, he had an iron will. He had determined to gain a place nearer that lovely woman, and it was for her sake that he had gone to ask protection of the fool, and for her sake he was ready to bear still greater humiliation.

Cosel, intoxicated by her love for the beautiful Augustus, had not forgotten the boy who, when she was at Laubegast, used to stand up to his neck in the water in order to catch a glimpse of her. She smiled at the reminiscence, about which she had never said a word to any one. He excited her curiosity, that was all, and she frequently looked after him as he stood among the crowd.

Augustus' love for the beautiful Lady Cosel did not cause him to give up drinking with his friends. For many reasons this became more necessary to him. Amidst his drunken courtiers he could sow discord, which he used as a tool to support his own power.

That day was a day of revelry in the castle. Augustus was in an excellent humour, and was planning how he might best surround his favourite with entertainments, magnificence, and luxury.

Hoym, who still retained his position as Secretary to the Treasury, and whose tears for the loss of his wife the King had dried by a present of fifty thousand thalers, was again among those who came to drink with the King. Hoym was more necessary to Augustus than any of the others, for money was necessary to him, and the secretary knew how to provide it.

But the most clever methods of obtaining it had been almost exhausted, and now they would be obliged to employ some extraordinary means by which they might obtain the required gold. Augustus, like many of the rulers of his day, believed in alchemy. They did not doubt but that there existed some marvellous mixture which could change any metal into the gold that was so necessary to happiness.

At times no other subject was mentioned at Court than how gold could be made. Every one had a laboratory. Chancellor Beichling would not have been sent to Königstein had not Fürstenberg persuaded the King that he could find a man capable of making gold, and much more gold than Beichling could squeeze out of the country.

The savant on whom Fürstenberg depended was a simple apothecary, by name Johan Friedrich Bottiger, born at Schleiz, in Saxony. He had been manufacturing a gold-making mixture in Berlin, and Frederick I. had wished to keep him for himself, but Bottiger succeeded in making his escape, and came to Saxony, where he received a warm welcome, and was shut up in a castle and ordered to make gold for King Augustus II.

Fürstenberg was working with him, and the King firmly believed that any day they might produce as much gold as they wanted.

They flattered Bottiger, they surrounded him with luxury, but they kept him securely guarded. Years passed by, and yet the apothecary had not been successful in making his mixture. They sent the King many things with which to make gold, but in every case it was necessary before using them to prepare oneself by prayer, and to have a pure heart. Augustus prayed, confessed, sat by the crucible, but he could not make gold. Fortunately a dog overturned the mercury sent by Bottiger, and they were obliged to use other, and so the ill-success of the work was attributed to the dog. Bottiger was kept in constant confinement in Fürstenberg's castle, and, despite all the comforts with which he was surrounded, he nearly went mad, but still he did not succeed in making gold. Bottiger used to give balls and dinners in his prison, and during the past few years had cost the King forty thousand thalers.

When Lady Cosel succeeded Princess Teschen the famous alchemist was confined in a tower in the castle, where he busied himself preparing prescriptions for making gold. Great was the expectation of the Court, and none doubted that Bottiger would succeed at last.

The evening of the day on which Zaklika sought the protection of the fool the King, accompanied by Vitzthum, Fürstenberg, and the Countesses Reuss and Vitzthum, supped with Lady Cosel.

After supper, Frölich, being called to entertain the company, imitated the alchemist, and brought in some dirt in a crucible. Such a joke caused Augustus to look gloomy. Cosel, who had heard something about Bottiger, began to inquire about him in a whisper. The King was unwilling to speak of the matter, but to please his favourite he told her all about the alchemist, what a valuable man he was, and how they always kept watch over him, lest he should escape.

"Your Majesty," said Frölich, "so long as he is not watched by a very strong man, the possibility is that he will escape. Your Majesty alone would be a proper guard for him, or a man equally strong—but such an one it would be impossible to find, did we search throughout the whole world."

"There you are mistaken," said Augustus; "I have at my Court a man as strong as myself."

"I have never heard of him."

It was in this way that Augustus was reminded of Zaklika.

"And what does this Hercules look like?" inquired Cosel.

"Summon him," commanded the King.

Poor Raymond, directly he entered the King's presence, made use of the opportunity to ask for his discharge, but Augustus shook his head.

"I cannot discharge you," said he, "for I have need of your services. I have a treasure which I intend to trust to your strength and honesty. From this moment you belong to the court of Madame Cosel; you will watch over her safety, and risk your life for her if necessary."

Zaklika could scarcely believe his ears; he blushed, and said nothing. Chance had served him better than the fool.

Madame Cosel was much surprised, and she also blushed, for she remembered her meetings with him at Laubegast. However, she was careful not to say a word about them, and so Zaklika obtained the position he had so coveted.

The reign of Countess Cosel (she had already obtained the title of Francis I.) promised to be a long one. Having obtained a written promise of marriage from the King, she considered herself a second Queen, and as such she acted. She was almost always in Augustus' company, and she was ready alike for a journey or for war. No peril caused her the least alarm.

Soon she knew his character, and was able to discern all the threads of intrigue. She kept him constantly entertained by her calmness of mind and unfailing gaiety; she ruled over him, and gained fresh influence over him every day.

It was soon clear to every one that Cosel was invincible. If the frivolous King forgot her for a few moments, she knew perfectly how to hasten out to meet him and within a few hours had regained her former influence over him. Her beauty seemed to increase rapidly. In vain did jealous women look for some change in her appearance, for some weariness in her manner, she bloomed continually, as though perpetual youth had been granted her.

The following year, the King ordered a palace to be built for her, near to the castle. This building was a masterpiece of art. It was called the Palace of the Four Seasons, for there were different apartments for the different seasons; cool rooms for summer, and bright, warm, and sunny ones for winter. The former were adorned with marble, the latter with tapestry. The most costly and valuable articles that Europe could supply in the way of furniture, trinkets, carpets, dresses, &c., were to be found here. The army could not be paid, but the palace was marvellous.

A splendid ball was given as a house-warming, and Countess Cosel, covered with diamonds, victorious, and looking like some beautiful goddess, leaned on the King's arm, whom, in secret, she called her husband. Frivolous Augustus, although not entirely faithful, yet loved Cosel best of all. She was indeed most bewitching, and foreigners who saw her at the zenith of her glory spoke of her with enthusiasm.

Cosel extended her influence, and made friends with great ability, but she could not overcome the jealousy and fear of those who had any reason to be afraid of her. In vain the clergy, scandalized at the King's open attachment to her, began to preach against beautiful Bathsheba, and one day Gerber, a famous preacher of those times, spoke against her so strongly that there was murmuring in church.

Throughout the whole day nothing was spoken of but Cosel Bathsheba. In the evening the King's favourite was informed of the attack that had been made on her by the preacher. Augustus, coming into her apartment, found her weeping.

"What is the matter, my beautiful goddess?" he exclaimed, seizing her hands.

"Your Majesty, I beseech you for justice," she replied, sobbing. "You say that you love me, then protect me from public insult."

"What is the matter?" asked the King uneasily.

"I ask for the punishment of Gerber! An example must be made of this arrogant priest, who does not even respect the crown. Gerber said I was Bathsheba."

Augustus smiled.

"I am not Bathsheba, I have no wish to be her! I am your wife, my lord! You must punish him," cried Anna, kneeling before him.

But Augustus only answered kindly,—

"A priest can say anything he likes once a week, and I can do nothing to prevent him. Did he pronounce a single word outside the church, I would punish him. The church shelters him."

Gerber was not punished, but he made no further mention of Bathsheba.

During those most disastrous years that followed, the King's love increased. The wild Charles XII., a severe and merciless soldier, with hair cut short, and wearing enormous boots that reached higher than his knees, persecuted the King covered in velvet and lace, who skirmished against him clad in golden armour.

Many marvels were told about him. Augustus listened, and was silent. The Saxon Army was defeated. Despite the exertions of Flemming, Prebendowski, and Dombski, the prestige of the most magnificent monarch in Europe was diminishing in Poland. Countess Königsmark, a former favourite, sent over a secret mission, but could accomplish nothing. Charles

XII. had no desire to speak either with her or with any one else. Good fortune abandoned Augustus II. Bottiger could not make gold, Hoym was unable to supply it, and Cosel wanted millions. The people, not wishing to serve in the army, ran away and hid themselves in the mountains, whilst the preachers vehemently denounced the robbery of the country.

The nobility, although very respectful, resisted paying such heavy taxes.

The King was frequently in a very bad humour, but it never lasted long, for Cosel smiled and her lord's face brightened. Countess Cosel had no allies, but she did not want them, she felt she was stronger than them all. The courtiers were frightened.

Vitzthum alone still enjoyed the favours of the King and his favourite, for he cared not for politics, and loved Augustus like a brother.

The years passed one after the other, full of various incidents. Fortune was not yet tired of persecuting this most magnificent of monarchs. The Swedes were victorious, and threatened to drive him from his throne. Augustus resisted as best he could, grieved, and endeavoured to counterbalance adversity by indulging in merry-making.

But hunting parties, banquets, balls, masquerades, and theatres, all were suddenly interrupted by the news that the Swedes had invaded Saxony. Charles XII. had pursued the enemy into his own country. Fear seized on every one.

After the defeat at Frauenstadt isolated groups of deserters returned, and these were captured and hanged, or shot down, for not having done their duty. On September 1st Charles XII. invaded Saxony at the head of twenty thousand men. It was impossible to fight against them, so they were obliged to feed them. Augustus' small army escaped to Würzburgh. Dresden, Sizendorf, Königstein, and Sonnenstein had garrisons.

With Charles XII. came the new King of Poland, Stanislaus Leszczynski. Dresden was deserted. The Queen went to her family at Bayreuth, her mother went to Magdeburg, and then to Denmark.

Augustus was obliged to resign the crown of Poland in favour of Stanislaus Leszczynski, and in 1706 a treaty was signed at Altranstadt, but the Swedes did not leave Saxony.

During the war, and all the bloody horrors that accompanied it, Augustus remained still the same; love played the most important part in his life. He lost kingdoms, but he conquered hearts. He still loved the Countess Cosel, but whenever he was absent from her, he led a life of dissipation. Now, more than ever, he required distraction, and his courtiers, who wished to get rid of Cosel, did everything they could to displace her in his affections.

Fürstenberg, Countess Reuss, and the whole clique of her enemies, disappointed in their ambitions, did their best to procure her downfall. But, confident in her beauty, Cosel cared nothing for their efforts. She only smiled at their vain attempts. Her relations with the King were by this time further strengthened by the birth of a daughter. The proud woman persuaded herself that Augustus could not find another like her; she alone was capable of participating in his pleasures, and, besides, she was afraid of neither firing, mad riding, nor campaigning.

Yet, while she was with him in Warsaw, the King betrayed her with the daughter of a French wine merchant. Having learnt what had occurred, Anna threatened the King that she would shoot him, but Augustus only laughed, kissed her hands, and obtained forgiveness. In truth, despite his side wooings, the King loved Anna best, she alone was able to amuse him, and he was happiest when with her.

The war, the devastation of the country, the loss of the Polish crown, did not diminish any portion of Cosel's luxury. Amidst all these calamities the King played the rôle of demi-god with a serene countenance. From the clatter of arms, Augustus, after having signed a shameful treaty, returned to Dresden, and the carriage had scarcely stopped in the courtyard of the castle, when he sprang out and rushed to Cosel's apartment.

At the door of her room he found the faithful Zaklika, leaning against a chair, plunged in deep thought. Seeing the King, Raymond sprang to his feet, and stopped him.

"Your Majesty, the Countess is ill; she expects to be delivered."

The King pushed him aside and entered.

There was silence in all the rooms. At the door of the chamber Augustus heard the sound of a baby crying. Cosel, white as marble, exhausted by suffering, and unable to utter a word, stretched forth both her hands and pointed towards the infant. The King took it in his arms, and kissed it. Then he sat down beside the bed, and covered his face with his hands.

"Anna," said he, "the world will look on me with contempt, and will cease to love me. Good fortune has deserted Augustus; I am conquered, defeated!"

"Augustus," said Anna, sobbing, "I shall love you more than ever, now you are unhappy."

"I need such a consolation," rejoined the King gloomily. "My enemies pursue me, my allies are helpless. Every one bows to the victors. I am indeed most miserable."

Thus an hour passed; the sick woman needed rest. The King left her, and was speedily surrounded by generals and ministers, Flemming, Fürstenberg, Plug, Hoym, and others, who all rushed to him, terrified at the calamities that had fallen upon Saxony. They all looked at him, searching for traces of grief. But egotism had stifled all feeling in him; so long as he himself was well, he cared nothing for the rest; he did not even blush.

On the 15th of December Augustus disappeared. He, Plug, and one servant rode to Leipzic to see Charles XII., for the King was convinced that if his stern adversary saw the serenity of his face and the magnificence of his apparel, he would grant him better terms.

There could not have been a greater contrast than that presented by these two enemies. Charles XII. looked like a Puritan, Augustus like a courtier of Louis XIV. They saluted with great cordiality, and kissed each other. Their private conversation lasted for an hour, and by the time it was ended Augustus looked pale and exhausted.

That day spent with Charles XII. weighed heavily on the King, and he never spoke of it to any one. The following day Charles returned his visit; the treaty, however, remained unchanged.

The year that followed was a very hard one for the King, who was anxious to get rid of the Swedes, even at a great sacrifice. Augustus spent many weary days, travelling between Altranstadt, Moritzburg, and Leipzic, trying to obtain the ratification of the treaty.

Augustus and Charles met frequently, but the latter never wished to talk about politics; his secretaries, Piper and Cedermhiolm, were for that.

The treaty was eventually ratified, but still the Swedes did not think of leaving the country.

Without counting the burden of the enemy camping in his country, the poor King really had a great deal to do. He hunted, loved, and entangled himself in the intrigues of his courtiers in order to forget his own misery.

But from time to time his serenity was clouded by Cosel's outbursts of jealousy.

One day during her confinement, as the King was sitting by her bedside, a servant came with the news that letters of importance had just arrived. Augustus wished to go and read them, but Anna, ill and capricious, prevailed on him to stay with her, and to allow the Secretary, Bose, to come to her chamber and read them. The King yielding to her despotic wish, Herr Bose was introduced.

He began by making His Majesty such a profound bow that his wig touched the floor. He paid the same mark of respect to the sick lady, who, wrapped up in lace, looked like a pale pink rose among snow.

Herr Bose whispered to the King,—

"Urgent, from Warsaw."

They both went to the window. Cosel, who had caught the word Warsaw, looked at the King's face intently, trying to read there the contents of the papers. With great respect, Herr Bose handed the King letter after letter. At first they were all large, and sealed with great seals. Cosel did not budge, but remained with her head resting quietly on both her hands.

Suddenly Bose whispered to the King, and handed him a small letter. The King opened it, read it, smiled, blushed, and then glanced involuntarily at Countess Cosel.

Anna was sitting up in bed.

"What is in that letter?" she asked.

"State business," replied the King.

"May I see it?"

"No!" said the King coolly, continuing his reading.

Anna's face flushed, and, forgetful of the Secretary's presence, she sprang out of bed, and seized the letter. The King grew confused, and looked at the old man, who was likewise greatly embarrassed. This violent scene so surprised him that he knew not what to do.

Cosel devoured the letter with her eyes, and then tore it into fragments. Her presentiments were correct; the letter was from Henriette Duval, for whom the King had betrayed Cosel at Warsaw. She had written to her royal lover, telling him that she had been delivered of a daughter, who afterwards became the famous Countess Orzelska. The mother ended the letter by asking what she was to do with the child.

"Drown her!" screamed Cosel.

The King laughed, Anna wept, Bose bowed and began a retreat towards the door.

"Cosel, for Heaven's sake, be quiet," said the King, coming over to her.

"What?" she screamed. "You dare to betray me; you to whom I consecrated everything!"

It was not the first scene of the kind, but this time it lasted longer than ever before. It was in vain that Augustus kissed her hands, promising everything.

"What is it you wish me to do?" he exclaimed.

"If you write a single word to that impertinent woman, I shall take the post, and go straight to Warsaw. I will kill both mother and child. I swear I will!"

To pacify her, the King promised everything. He would have nothing further to do with her; would forget her existence; would leave the unfortunate woman to the caprice of fortune.

No one would ever have known of that scene, for it was Bose's policy always to keep his tongue behind his teeth, had not the weary King gathered a few of his companions together, that he might find distraction in their conversation. After drinking a second and a third bumper, the King began to laugh and look towards Fürstenberg.

"What a pity," said he, "that you did not bring those papers this morning, instead of Bose; perhaps you would have made it up with Cosel had you seen her as that old man had the good fortune to do."

"But the Countess has not yet left her bed," returned the Prince.

"She sprang from her bed, though, to tear the letter poor Henriette had sent me, from my hand. She is so jealous, that I should not be surprised if one day she were to shoot me."

Fürstenberg looked round cautiously, that he might be sure that only those who hated Cosel were present, then he said,—

"Your Majesty, if the Countess Cosel is so jealous, she should be careful to give you no cause for jealousy."

The King slowly raised his head, frowned, thrust out his lips, and replied coldly,—

"The person who dares to make such assertions should weigh his words well, and carefully consider the consequences. You must explain yourself."

The Prince glanced round at his companions.

"I am ready to justify my words. All of us here present have seen how the Countess conducted herself during your Majesty's absence. The palace was always full of guests and admirers, amongst whom the Count Lecherenne enjoyed especial favour. Sometimes he was seen leaving the palace about midnight."

The King listened with apparent indifference, but those who knew him well, could see that the dart had stung him.

"It is the voice of jealousy speaking through you," said Augustus. "You do not like Cosel, and you would be glad to see her shut up in one room. Naturally she longed for my return, and required some distraction, and you must allow that Lecherenne is amusing."

"Your Majesty," said the Prince, with well-feigned simplicity, "I had no intention to be an informer. I enjoy your Majesty's favour, and I do not care much about that of the Countess. But, being your Majesty's devoted servant, I should be deeply grieved to see your great love repaid with ingratitude."

Augustus looked gloomy. The wine cups were full, but no one raised one to his lips; the conversation stopped, and the King rose.

Fürstenberg understood that he had gone too far. Whenever Augustus wished to get rid of a favourite, he was glad to hear something against her. His anger on the present occasion was a proof that as yet Cosel was not an object of indifference to him.

Not wishing to talk any more, Augustus nodded to his guests, and retired to his chamber.

Fürstenberg and the other courtiers regarded each other sorrowfully—they feared the consequences of such a bold attack.

But an unseen witness had overheard the conversation; this was none other than Zaklika, whom Countess Cosel had sent with a letter to the King. Wearying of her solitude, she had written to the King, begging him to come and see her, and had sent the faithful youth with the message. No one save Zaklika was allowed to enter the room while the King was merrymaking; unseen, he had entered the room, and stood behind the great side-board, waiting until the conversation was ended to deliver his letter. Thus he had overheard everything. The danger threatening Anna gave him sufficient courage to leave the room without handing the King the letter; he rushed back to his mistress's palace, and tapped at the door of her chamber. She had just risen for the first time. The moment he entered, she knew by his pale face that something had happened.

"Speak!" she exclaimed. "Has something happened to the King?"

"No," replied Zaklika, and then he repeated all that he had heard.

Cosel listened, blushing, confused and offended; when he had finished, she took the letter from him, and signed to him to withdraw. She left her chamber and entered the drawing-room, the walls of which were covered with pictures representing scenes in the life of the King. One of them was a picture of the King's coronation.

As Cosel was gazing on it, her eyes filled with tears, steps were heard approaching—it was Augustus. He walked quickly, and looked pale and angry.

As though she had not noticed his entrance, Anna rose and approached the picture.

"Well," said he angrily, "so you condescend to look at my portrait? Surely it is a mistake? I cannot believe that I still receive such honour."

"Your Majesty," replied Anna calmly, "it would be ridiculous to suppose, that, being aware of all that makes you superior to other men, any one else should attract my glance after you. The most frivolous woman would be incapable of doing so. How could your Majesty have such suspicions?"

"Yes," interrupted the King with trembling voice, "until today I flattered myself, I thought—but appearances are deceiving, and the caprices of a woman are in most cases difficult to understand."

The King's angry tones rejoiced Anna, for she was sure his jealousy meant that he still loved her, but she pretended to be offended.

"I do not understand your Majesty," she said. "Will your Majesty please to speak clearly, so that I may have a chance of justifying myself?"

"To justify," interrupted the King passionately, "there are some deeds that cannot be justified. You wish to deceive me, but I have proofs."

"Proofs against me!" exclaimed the Countess, wringing her hands. "Augustus! You torture me! Speak! I am innocent."

She threw her arms round his neck; he tried to push her away, but she grasped his hand and began to weep.

"Have mercy upon me! Speak! Let me at least know why I suffer. Who has dared to slander me?"

It took quite a long time to pacify the King, but her tears softened him, and he made her seat herself beside him.

"Very well, then," said he, "I will tell you everything. Fürstenberg told me that the whole city was scandalized at your conduct towards Lecherenne, whom you received every day, during my absence; he used to spend whole evenings with you."

Cosel put on the air of an offended woman.

"Yes," she replied, "it is all true, Lecherenne is in love with me, but I laugh at him. He amused me with his love, but I do not think I sinned in listening to him. Your Majesty is mistaken in thinking that it is enough for any one to be in love with me, to have my love in return. But it is dreadful," continued she, wringing her hands again, "to think that such a person as Fürstenberg can shake your Majesty's faith in my love."

She sank back on the sofa, weeping bitterly. The King was completely disarmed; kneeling before her, he began to kiss her.

"Cosel, forgive me," he pleaded, "I should not be jealous, if I did not love you. Fürstenberg is the most poisonous snake at my court. Forgive me! but I do not like your being even suspected."

Anna continued to weep.

"Sire," said she, sobbing, "remember that if you do not punish the slanderers, they will soon attack your own person, which is so sacred to us."

"Be content," replied the King. "I give you my word that I will not suffer any one to slander you, my dearest."

Thus the scene ended. Cosel was obliged to promise that she would not let Fürstenberg know that she had learned of the accusation he had made against her.

Thanks to Zaklika, Cosel was victorious.

The pacified King returned to his castle, but throughout the next day he did not speak a word to Fürstenberg. The Grand Master of the court, Augustus Lecherenne, received an order to leave Dresden within twenty-four hours.

This was such an unexpected blow to the young Count, that he was unable to believe the tidings. He rushed immediately to see Countess Cosel. When Zaklika went to announce his arrival to her, she blushed from fear and uneasiness.

"Tell him," said she calmly, "that I cannot receive those whom the King has banished—tell him, also," added she, lowering her voice, "that I am sorry he has to go."

Saying this, she pulled from her finger a diamond ring that had been given her by the King.

"Give him this ring from me," she whispered, turning her eyes away from the faithful servant.

Zaklika turned pale.

"Countess," he ventured to say, in a muffled voice, "kindly excuse me, but this ring is from the King."

Cosel, who could not brook the slightest contradiction, turned towards him with a threatening glance and frowning brow.

"I do not ask you for advice, I give you an order and you have to execute it," said she.

Zaklika left the room, confused; he waited for a few moments behind the door. A few years back, a Bohemian noble had given him a costly ring, similar to the one he now held, as a reward for his great strength. Some presentiment caused him to change the rings; he gave his own to Count Lecherenne, and hid the ring the Countess had given him, close to his heart.

A few days later, the King entered Cosel's room while she was dressing. As it was always her custom to wear that ring, the jealous lover immediately noticed its absence.

"Where is my ring?" he asked.

Cosel began to search for it, while the King's face grew crimson.

"Where is it?" he repeated.

Cosel turned to her servant.

"I have not noticed it on your finger for four days," whispered the maid.

Augustus counted the days. It was exactly four days since Count Lecherenne had left Dresden, and had gone to the palace to take leave of Cosel, a fact of which the King had been duly informed.

"Do not waste time searching for it," said he ironically, "I can tell you where it is."

Cosel looked confused. The King broke forth in fury. He did not wish to hear any explanation. The servants rushed out terrified, for the King's voice resounded loudly throughout the palace. Fear took possession of every one.

Cosel was just ready to faint, when a knock was heard at the door, and, looking up, she saw the pale, sad face of Zaklika.

"I beg to be excused for entering," said he, "but the servants have informed me that they cannot find the ring, which about an hour since I picked up on the floor, and which I was only waiting for a proper opportunity to return."

The King glanced at the ring, and was silent.

Cosel did not even look at Zaklika, she said not a word to Augustus, but, placing the ring slowly on her finger, she cast an angry glance at her lover, and walked into another room.

That was quite sufficient to calm the King, and make him seek her pardon on his knees. He remained the whole day at the palace, thereby hindering Cosel from summoning Zaklika, and demanding an explanation.

It was almost midnight when the King retired to his cabinet, where his ministers were awaiting him. The King had barely quitted the palace, before Cosel rang the bell, and ordered the servant to send Zaklika to her.

As was his wont, the faithful Raymond was sitting in the ante-room, reading a half-torn book. On seeing the servant he shivered. He had saved Cosel, but he knew his action would be regarded as a sin. Tremblingly he entered the lady's room. Cosel, beautiful as a goddess, and proud as an absolute sovereign, was pacing up and down the room. She frowned on seeing Zaklika, and stood before him threateningly.

"Who gave you permission to alter my orders?" she inquired.

Zaklika stood for a few moments with his eyes drooped, then, raising them towards the Countess's face, he replied,—

"I am guilty, Madam. You remember Laubegast, and the devotion with which I gazed on you from afar. This sentiment, cherished until now, explains everything to you. I desired to save you."

"I require help from no one!" exclaimed Cosel severely. "I required you to obey me, that is all, and I despise the sentiments of a servant! They are offensive to me."

Zaklika's head drooped.

"Who told you that I cared more about your helping me to get out of trouble than I did about Count Lecherenne not receiving the ring?"

97

"The Count received the ring," replied Zaklika, although he suffered dreadfully at receiving such hard words.

"What ring?" demanded Cosel.

"One similar to yours. I had received one from Count Starenberg, and I gave it to the Count!"

Cosel was astonished.

"You deserve some reward," she whispered.

"Not a reward, but forgiveness," said Zaklika. "I could not accept a reward."

He retreated towards the door, and stood leaning against it. Cosel watched him for some time. Evidently some change had come over her sentiments, but pride prevailed.

She approached Zaklika, and handed him the ring that had been intended for Lecherenne.

Then Raymond woke, as from a dream, and seeing the ring in her white hand, he said,—

"I cannot accept it! It would always remind me that you were cruel to me."

The ring disappeared, and instead, the white hand approached Zaklika's lips.

He kissed it rapturously, and then rushed from the room like a madman, and Countess Cosel was left alone, thoughtful, and with tears in her beautiful dark eyes.

"It is thus that poor men love," said she to herself. "Kings are different."

All this time the Swedes were still in Saxony. Charles XII. was heartless and sardonic towards the King; severe towards the nobility; and a grievous burden to the country, for his soldiers went about catching men and enrolling them in the Swedish army. The treaty of peace had been signed, but Charles XII. would not leave Saxony.

So many humiliations, so many sacrifices, exhausted the patience of all, and caused despair in every heart. The arrogance of the Swedish monarch, who rode through the country attended by twenty or forty soldiers, disgusted every one.

One morning, when the King was busy presiding over a council of his ministers, Count Schulenberg was announced. The old man was invited to take part in the council, but he had no desire to speak, and begged a private audience.

When they were alone, the King inquired,—

"General, do you bring me the good tidings that the Swedes are going to leave us?"

"I am sorry that I cannot bring your Majesty such good tidings. But there might be a way of getting rid of them."

"The only way I know of would be if Heaven sent us its army, with the archangel Michael at its head."

"Your Majesty," interrupted Schulenberg, "I am sure that with a little desperate courage we could rid ourselves of them, without the help of the angels. There are twenty thousand Swedes scattered throughout Saxony; it is but a mere handful, that one man's daring renders terrible. Let us catch him, and the rest have lost their value."

"How can you say that? Catch him during peace, when he trusts us?"

"That is what makes our vengeance possible," replied Schulenberg. "I have reconnoitred his quarters. They are very badly guarded. I could attack them during the night, and seize him. I will convey him to Königstein; if they besiege me, I shall not surrender. Then the King's head will answer for my safety, and he will sign the treaty, as we wish it to be signed."

Augustus listened attentively.

"Suppose you should not succeed?" he asked.

"In that case, the blame will fall on me, and not on your Majesty," replied the General. "I desire to save my country from the invaders."

"General," said the King, "I think you are dreaming. You know that I respect knightly customs, and I cannot consent to your plans—I cannot! I hate him, I should like to strangle him if I could get him into my hands, but I cannot allow him to be attacked during the night. General, this is not a business for Augustus the Strong!"

Schulenberg looked at him gloomily.

"Have they always acted in a knightly fashion towards your Majesty?"

"Ruffians such as they can do what they please; they are barbarians. But Augustus, whom people call the Strong, and whom monarchs style the Magnificent, will not stoop to employ such means."

The old soldier twisted his moustache, and saluted.

"But suppose some insubordinate soldier were to do it?" he asked.

"I should be obliged to defend my enemy, and to release him," exclaimed Augustus.

"That is very noble and knightly," said Schulenberg sarcastically, "but—"

He did not finish, but saluted respectfully.

The King took his hand.

"My dear General, give up that idea, and do not say another word about it. I do not wish for victory at such a cost."

Schulenberg looked at him with his pale blue eyes, as though he would ask whether the imprisonment of Imhoff and Pfingstein, and the surrender of Patkul, about which Augustus had not hesitated, were nobler deeds than this. The King must have understood the mute reproach, for he blushed. After a moment of sad silence, Schulenberg said,—

"We must try and get out of this difficulty by some act of despair. We must risk our lives. We have nothing else to lose. We have lost a crown that has cost us millions; the other is almost broken—what can happen further?"

"What can happen?" said Augustus. "The arrogant youth will go further. A few victories have given him a mad boldness, and he will be crushed in some crazy enterprise for which he has not properly calculated his strength. Why should we stain our name by trying to hasten that which must most surely come to pass? Why should we not bear our adversity patiently, so that in the end we may profit by that which some one else has accomplished?"

"But in the meantime, Saxony suffers dreadfully," said the General.

"Yes, the poor people suffer," exclaimed the King. "But the people are like the grass that is trodden down by the cattle; it is greener the next year."

"But they are people," said Schulenberg.

"The crowd should not be taken into consideration," rejoined the King.

Silence followed, and the General took his leave. When he was gone, the King threw himself into a chair, and was soon deep in thought.

After the surrender of Patkul his chivalrous sentiment was at the least very peculiar.

Charles XII's defiant wanderings through Saxony had given Cosel the idea of seizing him, and thus avenging the humiliations of her oppressed country. It was she who had suggested the idea to Schulenberg. She did not mention it to the King first, for she was sure he would not listen to her plans. She therefore was obliged to plot alone. She gained Flemming over to her side, and although he disliked the favourite, he nevertheless promised to aid her patriotic plan. Schulenberg promised it the support of his cavalry.

Cosel declared that once the deed was accomplished, although Augustus might be indignant at first, he would soon be obliged to give way. Still Schulenberg was commissioned to find out what Augustus would think of such a scheme.

Although he said not a word to any one on leaving the King's presence, they could see by his face that the plan had been rejected.

But in spite of this, Cosel was not discouraged. She felt strong enough to fight the King himself.

Augustus had no secrets from her, and the same evening he told her of his conversation with Schulenberg. Hearing which, the Countess exclaimed,—

"What? Your Majesty does not wish to avenge his wrongs?"

"Let us talk no more of the matter," said the King, frowning.

Seeing it was not a good time to press the subject, Cosel turned the conversation, and told him all the court gossip.

For a long time she had been urging the King to take her to see the alchemist. Bottiger was at this time shut up in a tower of the castle, but although kept in perpetual imprisonment, he was always treated with the respect due to a man from whom gold is expected.

Fürstenberg was for ever persuading the King that their object would soon be accomplished, and he was always at work with the prisoner, either in his own laboratory or in that of the alchemist. Bottiger's lodging was very comfortable, almost magnificent. He had a garden filled with flowers, and there were plenty of silver dishes on his table, at which he frequently entertained his numerous guests. Seeing he could not possibly escape, he succeeded in making Fürstenberg believe that he was seriously thinking of how to manufacture gold. He exhausted all his formulas, read all the books on alchemy,—but every effort proved fruitless.

Knowing the great influence Cosel possessed, the prisoner sought to gain her favour, sending her every day the most beautiful flowers from his garden.

The Countess was anxious to see him—the King postponed the visit. But that day she was so persistent, so tender, and, at the same time, so beautiful, that Augustus rose, and offering her his arm, said,—

"Come, let us go and see Bottiger."

There was no one at hand who could be sent to announce the King's visit, but, chancing to look through the window, Augustus saw Frölich the fool, who was trying to rid himself of the courtiers, who were bent on teasing him.

The King called him.

"A most suitable messenger," said he to Cosel. "I will send him on before us, so as to give the alchemist a chance of dressing decently; and also to make sure that we do not find him in improper company."

Bottiger, whose good graces were considered most important, received even the fair sex.

Frölich appeared on the threshold.

"I appoint you my chamberlain until the evening," said the King, laughing, "so you must not say that you carry the key in vain. Go and tell Bottiger that the goddess Diana will visit him today."

"In company with Apollo," added Cosel.

Frölich went out with much gravity, and proceeded by way of the balcony to the corner tower.

A gay company was assembled round the alchemist's table that day. Glasses and witty sayings were circulating freely. Amongst the guests were Prince Fürstenberg, Secretary Nehmitz, and an ardent admirer of alchemy, Tschirahaussen. The thick walls of the tower were covered with silk brocade, brightened by many mirrors, and enriched by gilded furniture and bronzes. A small staircase connected this room with the laboratory beneath, and with the sleeping room above.

Bottiger was distinguished among his guests by his beautiful figure and merry face, on which intelligence and wit were plainly visible. He was carefully dressed, and looked more like a nobleman than a man who was shut up in prison and obliged to wither over crucibles. He was a most jovial companion at the dinner-table, a most eloquent wit in society. The company was just drinking his health, and the apothecary was ready to respond to the toast, when the King's ambassador, with his pointed hat, and this day a red swallow-tail coat, appeared on the threshold.

"Ah! Frölich," exclaimed the party.

"What do you want?" inquired Bottiger.

"I am not a common Frölich today," replied the fool gravely. "It has pleased His Majesty to appoint me as his chamberlain for four-and-twenty hours, and in fulfilment of my duties I am come to announce to you that Diana, accompanied by Apollo, will honour Herr Bottiger with a visit. Dixi!"

He rapped with his stick. All the guests sprang to their feet. Bottiger and Nehmitz began to clear the table. The window was thrown open, and a servant despatched for fresh flowers. The guests disappeared by the side balconies, for they knew that the king would come by way of the back balcony. The alchemist, Fürstenburg, and Nehmitz alone remained to greet them.

The furniture was hastily placed in proper order, the floor was strewn with flowers, and Bottiger stood on the threshold with a bouquet.

Soon the room was brightened by the arrival of Cosel in the full splendour of her beauty. The prisoner knelt.

"We always receive a goddess kneeling," said he, "and the best sacrifice we can offer her is scented flowers."

Cosel smilingly accepted the flowers her host offered, and then looked around inquisitively, wondering that there was not the least indication of the great work that was in progress.

The King followed her, and explained that they were not in the laboratory.

"But I should like to see that mysterious sanctuary," said she.

"Madam," replied Bottiger, "it is such a fearful den, the air is so unhealthy, and the aspect so sad, that a goddess should not descend into such a hell."

"But woman's curiosity!" sighed Cosel, and looked at Augustus. The King looked at Fürstenberg; but the Prince only shrugged his shoulders.

"The Countess is not accustomed to such dark stairs," added the alchemist.

But Cosel replied,—

"The goddess commands, guide us!"

Saying this, she turned towards the door; but Bottiger pressed a button in the opposite wall, and immediately a secret door flew open, and beside this the alchemist stood, candelabra in his hand.

Augustus offered no opposition, and they all descended the dark, narrow stairs, and entered a room, the walls of which were black with smoke. Against its thick walls were several stoves, on which stood cold retorts and crucibles; there were several articles of furniture of strange shapes, and a number of bottles and jars. On the tables lay large folios with brass clasps, rolls of parchment, and various kinds of tools.

The apartment had such a strange, gloomy, and mysterious aspect that it frightened the Countess, who was leaning on the King's arm.

Having raised the light, Bottiger stood silently watching them. Augustus looked round the laboratory that contained such wonderful hopes with a certain degree of respect. Suddenly he advanced to the table, and his gaze rested on an object that lay among the papers.

It was a cup of the colour of jasper. The King, who was a great admirer of china, thought it a product of Japan.

"Bottiger," he exclaimed, "that looks like Japanese china, although it is of a different shape to theirs."

"Your Majesty," replied the host, bowing reverently, "that is my plaything. I tried to make china from the lime they brought me wherewith to make gold."

The King took the cup, examined it carefully, and then held it against the light.

"You say you made this?"

Bottiger bent down and picked up several fragments, then from beneath the papers he drew forth several saucers, which he handed to the King and Cosel.

"Why, it is the most beautiful china in the world!" exclaimed Augustus.

Bottiger was silent.

"You are truly a discoverer! You have found out a wonderful secret! For God's sake, make porcelain for me! I paid fifty thousand thalers for one Chinese service. The Prussian robbed me; he took away a company of my best-looking soldiers: you can make porcelain, and you say nothing about it!"

"It was only an experiment."

"A most successful experiment! Bottiger, you shall make the first service for Diana!"

Seeing the King's enthusiasm, Fürstenberg and Nehmitz both approached to look at the wonderful discovery, but the Prince was dissatisfied, for he feared the alchemist would neglect the gold for the porcelain.

The King rejoiced more over this discovery than he would have done had he been told that the Swedes had left Saxony. He took the cup, and, after again expressing his great satisfaction, turned towards the door. To save the King and Cosel the trouble of ascending the narrow stairs, Bottiger opened the door that led directly into his garden, from whence they returned to the back balcony.

That was a memorable day in the history of Saxony, which in Bottiger's accidental discovery of an art which had long been kept secret under pain of death, had indeed gained a veritable gold mine.

A few days later, news of a more dramatic character shocked the whole of Dresden. Although Schulenberg had given up all idea of seizing the person of Charles XII., the more daring Cosel, assisted by Flemming, had not the slightest intention of relinquishing it. Every day, the King of Sweden gave them an opportunity of carrying out their bold plan; but the number of persons necessary for its satisfactory accomplishment was lacking.

On September 1st, the same day on which he and the Emperor signed the ratification of the treaty granting freedom to Protestants, Charles XII. left Altrandstadt. He journeyed towards the North, following his army, which, under the command of Rhenskyold, had begun to leave Saxony for Silesia and Poland. The greater part had already left Saxony, but a few regiments still remained at Leipzic.

By September 6th, Charles had reached Oberan, near Meissen. It was such a beautiful day that he went out riding; as they ascended a hill, one of his followers directed his attention to the spires of the Dresden churches.

For some time Charles remained gazing at them, thoughtful and silent, then, addressing the few officers who accompanied him, he said,—

"It is so near, we must go there."

It was between three and four in the afternoon when the unexpected guests arrived at the gates of Dresden. Finding the gate closed, Charles XII. told the officer in command that he had come with messages from the Swedish King. Hearing this, the officer conducted him and his suite to the guard-room. Now it happened that at the same moment Flemming passed by, and he was greatly alarmed at recognizing the King.

At this hour Augustus was usually to be found taking exercise in the armoury. This afternoon Countess Cosel was also there, admiring the skill and strength displayed by her lover in breaking iron. Her merry laugh was re-echoing through the hall, when a knock was heard at the door.

"Come in!" called the King.

He turned towards the door as he spoke, but started, and then appeared as though changed to a block of stone on seeing his enemy, Charles XII. Flemming, who followed him, made signs to Countess Cosel, that he only awaited her signal, to summon the soldiers and seize their important guest.

Augustus was still standing motionless, when Charles greeted him cheerfully, exclaiming,—

"Well, brother! how are you?"

Countess Cosel turned purple, and, seizing the King by the arm, whispered,—

"For God's sake, consent!"

It seemed as though Charles XII. had overheard her words, for his face grew stern, and Augustus, turning to the Countess, said stiffly,—

"I beg you; I command you to leave us!"

The Countess, with her accustomed vivacity, was about to make some reply, when the King, frowning angrily, exclaimed,—

"Go!"

Cosel withdrew, glancing angrily at Charles, who stood quietly looking at the armour. She took Flemming's arm; that courtier's eyes were also glowing with anger. He shrugged his shoulders. Augustus cast on them a glance that commanded them both to be silent, and then greeted his visitor politely,—

"We have heard much talk of your strength," said Charles, sneeringly, "and we should be pleased to see one of those miracles you perform so easily."

An iron rod lay on the floor; Augustus raised it.

"Give me your hand." said he, smiling, "and do not be afraid, I will not hurt you."

Charles extended his broad, rough hands. Twisting the rod with perfect ease, Augustus bound his enemy's hands. The two men looked into each other's eyes. Then Augustus broke the fetters, and threw them on the floor. The Swedish King did not utter a word, but began to inspect the armoury.

"You have plenty of arms," said the Swede laconically, "what a pity that you lack men to use them."

From the armoury, both Kings proceeded to the palace, as Charles wished to pay his respects to the Queen, for whom he had as great a respect as he had contempt for Augustus.

In the meantime, the news that Charles XII. was in Dresden spread rapidly through the city.

His name always excited great interest. The Protestants, knowing what he had done for their coreligionists in Silesia, were anxious to see him. That young King, a few years over twenty, was the wonder of all Europe.

Count Flemming and all who were attached to Augustus II. were indignant at the boldness of the young hero, who thus set the conquered King at defiance, by coming unarmed into his capital. Flemming and Cosel were furious, and uttered threats of vengeance. The former ordered some of the soldiers to be fetched from the garrison, and wished to capture the enemy, despite the King's prohibition. Anna seized a pistol, and declared she would follow him down the street, and shoot him.

The excitement was considerable and universal, and could not fail to be noticed by Augustus and Charles as they passed to the palace. The King alone was perfectly calm, and by his manner commanded every one to keep quiet. He, as well as Charles, noticed the preparations that had been made, but the Swede's courage did not fail him for a moment, neither did he lose his self-possession. He made no attempt to shorten his visit, and as Augustus was pleased to entertain him, perhaps to test his courage, his visit was a long one. He remained for half an hour at the castle, and this gave Flemming plenty of time to collect the soldiers and place them in readiness; then, fearing the King would not consent to his enemy being captured in Dresden, he despatched a detachment of cavalry to capture him on his way to Meissen.

While Charles XII. was talking with the Queen, Flemming succeeded in calling Augustus from the room. "Your Majesty," he exclaimed vehemently, "this is the only moment in which we shall be able to avenge all our wrongs. Charles XII. is in your Majesty's hands."

"Trusting to my honour," replied Augustus, "therefore not a hair of his head shall be hurt."

"It would be ridiculous to show magnanimity to a man who has brought such calamities on your Majesty. I shall capture him, even if I am beheaded for so doing."

"There is something far more important than your head to be considered in this matter," replied the King, "and that is my honour as a King. Do not dare to do anything of the sort!"

"Then there is nothing further for me to do than to break the sword with which I have served your Majesty." He made a movement as he spoke, as though about to carry out his threat, but Augustus stopped him.

"Flemming," said he, sternly, "do not forget that I am here; that this is my business, and that no one commands here except me!"

Flemming's wrath was extreme.

"Your Majesty will lose another crown by acting thus!"

With these words he rushed away, and the King returned quietly to the Queen's apartments, where he had left his guest. Charles XII. did not even look at him as he entered, although he guessed that outside the door he had been the subject of conversation.

While this was taking place at the castle, Cosel was watching in the street, waiting to fire at Charles XII. as soon as he appeared. Zaklika endeavoured to dissuade her from her purpose, telling her that the populace would immediately rise in his defence, for Charles was a staunch protector of the Protestants. And indeed this would have been the feeling among the greater portion of the crowd now waiting in the streets.

When Charles XII. was ready to depart, Augustus ordered his own horse to be brought, so that he might accompany his guest. The streets were thronged with people, the windows were filled with curious heads, a profound silence reigned, as the two Kings rode along the streets; it seemed as though the waiting multitude held their breath, in their anxiety to catch the conversation of the riders. All eyes were turned towards Charles, who rode calmly along without exhibiting the least sign of feeling or emotion. Beside him rode Augustus, looking gloomy and thoughtful, but at the same time majestic. They turned towards the gate leading to Meissen. The King had sent orders that three cannons should be fired in honour of the Swede. When the first shot was fired, and Charles turned to express his thanks, Augustus touched his hat, and smiled indifferently. At the gate, the cannon were fired a second time. Charles now wished to take leave of his host, but Augustus knew Flemming and his people too well not to suspect that they had prepared some ambush. He knew also that the only way in which he could protect the Swede was by accompanying him until he was out of reach of danger.

Augustus accompanied his guest to Neudorf; here they shook hands and parted. Charles XII. galloped on his way, but Augustus sat motionless for a few moments, gazing straight before him, wondering whether after all he had done well in listening to the dictates of honour.

He was still waiting there, when Flemming arrived foaming with rage. "Your Majesty," said he, "doubtless thinks that Europe will admire your magnanimity, but if you imagine that it will counterbalance the imprisonment at Patkul, you are greatly mistaken. The people will laugh at such heroism."

"Silence, Flemming," cried the King threateningly, then turning his steed, he galloped away alone in the direction of the city.

He dismounted at the Palace of the Four Seasons, where he found Cosel even more indignant than Flemming.

"Do not come near me!" she exclaimed, sobbing. "You have made a grievous mistake. I do not wish to see you any more. Twenty millions of money, hundreds of thousands of soldiers, the death of your officers, your own shame, all this you might have avenged, and you would not. You were afraid!"

The King threw himself on the sofa, and allowed the Countess to storm as she pleased—he did not utter a word. Only when, exhausted by passion, she sank into an arm-chair, he remarked coldly,—

"I had no wish to stain my honour with such a revenge!"

The next day, seeing that every one reproached him for his lenity, he summoned a council of war, which being presided over by Flemming, declared that it would have been right to imprison the Swedish King, and force him to sign a fresh treaty, seeing he had so frequently violated all the laws of nations.

The King heard them in silence.

The Swedish envoy at Vienna, having heard of the council, remarked contemptuously,—

"These people decide on the second day what they should have done the day before."

The Swedish King had not yet left Saxony when Augustus began giving splendid festivals, for which he had plenty of time, although not much money. Naturally, Cosel was first at all entertainments, and she ruled King and country despotically.

When weary of balls, tournaments, and carouses, Augustus was fond of taking excursions through the country.

In Nizyca, in the old Slav lands of Luzyce, there is a very old settlement, situated at the foot of a mountain, called Stolp. This mountain was pushed from out the bowels of the earth by some strange phenomenon of Nature, and its enormous rocks of black basalt stand boldly forth, looking as though they had been hewn by the hands of spirits. On these rocks, which were so hard that iron could not break them, there was built, many centuries ago, a castle, whose business it was to dominate and defend the borough that lay at its feet. From this mountain a wonderful view is obtained; afar to the south, one sees the Saxon and Bohemian mountains covered with forests; to the west, there stand forth the copper mountains of Saxony; nearer are visible those gigantic heights, in form like the pyramids, on which are seated Ditterzbach, Sonnenstein, and Ohorn; to the East one sees the forests and mountains of Hochwald—whilst in the far distance Bohemian villages and towns are visible.

In days of yore, the old castle of Stolpen was the property of the Bishops of Meissen, and stood forth to view, magnificent though gloomy, with its pointed towers, which not even thunderbolts could destroy. This castle was surrounded by enormous walls, near it was a large park, and in the adjoining forest game was to be found in abundance.

One beautiful day in July, before the heat had set in, horses stood ready before the castle of Dresden. One of Augustus' courtiers had told him of the strange mountain, composed of iron-like rocks, on which the castle of Stolpen stood, and the King, recollecting it, longed to see it.

The dew was still wet on the grass and trees, when the King came forth to mount his charger. At the same moment Zaklika appeared with a message from Cosel, inquiring where His Majesty was going.

"Tell your mistress," said the King, "that I am going to Stolpen, and that if she choose, she may overtake me; but I am not going to wait until the heat of the day has set in; this will be the case long before she has finished dressing."

Cosel had just left her bed, she was angry that the King had not notified her of this excursion; and when Zaklika returned with the answer, she felt hurt that the King was not willing to wait for her. Still she gave order that the horses should be saddled, and some young nobles invited to accompany her. Everything was to be ready in half an hour, for Cosel was determined to show the King that she did not require to take a long time dressing, in order to appear beautiful. She wished to overtake him before he could reach Stolpen. In half an hour the gentlemen invited were ready, and Cosel's white Arab steed, its saddle covered with crimson velvet ornamented with gold, was neighing impatiently. Then the beautiful lady came forth to the astonishment of her admirers. She wore a wonderfully becoming dress. Her hat was blue with white and azure feathers; her bodice was blue embroidered with gold, and a full white skirt, likewise trimmed with gold, completed her costume. She sprang on her horse, impatient to start as soon as possible. Then she welcomed her guests with a gracious smile.

"Gentlemen," said she, raising her small hand, in which she held a riding whip whose handle was set with precious stones, "the King has challenged me to race with him. He started half an hour ago, but we must overtake him, even though our horses should die in the attempt, or we should break our own necks. He who cares for me, will follow me!"

Having said this, the bold amazon turned her horse towards the gate, and galloped madly down the street. Zaklika and an equerry followed her closely, to be in readiness in case of accident. The others followed after. With the white Arab keeping well ahead, they passed through the old city, and turned to the left towards Stolpen. Fortunately for the party, the high road was broad and sandy, the morning refreshing, and the horses strong and fresh. In silence, the Countess's brilliant cavalcade flew along the road, as though carried by the wind.

They passed mountains and groves, meadows and fields. Through the orchards they could see the villages of the Wends, with their houses surrounded by wooden piazzas, and covered with high roofs. From time to time they met a peasant coming along the road, who doffed his cap respectfully at sight of the marvellous apparition, but before he could open his mouth to reply to the question whether he had seen the King, the riders who had asked it had disappeared in clouds of dust.

The horses were covered with foam, and, after an hour of mad riding, the equerry besought the Countess to stop and rest. At first she would not listen to him, but in the end she slackened her pace, and the horses stopped in front of an old house. The poor animals were panting and snorting. In the doorway stood an old, yellow-faced, miserable-looking woman, leaning on a stick. She glanced at the riders with indifference, and then turned her face from them.

Only once Countess Cosel's eyes and hers met, and the beautiful lady shivered.

They asked the old woman about the King, but she only shook her head.

"We don't have any kings, our kings are dead!"

She spoke slowly and with indifference, and her accent was that of a foreigner.

At that moment, a middle-aged man came out of the house; he had long hair, and wore a blue jacket with silver buttons, knee breeches, and stockings. Taking off his hat, he welcomed the guests in pure Saxon German.

He told them that it was three-quarters of an hour since the King had passed the house, but that he was riding so fast that it would be impossible to overtake him.

Cosel then inquired if there were not a shorter way, but finding there was none, she dismounted, and expressed her intention of resting for a few moments. Thereupon the German offered the company some beer.

"Who is that woman?" inquired Cosel, pointing towards the beggar.

The German shrugged his shoulders contemptuously:

"She is a Slav, a Wendish woman! I cannot get rid of her. She claims that this property used to belong to her father. She lives not far from here in a hut built at the foot of the mountain. I don't know what she lives on; she wanders across the fields muttering, and who knows but it may be some devilish incantations, for she must be a witch. Sometimes of nights when the storm howls she sings, and then we shiver. I cannot chase her away, for she knows how to conjure up devils, who serve her."

Then with a sigh, he added,—

"She foretells the future, and she is never mistaken."

Cosel turned and looked at the old woman; then she went over to her. She was the only one of the party bold enough; her companions, hearing witchcraft mentioned, had withdrawn to a distance.

"What is her name?" she asked the German.

The man hesitated, then whispered so low that even she could scarcely hear what he said,—

"Mlawa."

The old woman made a movement as though she heard her name; she raised her emaciated head proudly, shook her long, hanging, grey locks, and looked around, as though searching for the bold person who had dared to mention her name.

Unheeding the woman's strange manner, Cosel, to the surprise of her companions, went up to the old beggar. For a moment the two women looked into each other's eyes.

Cosel was the first to speak.

"Who are you?" she asked. "Tell me why you are so poor."

Mlawa shook her head.

"I am not poor," she replied proudly, "for I have memories of happy years. I am here still on the land that belonged to my family. I am the Queen."

"You are a Queen?" laughed Cosel.

"Yes, I am a Queen! for the blood of the kings of this land flows in my veins. All things are possible in this world. You, though today you are almost a Queen, by tomorrow may be as miserable as I."

"Of what kings are you speaking?" inquired Cosel thoughtfully.

The old woman raised her hand and pointed to the surrounding country.

"All that was ours—all, until you came and took it, and slew us as though we had been wild beasts. We were good; we came with bread, and salt, and song; while you came with iron, fire, and slaughter. And the German race multiplied, and pushed us out of our land. It's my land, and I must die here. From this place my soul will find its way back to my people."

"Are you able to tell fortunes?" asked Cosel, urged thereto by feverish curiosity.

"That depends," said Mlawa indifferently.

"Would you do it for me?"

The old woman looked on her pityingly.

"Why do you wish your fortune told?" asked she. "Whoever rose as high as you have done can only fall; better not ask!"

Cosel paled, but anxious to show that she was courageous, she smiled, though her lips trembled.

"I am not afraid of anything," she said, "I can look at happiness, as I can look at the sun; and I shall be able to look into the darkness also."

"But suppose the darkness lasts too long?"

"It cannot last for ever," rejoined Cosel.

"Who can tell?" whispered Mlawa. "Let me see your hand!" she added, stretching forth her own.

The Countess retreated a few paces, feeling rather afraid, for in those days every one believed in witchcraft.

"Don't be afraid, my beauty," said Mlawa calmly. "I shall not soil your white fingers, I shall only look at them."

Cosel drew off her glove, and exhibited to the old woman, a beautiful white hand, glittering with rings.

"What a beautiful hand! Worthy to be kissed by kings; but, my child, there are dreadful signs in it. That hand often touched the face that looked on her boldly. Am I right?"

Cosel blushed; Mlawa was thoughtful.

"What are you going to tell me?" whispered Cosel uneasily.

"You are going on towards your destiny. Who has ever avoided his fate?

Who has ever seen its precipices? After long happiness, there awaits you a still longer, oh, far longer season of penitence, a rigorous captivity, sleepless nights, unaccustomed tears. Having children, you will be childless; with a husband, you will be a widow, you will be an imprisoned Queen; you will be free, but you will throw away your freedom—you will be—oh! don't ask me—"

Cosel was as white as marble, but still she tried to smile.

"What have I done to you," she asked, "that you wish to terrify me?"

"I pity you!" said Mlawa. "Why did you wish to look into my soul? Wormwood grows there! Bitterness flows through my words. I pity you!"

The old woman's head drooped.

"You are not the only one! Thousands have suffered in this world, and have died, and their ashes are scattered by the winds. Like you, thousands are moaning in slavery—my forefathers, grandfather, father, kings. I am the last of their race. The German has driven me from my home."

Cosel drew a gold coin from her purse, and handed it to the old woman.

"I don't take alms," said she; "you will pay differently; everything is reckoned above."

And raising her hands, she walked into the meadows.

During this conversation, Cosel's companions had been standing at a little distance, admiring her courage. Now none dared ask why she looked so pale and thoughtful. She mounted her horse, but she dropped the rein and allowed the animal to guide her.

They continued to ride forward, but slowly. Then from afar high towers appeared in sight.

"That is Stolpen," said the equerry.

An hour's more riding and they reached the castle. The King's cavalcade was standing opposite the rock of basalt, waiting for the Countess, whom they had seen while she was still at a distance.

Augustus advanced to meet her with a smile of welcome.

"I have been waiting for you an hour," said he.

"Yes, for I lost half an hour over some fortune-teller," replied the Countess.

The King looked surprised.

"Well, what fortune did she prophesy for you?" he inquired.

Anna looked at him, and her beautiful eyes filled with tears. Augustus grew confused and alarmed. Then he strove to chase away her sadness, and was gallant and witty.

"What a magnificent castle these Bishops of Meissen built!" he said.

"It is dreadful! Fearful!" said Cosel shivering. "I am surprised that the King should come for pleasure to a place where memories of torture and cruelties reign supreme."

"Why, my lady," interrupted Augustus, "your beautiful eyes can make bright the gloomiest spot. I am happy everywhere with you."

He offered her his arm and she leant on it. Thus they went round the dreadful castle. The Countess was silent, the King serene. Perhaps he was thinking that when his prisons at Königstein and Sonnenstein were full, he would be able to shut up a few prisoners here. He wished to see the interior of the castle, but Cosel remained outside, looking at the black towers and walls. The King went on further and examined the prisons, called "Monchlock," where the monks were kept, then the "Richter-gehorsam," and a pitch dark "Burguersiess," into which the prisoners descended by means of a ladder. Although empty, everything was in good order. Augustus looked at everything with eager curiosity, and as though he were searching for traces of the old tortures. At length, having looked at the walls of the fortress, he left the castle.

Outside he found Cosel just where he had left her; she appeared gloomily thoughtful.

"What a dreadful place!" she repeated. "It seems as if I could—can hear the moans of those who have been tortured here."

"We cannot be tender towards every one," said Augustus, indifferently. "But how is it you have such gloomy thoughts? Let us leave the castle and go into the park. I have ordered them to have lunch ready. Soon they will drive up some game, and we shall be able to admire your skill in shooting them."

In the park, under a magnificent Turkish tent, they found lunch all ready prepared for them. The sun was scorching, the heat was overpowering, so that none of the company were very animated. Even the witty Kyan sat silent in front of his full glass. Augustus did not like silence, so he ordered the servants to serve quickly, and then fetch the rifles.

Luncheon ended, all went into the park. Cosel followed the King, but she felt very sad, for Mlawa's words, foretelling the dreadful fate that awaited her, still rang in her ears, though at present no signs of such a fate were visible. Augustus, on the contrary, was merry.

Towards evening, having killed a few deer and boars, Augustus mounted his horse. Cosel rode beside him. As they passed the house where she met Mlawa, Cosel searched for her with her eyes, but she was not there. A little further on they saw her standing leaning on her stick, as though she were waiting to see the King. She glanced at Cosel and smiled, as though recognizing an old acquaintance. Augustus turned from the sight of her in disgust.

Prince Fürstenburg and Count Flemming had made a compact to get rid of Countess Cosel. She ordered them, as if she had been a Queen, she treated them proudly, and she squandered money like a child who is ignorant of its value. The influence she had acquired over the King alarmed every one. None of the King's favourites had had such power, such faith in herself, and none of them had been able to keep the fickle Augustus so long at her side. The whole court longed for her downfall; the number of her enemies increased daily. But the Countess heeded them not, and when the faithful Zaklika told her things that he had overheard, she only laughed contemptuously. Slowly yet surely the forces of her enemies were gathering together against her, but as yet they did not venture to declare open war. They were waiting for certain symptoms that would lead them to believe that the King was tired of her, and would indicate that the fight would be crowned with victory.

On the one side were adroit and clever courtiers, drilled from childhood in the art of intriguing, and aided in their enterprise by corrupt and cunning women; on the other side was Countess Cosel, proud, intelligent, trusting in her beauty, in her imaginary title of wife, in the knot that had been made fast by having her children acknowledged, and a few friends without influence, and a few double-faced people, who were eager to be on the victorious side, and only waiting to see which side had the greatest power. The prospect was that the war would be long, but Cosel's adversaries were patient, and, knowing the disposition of the King, felt confident of an ultimate victory.

They knew that sooner or later Cosel must weary the King by her fancies and by her insatiable desire for luxury as well as by her pride and impetuosity. Until the present these had amused the King, but at any moment the scale might turn.

Every one of importance at Court was against Cosel, profiting by the King's absence in Flanders, whither he had gone to fight against France, in the hope that by some deed of daring he might brighten his fame, so clouded by the Swedish defeat. Fürstenberg and Flemming wished to shake the King's love by writing to him about the Countess's extravagant luxuries. So black did they succeed in painting her, that the King gave orders that she should not be furnished with too much money. Fürstenberg seized on this order to refuse Cosel money several times when she required it, for which insult the Countess threatened to give him a slap in the face should she come across him.

But when the King arrived in Dresden, he had not a single look for Fürstenberg, instead, he went straight to the Palace of the Four Seasons, where again he found Cosel just leaving her room after another confinement. She was more beautiful than ever, and, although weeping, received him most affectionately.

"Ah! my lord!" she exclaimed, throwing her arms round his neck, "you know that I am always eager to see you as soon as possible, yet, perhaps, never have I longed so much for your return as at the present time. Deliver me from persecution! Am I still the mistress of your heart or not, that these men humiliate me so cruelly?"

"Who?" inquired the King.

"Your best friends; that drunkard, Flemming, and that perverse hypocrite, Fürstenberg, have made me a laughing-stock. My lord! deliver me from them."

After long separation, Cosel had regained her power over the King, who had begun to cool towards her.

"I will scold Fürstenberg and Flemming severely," said he.

By the time he left the palace, he was once more under the influence of her charms, and when Fürstenberg and Flemming came to him with an accusation against her, he told them both to go the next day and beg the Countess's pardon.

"You are both wrong. I dislike quarrels, and you must make it up with the Countess."

"Your Majesty, it would be too humiliating for me," said Flemming.

"It must be done, otherwise you would be obliged to leave the Court."

The next day the King sent for them to come to the Palace of the Four Seasons. Cosel was crimson with anger, and proud as a Queen.

"I suppose," said the King, "that a mutual misunderstanding was the cause of the quarrel. The Countess will forget the past, and you, gentlemen, ever indulgent to the fair sex, you will overlook it if she has ever said any bitter words about you."

All the while the King was speaking, Cosel's look was full of anger, Fürstenberg's of hatred, and Flemming's of irony. Yet when he had finished, they bowed politely, and their indistinct mutterings might have been taken as begging pardon.

Neither side was deluded with the idea that the reconciliation was sincere.

Soon after this her cunning enemies again tried to make the King quarrel with the beautiful Cosel, who seemed to be one of those wonderful creatures who are always young. Passing through Brussels on his way from Flanders, the King met a beautiful dancing girl, called Duparc, and invited her to come to Dresden. Cosel's enemies knew how jealous she was, and they employed the Baroness Glasenapp to carry out an intrigue. When inviting Duparc to Dresden, Augustus did not tell her that he was the King; he was travelling then under the name of Count Torgau. On her arrival in Dresden, she failed to find a Count of that name. However, she had an aunt in Dresden, who was in the theatre, and this aunt took her to Chamberlain Murdachs, who was at that time director of the royal entertainments. He knew all about Duparc, and to her great surprise received her very well, expressing a wish that she would appear in the ballet, called "The Princess Elida," that had just been prepared to celebrate the King's return. All this was the work of Count Torgau, and both the women guessed that he must be the King, and their suppositions were rendered more certain by the anonymous presents received by the dancer.

During the ballet the King sat in the box with Cosel; when Duparc noticed him she fainted from emotion. The King ordered his doctor to go and attend to her, and this seriously displeased his jealous favourite.

"It seems to me," said she, "that your Majesty is too good in taking such interest in an unknown dancer, who probably does not deserve such a favour."

Augustus was offended, and replied drily,—

"It is true that I should often be accused of showing too much favour to persons who only abuse it! I hope that Duparc will be less exacting."

Cosel, unable to control either her voice or her movements, withdrew to the further end of the box, exclaiming,—

"Your Majesty has a peculiar taste for the street women."

Fearing a further outburst of passion from her, the King left the box.

Cosel was thus exposed to the ironical glances of the whole Court; she remained for a short time longer, then making believe that she was unwell, ordered her litter, and returned home.

The Countess's enemies thought that by exciting her jealousy, they would succeed in making her quarrel with the King; and with this end in view they sent the Baroness Glasenapp to call on her. She found Cosel in tears and at once began to prattle.

"You cannot think how I pity you. I know everything, and I am indignant at it. You do not perhaps know that the King has taken supper with Duparc?"

Cosel listened quietly to her gossip, then she said,—

"Do not think that I am jealous; I only grieve for the King, who wrongs himself more than he does me."

Having said this, she rose, wiped away her tears, and, suspecting some intrigue, tried to appear indifferent.

Glasenapp did not succeed in making her angry. Cosel could control herself at times.

The King did not come to see her the next day, he was afraid of her impetuosity. Instead he sent Vitzthum to reconnoitre. Cosel and he had always been good friends. Apparently, he came of his own accord, to inquire after her health, and did not in anyway allude to the events of the preceding evening.

"As you see, I am quite well," said Cosel with a sad smile.

"You are always beautiful!"

"And you are always good-hearted and polite."

They talked awhile on indifferent subjects, and then Vitzthum returned to the King and told him Cosel was very reasonable.

The whole clique of her enemies now waited impatiently for the dénouement. Towards evening Augustus himself repaired to the Palace of the Four Seasons.

The news spread, and faces grew sad in consequence.

The King had become accustomed to Anna, and did not wish to abandon her; although his passionate love for her had passed, the habit still remained. He was ashamed of Duparc and proud of Cosel. Cosel on her side was determined to be as reasonable as the Queen herself.

"I do not like public quarrels," said the King, "they do not become either of us."

"Your Majesty, it is my love for the King."

"It must be reasonable," interrupted Augustus.

"It is characteristic of love that it cannot be reasonable."

"But you must try not to be jealous."

"Why, your Majesty, should you give me any reason for jealousy?"

The King shrugged his shoulders, and replied,—

"Childishness."

Cosel refrained from another outburst; she knew that she was not threatened by anything.

The relations between her and the King were not at all changed, only they had become less cordial; a ceremonious gallantry was now substituted for his former passionate love.

The best proof that the Countess had not lost her lover's heart was furnished by the visit of the Danish King, Frederick IV. Augustus, who was always glad of an opportunity for festivities and entertainments, by which he might astonish Europe, received his nephew with great splendour, and in all the festivities Cosel played the leading part, for by her beauty and majestic mien, she was superior to all the women at Court. It seemed as though the King should be excused for admiring such an exceptional being.

After the balls, tournaments, shooting parties, there came the day when the Danish King must take his departure and set out on a journey to Berlin, whither Augustus was to accompany him. After a splendid supper, Cosel returned to her palace. Her face still glowed with triumph and enthusiasm, but at the same time she felt exhausted. She threw herself down on the sofa to rest.

In the palace perfect silence reigned, and this quiet, following on the noise of the entertainment, acted on her most strangely. She was seized with a most unjustifiable fear.

During the hour of her triumph, she had several times encountered Flemming's ironical glances, in which there was an expression of menace, which she alone could understand. Those looks stung her to the heart and made her sad.

In vain she tried to brighten her gloomy thoughts, by recalling all the marks of favour shown her by the King; she could not succeed, and even in the hour of her triumphs, she was haunted by the presentiment of a miserable future.

She did not expect to see the King that day, for the next morning he set out for Berlin.

Suddenly the sound of footsteps was heard coming along the corridor that connected the staircase with the gallery leading to the castle. It could be no one but Augustus, and Cosel sprang to her feet and hastened to the mirror, to assure herself that her hair and dress were in proper order.

Her first glance told Cosel that Augustus was in a state in which she had but seldom seen him.

The leave-taking of his nephew, whom the courtiers had respectfully carried to his bed, had been celebrated with bumper toasts. The King, although accustomed to these feasts, had not come out victorious. It was true that he was able to walk with the assistance of his chamberlain, but that minister only accompanied him to the door, and as soon as he was in Cosel's room he threw himself immediately on the sofa. His face was crimson, his eyes misty, and his speech indistinct.

"Anna," said he, "I wished to bid you goodbye. Well, today you were triumphant, as women very seldom can be. At least you will thank me for it."

Cosel turned towards him—she was sad.

"Alas! my lord," she replied, "I have not sufficient words to express my gratitude. But had you seen the jealous glances cast at me, you would understand why I have returned sad."

Augustus smiled.

"The tragi-comedy of life," he returned indifferently. "I had my Charles XII.—you have your Flemming! Every one has some pain, and life—is life. Be merry for my sake."

"I cannot," she said.

"For me!" repeated Augustus.

Cosel looked at him, then she smiled, though rather with an effort than from the heart.

"Could I always look on you, my lord," said she, sitting down beside him, "then I should be always most happy. But unfortunately you are going away, and who can tell how you will return?"

"Probably not so drunk as I am tonight," rejoined Augustus, with a cold smile. "I like wine, but I hate its dominating over me."

"And when will my lord return?" inquired Cosel.

"Ask the astrologers that question, I do not know. We are going to Berlin. But there is one thing I am glad of, Brandenburg will look rather meagre when compared with our festivities. Frederick will show us his soldiers instead of giving us a good dinner. Berlin after Dresden, ha! ha! ha! I am going on purpose to see my triumph."

"But will your Majesty return faithful to me?" asked Cosel, with whom this was now a constant thought.

"From Berlin?" laughed Augustus. "It is one of the most tedious courts in Europe. There is no danger there either for me or for you."

"And Dessau?" whispered Cosel.

"That is true!" said the King, making a movement with his head. "She was pretty, but she did not understand gallantry. She was offended with half a word. No, I do not like such women."

Then kissing her hand, he said,—

"My dear Anna, I should like to ask you a favour. I should be glad if you and Flemming would not devour each other."

Anna frowned.

"Your Majesty must kindly say that to Flemming, not to me. He is lacking in civility to me, to Cosel, to Augustus' wife."

At these words a strange smile passed over the King's face and his eyes shone fiercely.

"But I dislike wars," said he.

"Then command him to respect and obey me, your children's mother; that will be the best way of keeping peace."

The King made no reply to this, but began to take his leave. Cosel hung tenderly on his neck, then she conducted him to the door, behind which the chamberlain was waiting. The King was gloomy when he left Cosel.

Who could tell the thoughts that then filled his mind? The same evening he summoned Flemming. He was sarcastic and irritable.

"Old man," said he, jokingly, "Cosel complains of you. You must endure it; you must not pay attention to many things, the others you must forgive. You know I bear a great deal from her."

"Countess Cosel pays your Majesty with her love," said Flemming familiarly, "that is quite different."

"Well, get on well with Cosel," added Augustus.

"It will be difficult; I cannot be her courtier; I can neither lie nor flatter, and it is no easy matter for me to bow, for my back is old."

To this the King replied, laughing,—

"It is true, she does not like you either. She says that you look just like a monkey."

Flemming's eyes gleamed, he muttered something between his teeth, and then relapsed into silence.

Had the King desired to make them implacable enemies, he could not have employed better means.

Whilst Augustus was enjoying himself with the indifference of a man who believes in destiny, Charles XII. was also hastening to his fate. In a strange country, with a handful of men, he hurled himself against an unknown power; and, with the bravery of a lion and the recklessness of a young man, he accepted battle on the plains of Poltowa.

This battle was decisive for many countries, and for a still greater number of persons.

Augustus was returning from Berlin well satisfied that he had not been surpassed by that Court, which did not care for splendour or luxury. On his way he was overtaken by a courtier, sent from Warsaw by Princess Teschen, who, on being deserted by Augustus, had returned to her own country, although she still preserved some sentiments of affection towards her royal lover.

The Princess was the first to notify him of the fact that Charles had been defeated. It was a great surprise to the King, who now, for the first time, realized the mistake he had made in resigning the Polish Crown. But, at the same time, he wished to keep his word in the face of Europe. While he still hesitated, Flemming arrived.

"Your Majesty," said he, "treaties obtained by force are not binding. We must return at once to Poland. Leszczynski is not a King. Your Majesty will find thousands of loyal hands ready to defend your rights. We have only to go, and the victory is ours."

The crown, relinquished after such heavy sacrifices, was very tempting to the Kurfürst. He had planned to create a great and hereditary monarchy there. Even were he obliged to give up one of his own provinces to his envious neighbours, Poland united to Saxony would be a very powerful state. He must, therefore, hasten to win back the crown, and change it from an elective to an hereditary one.

Augustus accepted Flemming's advice, and decided to return to Poland. Flemming had many connections in Poland, in consequence of one of his cousins having married the Castelane Przebendowska, and all his friends had promised to help him—there could be no doubt of a happy termination. From Poland there also came Denhoff, and the Bishop Szaniawski, both of whom invited Augustus to return. While the King of Denmark was at Dresden, Augustus had concluded an alliance with him, and to it was now added Frederick of Brandenburg.

Augustus had now no time for love affairs. Immediately on receiving the news of the battle of Pultowa, he returned to Berlin, to come to an understanding with its sovereign. He had barely time to see Cosel, whose quarrel with Flemming had considerably increased. Flemming felt himself strengthened by events. The Countess had sent to him several times, with different demands, but he always refused to carry them out, declaring that now he had more important business to deal with. He tore Cosel's letters in pieces and trampled on them, telling the messenger that he did not care for her complaints or her threats. Cosel could not put up with such provocation.

On the fourth day Flemming, who was riding, met her near the gates of the palace. Cosel leaned out of the carriage window, and, shaking her fist at him, exclaimed,—

"You must remember who you are, and who I am! You are the King's servant, and have to obey orders. I am mistress here. You wish for war with me, you shall have it."

Flemming laughed, and with apparent courtesy, touched his hat.

"I do not make war on women," said he, "and I do what I consider good for my master. I will neither bow to, nor gratify women's caprices."

Then, setting spurs to his horse, he galloped away.

War had now begun in good earnest between them. Cosel wept with anger, and awaited Augustus's return.

Augustus returned early the next day, and he had already been informed of everything that had occurred, for when Flemming met him on the road, he said to him,—

"I wonder that you, an old soldier and a diplomat, cannot live in peace with one woman."

"Your Majesty," returned the General, "I live in peace with many, but

I cannot with those who think themselves goddesses and queens. That woman ruins the country, and does not respect any one."

"But I love this woman, and I require her to be obeyed."

"No one slighted her, until she began to insult every one."

The King was silent, and Flemming added, confidentially,—

"She will ruin Saxony, and Poland too, and then she will not be satisfied. Your Majesty may be satisfied with her caprices, but with us who surround the throne, our duty is to free your Majesty from such fetters."

Augustus hastened to speak of other matters. On reaching the castle he went at once to Cosel, who was awaiting him with anger and reproaches, things that Augustus disliked exceedingly.

"My King! my lord!" she cried. "Help me! Flemming treats me as if I were the least among women. He insults me publicly; he tears my letters in pieces and tramples on them. He has threatened to drive me from this palace. Your Majesty must choose between him and me."

Augustus embraced her, smiling.

"Calm yourself, my dear Countess, you are excited. I need Flemming just now, therefore I must be kind to him."

"And I?" asked Cosel.

"You know very well that I cannot live without you. But if you love me, you will do something for my sake. You will be reconciled to Flemming."

"Never!" exclaimed Cosel.

"He will ask your pardon."

"I do not care about it. I wish never to see the man again."

Augustus took hold of her hand, and said coldly,—

"My dear Cosel, today you wish to be rid of Flemming, tomorrow you will ask to be freed from Fürstenberg, after that it will be the same with Plug and Vitzthum. You cannot live in peace with any one."

"Because no one is friends with me," replied Anna.

She began to cry; thereupon the King rang the bell, and, despite Cosel's opposition, ordered Flemming to be summoned.

After a long time, which Augustus employed in pacing furiously up and down the room, the General arrived. He did not salute Cosel on entering, but turned straight towards the King.

"My dear Flemming," said Augustus, "if you love me, you will ask pardon of the Countess. Shake hands both of you!"

"Never!" exclaimed Cosel. "I will not shake hands with that vile courtier, who has dared to slight a woman."

"Do not be afraid," said Flemming, "I shall not bother you by shaking hands with you. I do not know how to lie, and I shall offer no excuses."

The King had risen. He was angry.

"General, you will do it for me," he said.

"Neither will I do it for your Majesty. I should prefer to leave your service."

"You villain!" screamed Cosel. "His Majesty's favours have made you arrogant; but it is not far from Dresden to Königstein, thank God!"

"Cosel, for Heaven's sake!" interrupted Augustus.

"Your Majesty will permit me to be frank; for I likewise do not know how to lie. I must tell him what I think of him. He declared war against me, let him have it."

"I do not propose to make war against you, Countess," said Flemming. "I have something better to do."

"Leave my house!" screamed the Countess, stamping her foot on the floor.

"This house is not yours; there is not one thing that belongs to you; this is a palace belonging to my King and my lord, and I shall not leave it without his orders," replied Flemming.

Cosel began to weep and tear her dress. Then, addressing Flemming, the King said, gently and calmly,—

"General, I beg you to make peace. I love you both; I require both of you. Why must I suffer because of you?"

"Your Majesty does not need to listen to our quarrels; it were better to leave them to be decided by fate."

Having exhausted all her arguments, Cosel threw herself on the sofa. The King, seeing no means of reconciling them, either by calming Flemming or by softening the irritated Countess, extended his hand to the General and conducted him to the door. Then Augustus began to pace up and down; he was thoughtful, and it was evident that he was occupied with matters of greater importance.

Cosel loaded him reproaches.

"Alas! sire," said she, "then it has come to this, that your servants insult me. It is my fate. Flemming laughs at the one you say you love."

"Dear Countess," he replied calmly, "all that you say proves that you do not know how I am situated. At this moment I need Flemming more than I do my right hand: to make him angry is to renounce the crown of Poland. You cannot ask that of me, and if you did, as a King I should not do it. You know that I do not refuse you anything, but there is a limit to all things. I was a King before I was Cosel's lover."

Frowning, fearful, mad, Cosel rushed towards Augustus.

"Lover!" she screamed. "I have your written promise. I am not your mistress; I am your wife!"

Augustus made a grimace.

"All the more reason you should pay attention to the interests of my crown," he replied.

Again Cosel relapsed into tears. Augustus looked at the clock.

"I am not master of my own time," said he, "I have too much to do. I must leave for Poland shortly. Dear Countess, be calm, Flemming is impetuous, but he loves me, and will do what I ask him."

Cosel made no reply. She shook hands with Augustus silently, and he departed.

Soon after this scene they began to prepare for the journey to Poland. As she was enceinte, the Countess was unable to accompany the King on this expedition.

Cosel well knew the danger that threatened her. At Warsaw the King would meet Princess Teschen, and although in the whole of Augustus's life there had never occurred a reconciliation between him and a former favourite, Anna felt uneasy. Still she was more afraid of the other women whom her enemies put in the King's way, in the hope of inducing him to abandon her for a new favourite.

To save the Countess the unpleasantness of quarrels with Flemming, the King had determined to take him with him, and although Anna would rather have suffered his persecutions at Dresden, than have had him close to Augustus intriguing against her, she was powerless to prevent it.

The King was very kind towards her up to the last moment, and he assured her that he had strictly forbidden Fürstenberg to annoy her.

Having learned that Flemming was going with the King, and that the Countess would remain at home, Cosel's enemies grew hopeful that things would change, and that the combined influence of Flemming and Przebendowska would ultimately prevail, and a new favourite be substituted for Cosel.

Her downfall seemed to them certain.

The day of his departure, Augustus was as tender as possible. He spent the whole day with Cosel, whose state of pregnancy having made her weak, tried to arouse the King's pity by recalling old memories.

But this was the worst possible way she could have acted. Augustus was charmed by vivacity, gaiety, boldness, jealousy, daring—everything that acted on the senses; but sentiment was unknown to him; he played at it from time to time, but he never felt it.

To attempt to arouse in him tender feelings was the surest way to bore him. Cosel was greatly alarmed; she kissed the King; she wept; she entreated him not to leave her, not to forget her. Augustus replied in his choicest words, but his studied declarations were chilling.

Several years had passed; the enthusiasm of both of them had cooled. But in the woman there remained attachment, tenderness, gratitude; in the King a feeling of weariness predominated. Instead of pitying her sadness, he wished to escape from it as quickly as possible; her tears made him impatient, her grief bored him.

Cosel could no longer appear gay and cheerful as formerly, in the happy days when she used to ride out with the King to hunt the deer, or took her part in shooting at a target.

Her charms had not changed, but daily intercourse with her had made them appear common in the King's eyes. Grief had not dimmed her beauty; her eye had not lost its brilliancy; but neither her charming looks, nor her smiles, could now bring the King to her feet. Her power over Augustus was ended, the beloved woman had become common, because she no longer possessed for him the charm of novelty.

Never before, when the King departed, had the Countess felt as lonely as she did now. The palace, until then crowded, was suddenly deserted. Cosel had no one to be with her.

During the day, the gossiping Baroness Glasenapp would rush in, or the stern Baron Haxthausen, her only friend, would dine with her. This was all the company she had.

In the whole crowd, her most faithful friend was Raymond Zaklika, whose hand often trembled with the desire to attack some arrogant man who had offended the Countess. The slightest sign from her would have been sufficient for him, and the one whom he touched would have been a dead man.

Looking towards him at critical moments, Cosel had sometimes noticed him in such a state of excitement that she had been obliged to calm him.

Being a servant, Zaklika had no opportunity of expressing his feeling, but the Countess understood him perfectly, and knew that she could depend on his loyalty. Had she bidden him kill Flemming, he would have done so instantly, and would then have gone without a groan to the scaffold. In his eyes, she was always the same beautiful star that he had seen shining in bygone days among the linden trees at Laubegast. To him she even appeared more beautiful, and his whole happiness lay in the privilege of seeing her several times a day.

But whilst at Dresden all was sad and quiet, the King, in the best of spirits, and full of hope, was hastening to Warsaw. Flemming was with him, the Countess Przebendowska preceded him. It was an open secret that they wished to find a new lady for the King at Warsaw. They did not wish her to be as beautiful as Cosel, for beauty such as hers threatened a long attachment; neither must she be witty, for the King was content with giddiness, and she must not possess a heart, for it was only at the commencement that Augustus played a sentimental part.

Youth, great daring, coquetry, a good name, and good breeding were sufficient, and would counterbalance Cosel.

With these instructions, Countess Przebendowska started for Warsaw, where she was to choose. Flemming's cousin was a great friend of Countess Bielinska, whose two married daughters, the Countesses Denhoff and Pociej, both pretty, quiet and merry, could be placed on the list of candidates.

The first day after her arrival, Przebendowska paid a visit to her friend, who gave her a cordial welcome. She knew Przebendowska's influence over Flemming, and his power over the King.

"My dear," said Przebendowska, "I come to you with many troubles, and I hope you will help me."

"I will share them with you willingly," rejoined Bielinska.

"We are having great trouble with the King," continued Przebendowska. "He is in love with a woman who for several years has made him do whatever she pleases."

"I know Cosel!" interrupted Bielinska. "But why did not the King hold to Teschen?"

"He is never faithful to any one for long. We must get rid of Cosel, and find him some one else. The King is wearied."

Bielinska became thoughtful.

"It is easy enough to find some one else, but we must be careful not to put new fetters on him."

Countess Przebendowska stayed to dinner with her friend, whose two daughters were also dining with her. Both of these ladies were young, elegant in movement, and pretty. Countess Pociej was small and neat; she appeared frail, but her eyes lit up with fire, laughter was for ever bursting from her lips. Countess Denhoff was not tall either; she was gracious, and played the part of a melancholy person, although naturally she was flighty, and burned with a desire for gaiety. Her eyes sparkled with wit and malice, which she veiled under an exaggerated modesty.

Countess Przebendowska talked on indifferent subjects, but she never let the two pretty young ladies out of her sight for a moment. The dinner ended, the two old ladies were left alone.

Przebendowska knew well that Bielinska's affairs were in a bad state, and she at once began to condole with her about them. Presently her friend said,—

"You have seen my daughters. Marie is quiet, fresh, and pretty; she is also good-hearted, submissive, and easily guided. How do you like her?"

"She is charming."

"She is like quicksilver, and, although she seems delicate, she is really very strong and lively."

Then, lowering her voice, the mother continued,—

"We have been good friends since childhood; if some one must be so happy as to attach the King, why should we not introduce Marie to him?"

"I did not know if you would wish it."

"Why not? Denhoff is a bad husband, and he is not young, either; she is very unhappy with him. If he objects to have the King as a rival, Marie will obtain a divorce from him."

"But would she be willing?"

"I will persuade her," said the anxious mother. "It would really be a great blessing for us. Our affairs are in a shocking condition. Should my husband die, we should all be ruined."

Countess Przebendowska neither promised nor refused.

"We shall see, we shall see," she said; then added, "We must not say a word to Marie until we are sure she pleases the King. Cosel was jealous and arbitrary; after her, he will require some one who is gentle, merry, and submissive."

"He would not find any one who answered that description better than Marie does—that I warrant you."

After a long time spent in conversation, the friends separated, a good understanding having been established between them.

A few days later the King and Flemming arrived. Countess Przebendowska lived in the same house with her uncle, and they were able to talk freely even on the first evening. She at once mentioned Countess Denhoff to him.

The General made a grimace; he had heard a great deal about that lady and her giddiness; but after a pause he said,—

"The King is weary, and any woman can captivate him, so it may be better for him to have her."

The next day the General said that before deciding anything he must make the acquaintance of Countess Denhoff. Both the ladies were accordingly invited to spend an evening at Countess Przebendowska's palace. Flemming did not much like the candidate, but after searching about for several days they were obliged to decide on Countess Denhoff, she being less dangerous than any of the others. Having learned a lesson by his experience with Cosel, Flemming was afraid of an ambitious woman, or one who desired to rule. Countess Denhoff was giddy and coquettish, but she was not jealous, and never dreamt of influencing any one; she was simply fond of life.

The next day, Countess Przebendowska had an opportunity of approaching the King. She was merry and jocular.

"Your Majesty," said she, "it seems as though it should be Poland's turn now."

"Dear Countess, what do you mean?"

"After Lubomirska there was Cosel, and after her it seems necessary to choose some one from Warsaw."

"But I desire to remain faithful to Countess Anna."

"In Dresden," replied Countess Przebendowska; "but in Warsaw, and during her absence—"

The King smiled.

"Has your Majesty looked at the beauties in our theatres?" she continued.

"No, I have not!"

"Then I will take the liberty of attracting your Majesty's attention to one of them. There is not another here prettier or sweeter than she is. She is young, and has a beautiful hand."

"Who is she?" asked the King.

"Countess Denhoff, née Bielinska," whispered the lady.

"I do not remember her," said Augustus; "but being an admirer of female beauty, I promise you I shall take advantage of the first opportunity that offers to make the acquaintance of so charming a lady as you describe this one to be."

"If your Majesty will do me the honour to accept a modest supper at my house, tomorrow, perhaps I could succeed in presenting her to you."

The King looked at her, but it seemed as though she did not notice it, for, had she, she must have blushed, so ironical was his glance.

The same day Countess Bielinska was closeted with Countess Denhoff, and when they separated the latter was confused, but at the same time happy. Being accustomed to be regarded as a queen in her own little circle, and sure that everything she did must please, she was frightened at these preparations for a new fortune. She did not oppose her mother's will, but there was so much trouble, and the frivolous woman did not like too many ceremonies.

Flemming and Przebendowska knew that it was necessary that the King should be received with great splendour; the modest supper therefore was altered to a magnificent ball. When the King arrived, he found Countess Denhoff surrounded by many beautiful ladies. He went over to her and began a conversation, which did not succeed at all, and it was noticed that Augustus did not appear to be smitten by her beauty.

After supper the King danced with Countess Denhoff, who was still confused and awkward. The first impression was not such as Flemming's sister had expected.

After the reception the King said to Vitzthum,—

"Have you seen that they wish to seduce me here; but so long as women such as Denhoff wish to compete against Cosel, the latter is perfectly safe."

Vitzthum, who was in a good humour at the time, replied,—

"Your Majesty, it is not a question of Countess Cosel's happiness, for she can remain in Dresden, and Madam Denhoff at Warsaw. But it seems that the Poles complain that they are wronged by Countess Cosel, and wish you to select some one from among them. It would therefore be necessary to divide your Majesty's heart between Saxony and Poland."

The King laughed.

"It is all very well for you," said he, "but every day I receive letters full of reproaches, and then they try and tempt me here."

"The King should do that which pleases him."

Augustus did not need to be persuaded of that.

On Countess Bielinska's part, everything that might attract the King was attended to. The next day he was invited to supper, and Countess Denhoff and her sister amused him by singing to the harpsichord.

This evening Countess Denhoff was more daring, and while singing, she constantly looked across at the King, who liked to be provoked. Her mother and sister helped her, answering for her, and choosing merry subjects of conversation. The King soon grew to like the house and the people, and to visit them oftener; and it was not long before he became accustomed to the little Countess, and fell in love with her, as much as such a man as he was able.

The King was constantly receiving letters from Cosel, to whom her enemies purposely communicated everything: these letters were in consequence full of bitter reproaches. At first the King used to reply to them, but gradually he left them unanswered.

In a conversation with Vitzthum, the King had expressed a wish to get rid of Countess Cosel, whom he feared. Flemming determined to utilize the remark, and one evening when the King sighed, he laughed.

"I should like," said he, "to remind your Majesty of an old story which might perhaps be applied to present circumstances."

"For instance?" queried Augustus.

"In old times," said Flemming, "before he met the beautiful Aurore, the Kurfürst of Saxony was in love with Rechenberg. Soon he wished to get rid of her. Then the Kurfürst of Saxony asked Chancellor Beichling to help him. Beichling courted the lady, and the King was freed."

"I doubt if you would succeed in the same way with Cosel," said the King.

"One could always try."

"Whom do you wish to make happy with her?"

"I would leave the choice to your Majesty's penetration," said Flemming.

The King strode up and down the room, smiling ironically.

"It is difficult to choose, for Cosel has very few acquaintances who would even dare to approach her. Why not employ Baron Lowendhal, who, being her relation and protégé, can approach her more easily than any one else. If I could prove to her that she was unfaithful, I should have a pretext for breaking with her."

"I will employ Lowendhal," said the General. "She has done a great deal for him, but the King has done more; besides, he would not like to fail with Cosel."

"He will do what he is ordered."

As a result of this conversation, a letter was despatched to Dresden, to Lowendhal, ordering him to compromise Cosel.

Augustus wished to get rid of Cosel, but he wished to do it quietly. Sometimes he regretted her, but he was weak; he could not resist the intrigues. Fresh faces did with him what they pleased; novelty amused him, and he gladly entered on fresh amours, ended by laughter and gaping on his part, and tears on the part of others.

The example of Königsmark, Teschen, Spiegel, Esterle, and many more, who had been consoled, and provided with comforters, quieted his mind with regard to Cosel, although he well knew that there was a great difference between her and the others. But then she had threatened to kill him, and her threats were not vain. One might expect she would fulfil it. Orders were therefore given in Dresden that Cosel's movements should be watched; they feared she would come to Warsaw, and, knowing the King's character, Flemming was sure that did Cosel once make her appearance, she would regain her former influence over the King by her beauty and superiority.

It was important that Lowendhal should act speedily. Cosel was still young and beautiful.

One day Cosel's friend, Baron Haxthausen, found her weeping; she rushed towards him, wringing her hands with indignation.

"Could you believe it!" she cried, "that villain Lowendhal, who owes me everything, dared to tell me he loved me."

Haxthausen could scarcely soothe her.

"A few years back," she continued, "he would not have dared to insult me in that way. Have you heard about that Denhoff?"

"Yes! there are some rumours," replied Haxthausen.

"Through what mud will they drag the King!" said she sadly; then she was silent.

Flemming, who was managing the whole affair, came to Dresden. The King had ordered him to get rid of the Countess, but to treat her with great respect and delicacy.

At first his arrival alarmed Cosel, but after a few days, having persuaded herself that he seemed anxious to avoid fresh quarrels with her, she was reassured.

The King wished Cosel to give up the Palace of the Four Seasons, and Haxthausen was deputed to carry out this delicate mission. To his great surprise, Cosel replied,—

"The King gave it to me, and he can take it back. This house reminds me too powerfully of happy times. I could not live in it, and would move out willingly."

The news of her banishment from that paradise filled her enemies with joy. This must be a sure sign that everything was ended between her and Augustus. But Cosel kept on repeating to her intimate friends that she was the King's wife, and that he could not leave her thus.

In 1705, while he was still in love with Cosel, Augustus had made her a present of a lovely country house at Pillnitz, on the banks of the Elbe. The situation was very beautiful, but it was lonely, and quite a long journey from Dresden.

The King wished to show Denhoff the magnificence of his capital, but feared some outburst from Cosel. He therefore wrote to Flemming, telling him to induce Cosel to leave Dresden and take up her residence at Pillnitz.

Haxthausen was again chosen as ambassador, and the King's letter was shown to him.

"General," said Flemming, "the King wishes to visit Dresden, but he cannot come so long as Cosel is here. She has threatened to kill him so many times. And he never likes to meet those whom he has offended. I know that Cosel regards me as her enemy; she has made me momentarily angry, but I have forgotten all about it by now. I should very much dislike to push her to extremities. Be so kind as to go and induce her to leave Dresden. I should be sorry to be compelled to send her an order."

Having heard Flemming's sweet words, Haxthausen went. Cosel was in a very good humour; the General began by joking.

"I marvel at the King's bad taste," said he. "I do not know this Denhoff, but, from what I have heard, I am sure that you will return in triumph to your former position, provided always that you do not irritate the King."

Cosel guessed he had come charged with some errand.

"Do you bring me some command wrapped up in flattery?"

Haxthausen looked at her sadly, and nodded his head to signify that it was so.

"Then speak."

"Flemming has shown me an order from the King, saying that you are to leave Dresden and go to Pillnitz. I think it will be better for you; it will be more agreeable for you than to see—"

Tears dimmed her eyes.

"It is so hard! so very hard!" said she softly. "I know that you are my friend, and I can tell you that you have no idea what an effort it will cost me. Have you seen the King's order? Do they not lie?"

"Yes, I have seen it!"

She flushed, and then grew angry.

"They do not know me!" she exclaimed. "They will tease me until they arouse a fearful vengeance within me. They are mistaken in thinking that I shall respect the man who thinks that the crown gives him the right to scoff at sentiment."

Haxthausen listened in silence.

"And all this," she continued, "I have to suffer for such a woman as that Denhoff, who has already had several lovers. They wished to abase the King that they gave him such a woman as that."

She began to weep.

"Could I have expected this?" said she, sobbing. "He swore that I had his heart, he did not hesitate to give up everything for me, and I believed him; I was sure of the future. Three children unite us, he loved them, he acknowledged them; he was not ashamed of his love for me. I was faithful to him. I tried to please him in everything. I served him like a slave. And today, after so many years, I have to remain alone, driven out without a word of goodbye, without a word of sympathy. Alas! that man has my heart."

In such passionate outbursts half an hour passed; at length she sank on the sofa exhausted.

"Madam," said Haxthausen, "your anger is justifiable, but at present you

143

must be patient and cautious, so that you may not shut the door to a return. You know how changeable the King is; you must win him back, but you must be patient."

"Then give me your advice, my good friend," said Anna.

"Will you allow me to speak frankly?"

"Yes!"

"Flemming is better disposed to you than formerly. You must try and keep him in that frame of mind. Everything is changed at Court. You might be useful to him. If you act quietly now, the King will be grateful to you. They are continually frightening him by saying that you threatened to kill him. The King is afraid, and Denhoff will not venture to start for Dresden, being afraid for her life. As long as the King thinks that you are excited he will not venture near you. The best way, therefore, is to show that you are not vehement. Countess Königsmark has preserved her friendly relations with the King. Princess Teschen was not driven from Dresden, while Esterle, by her obstinacy, has closed the entrance to the palace to herself for ever."

"How dare you give me such examples!" exclaimed Cosel. "Esterle, Königsmark, Teschen, were the King's mistresses, while I am his wife! You must not compare me with them."

Haxthausen was silent.

"Still, you are right," she continued; "I must not make him angry. I will go tomorrow."

The envoy was about to depart with the good news, when Cosel broke forth again,—

"They would not dare force me! The King himself would not dare do that! It cannot be!"

Haxthausen tried to persuade her to be submissive, but no sooner had she agreed to follow his advice than she was again bent on resistance.

Three or four times she changed her mind. Finally she said,—

"I will not go! Let them use force if they dare!"

"Pray think it over! What shall I tell Flemming!"

"Tell him I do not wish to go!"

The Baron returned to the General, and told him of his conversation with Cosel.

Flemming was sorry he was obliged to use force: he went to her. She received him haughtily.

"You place me in a most awkward position," said he, "for I wished to save you unpleasantness. I have kept back the King's order for several days; now I bring it to you personally. Should you refuse to obey it, I shall be grieved, but I shall be compelled to force you to submit to it. The King does not wish to meet you in Dresden."

Looking from the window, Cosel saw a detachment of dragoons standing before her house. Her black eyes gleamed angrily, but she kept her anger under control.

She glanced at the letter.

"I am going at once," said she; "you can trust my word."

Flemming bowed and departed; the dragoons followed him.

An hour later, Cosel, hidden in a carriage, was journeying towards Pillnitz.

A few days later she had disappeared; she was on the road to Warsaw. Letters were immediately dispatched in great haste to Countess Przebendowska, notifying her of the danger.

Cosel's arrival would change their well-played comedy into a drama. The King was already in love, or rather entangled by those ladies, and they determined to act at once, in order to avoid danger. When the King came to see Countess Denhoff, he found her dressed in black, and weeping.

"What ails you, my beautiful lady?" he inquired solicitously, at the same time kissing her beautiful hands.

"Your Majesty," said Denhoff, "I am threatened by a great danger. I should not mind death, were I persuaded that your Majesty loves me; but, alas! they wish to take my life from me, together with your Majesty's heart. Cosel is coming to Warsaw; perhaps she is already here. Perhaps your Majesty has come to tell me that I must yield to my rival."

"From whence did you receive such news?" inquired the King in surprise.

"Still, let Cosel come; your triumph over her will then be more complete."

"No! no!" exclaimed Denhoff. "If she comes, I leave Warsaw."

The mother was listening at the door, waiting for an agreed signal to enter. Marie coughed, the door opened, and the Countess entered. She appeared much surprised at seeing the King.

"I am glad you are come," said Augustus. "You must help me to quiet your daughter."

"Why, what is the matter?" rejoined the mother, still pretending to be surprised.

The King repeated what Countess Denhoff had just told him. The mother listened, looking in wonder, now at her daughter, now at Augustus.

"I do not wonder that Marie is afraid," said she. "Every one knows of Cosel's threats, and how impetuous she is."

"Well," interrupted Augustus, "it is very easy to settle matters. If you wish, I will order Cosel to be sent back to Dresden."

The old lady replied to this with exclamations of gratitude.

"Marie, you may well consider yourself happy, having such a solicitous tutor."

Then addressing the King, she added,—

"I would venture to observe to your Majesty that Countess Cosel will not obey every one."

"Choose whom you please," replied the King, much bored by the scene.

The old lady recommended a Frenchman, by name Montargon, who had come over to Poland with Prince Polignac. Half an hour later he had the King's order that Cosel was to be sent back to Dresden.

"What am I to do, supposing she will not obey your Majesty's order?" inquired the Frenchman.

The King looked thoughtful; then, after a short silence, replied,—

"I will order Captain La Haye and six guards to accompany you; it seems to me that should be sufficient."

The captain was sent for, and given the necessary orders, and that same night the detachment of soldiers marched out against one unarmed woman.

Before starting on her journey, Cosel summoned the faithful Zaklika.

"All have forsaken me," said she; "I have none on whom I can rely."

Zaklika looked gloomy.

"Will you also leave me?"

"I? Never!" he replied shortly.

"I think I can rely on your noble character, and your devotion to me."

"Always!" said Zaklika, raising two fingers, as though he were taking an oath.

"I wish to entrust you with the most precious thing that I possess," said the Countess, lowering her voice, "but you must promise me that you will sacrifice your life, rather than give up that which I am about to give you; that you will guard my honour as—"

"As a holy relic," said Zaklika, raising his fingers a second time. "You may rely on me!"

"No one must know that you possess this thing."

"Do you wish me to swear?"

"No; I believe your word. But you must know what it is you have to guard. I said you would be the guardian of my honour. When the King granted me a divorce from my husband, he gave me a written and sealed promise that he would marry me, otherwise I should never have consented to such a life. They will try to take this promise from me. They may torture me, but I will never tell them where it is. I cannot conceal it here, for they can banish me, and it would not be safe to carry it with me."

She opened a mahogany box ornamented with gold, and took from it a small leather bag with a silk cord.

"You will not betray me!" said she, looking into his eyes.

Tears rolled down Zaklika's cheeks, as he knelt down before her and kissed her hands; then, suspending the bag round his neck, he said, in a voice full of emotion,—

"This shall only be taken from me with my life."

"We are going on a journey," said Cosel. "Things may turn out worse for us than we expect. You must have money."

She handed him a bag of gold.

A few hours later Cosel set forth, taking with her the loaded pistols which she always kept at hand.

Everything went well until they reached Widawa, a small town on the borders of Silesia. Here they were obliged to rest. Cosel put up at the best hostelry, at which there was a detachment of cavalry. Zaklika was at the door of the Countess's room, when Montargon and La Haye came to him with the request that he would announce them to the Countess, to whom, having met her on the road, they were anxious to pay their respects.

Cosel was much surprised at receiving such a message, as now every one seemed anxious to avoid her, still she suspected no danger, and ordered Zaklika to bring them in.

The Countess received the officers courteously, and as it was the hour for dinner, she invited them to share her modest repast.

Conversation flowed easily during the meal; Montargon told the Countess all the latest news from Warsaw; at length he said,—

"It seems to me that your journey is futile. So far as we know, it may make the King angry. You may meet with unpleasantness."

Cosel frowned.

"What!" she exclaimed, "you dare to give me your advice? You pretend to know the King better than I do, and to be a better judge than myself of what is fitting for me to do?"

Montargon looked confused.

"Pray excuse me!" he muttered.

"I will not excuse you!" exclaimed the Countess, "for it was impertinent, as well as in bad taste. Keep your advice for those that need it."

Montargon made a grimace.

"It is true," said he, "that you do not need advice from me, but suppose I have the King's order?"

"An order from the King?" cried Cosel.

"Yes."

"Even in that case I am not bound to obey," replied the Countess. "The

King is overpowered by my enemies, he is doing that which he has no right to do, and he will regret it afterwards. I am sure he will be glad that I have not obeyed him."

Montargon was a polite man, but the Countess's tone offended him, so he replied in a soft tone that made his words all the more offensive,—

"I should be greatly obliged to you, Countess, if you would spare me the unpleasantness of employing that most simple of all arguments—force."

"What?" exclaimed Cosel. "You would dare employ force against me?"

"I have a formal order to compel you to return to Dresden," said Montargon, "and I shall obey it."

Then the Countess's anger burst forth.

"Leave the room!" she cried, seizing a pistol. "If you do not go, I will shoot you through the head."

Zaklika stood ready on the threshold.

Montargon, who knew well that the Countess would keep her word, slipped out quickly. La Haye, who up to the present had not uttered a word, remained. The lesson his comrade had received had been good for him, and he now began very delicately,—

"Countess," said he, "ambassadors are never fired on; I pray you, calm yourself. We are not responsible for bringing such an unpleasant message. I should be in despair, should I incur your displeasure; but for Heaven's sake, consider; to a military man, the King's order is a sacred thing, and must be accomplished."

"Have you seen the King?" inquired Cosel.

"Yes; I received my orders from his own lips. I beseech you to give heed to it!"

This soft tone completely disarmed Cosel, she sank trembling into an arm-chair.

"Be calm," continued La Haye. "It seems to me that there is nothing serious for you in all this."

"And that Denhoff?"

"That is only a passing fancy," said La Haye; "something like the amour with Duval, which he has already forgotten. Moreover, Denhoff is married, her husband is in the country, and knows nothing of all this; should he learn the truth, there would be no chance of his allowing her to come to Dresden. But the King must return thither, then you will see him, and regain your former influence over him."

Cosel began to ask questions about everything, and La Haye laid the whole story before her in such a light, that he considerably modified the appearance of danger to herself. After a quarter of an hour's conversation, the Countess was persuaded that it would be better for her to return to Pillnitz.

Montargon did not show himself again, but sent a messenger immediately to the King with the good news. Being afraid, however, that Cosel might change her mind, he followed her with La Haye and the soldiers from afar, till they were sure she would not return.

In the meantime the Countess Denhoff began to attract attention by receiving the too frequent visits of the King. The respectable people were scandalized at the behaviour—at her dishonouring the good name of a married woman, during her husband's absence. They were much more shocked at the fact that her own mother was an intermediary agent, that her own sister was a witness, that they boasted of such conduct. Count Denhoff's whole family began to press him to call his wife to his country estate; and Denhoff sent her imperative letters, urging her to leave Warsaw immediately.

But the young woman sent her mother instead. When she came to her son-in-law's château, she said to him pointedly,—

"You must not plague us with these demands to return, for it cannot be done. We are not going to give up the happiness of our whole family for your fancies; the King is in love with Marie, and we intend to keep him. Do you wish me to bring her here for the sake of stupid prudery, and neglect our interests?"

Denhoff was a man of the old school, and he had already heard of his wife's flightiness.

"Madam," said he, "I am not inclined to share my wife's heart with the King; and, frankly speaking, there would remain very little of it for me, for, as it seems, many people court your daughter."

"Then," said the Countess, "you must either be silent, and thus assure for yourself the King's favour, or else consent to a divorce. The papal nuncio, Monsignor Grimani, is quite friendly towards us; he will secure the divorce in Rome."

"Deliver me from the King's favours; but if you would free me from my wife, I shall be only too thankful to you for it," said the Count.

The Countess was greatly astonished that her son-in-law should so readily give up all chances of the King's favour; but having received his written consent to the divorce, she returned with it to Warsaw. The nuncio wrote to Rome, and Clement XI. ordered the divorce to be granted.

There was thus no longer any objection to Countess Denhoff accompanying the King to Dresden; except, to be sure, that Cosel would be in her way.

In order to get rid of her rival, Countess Denhoff feigned that she lived in continual fear of her, and she incited the King to send her from Pillnitz, so that she would not be able to return to Dresden. Then Flemming helped her, reminding the King that he should take from her his promise of marriage, so that she would not be able to compromise the King. Augustus found he was right, and ordered Count Watzdorf to be written to, to try and obtain that document from Cosel and persuade her to leave Pillnitz.

Cosel was obliged to receive him, knowing that he came on an errand from the King.

"The best proof," said he, "that I wish you well is my coming here. I would like to help you to come to some understanding with the King; but you must show some goodwill, and finish peacefully like Aurore and Teschen."

Cosel blushed.

"Aurore and Teschen," exclaimed she, "were his favourites, while I am his wife. I have his written promise."

Watzdorf laughed.

"Ah! dear Countess," said he, with offensive familiarity, "it is an old story. You know well how tyrannical passion is; a man is not master of himself under its influence. Our King also signed the peace at Altranstadt, but does not consider himself bound by it; it is the same with his promise to marry you."

Cosel could hardly contain her indignation.

"No! I still believe he is an honest man who knows what he does, and deceives neither himself nor any one else."

She began to pace to and fro.

"Tell me, then, frankly," said Watzdorf, "what are your conditions? The King is willing to grant them to you, only you must not ask anything impossible or attach too much weight to trifles. You will give me back that paper."

Cosel turned towards him excitedly.

"Did you come for that?" she asked.

"Well, yes."

"Then return," said Cosel angrily; "for as long as I have life I shall not surrender that paper; it is a defence of my honour, and that is more precious to me even than life. Do you think I had consented, for all the King's riches, to stretch out my hand to him if he had not given me the promise of marriage?"

"But you well understand," said Watzdorf, "that it is of no value, for the Queen is living."

"Then why do you want it back?" asked Cosel. "You must be ashamed that the King has deceived me."

"I cannot hear any reproaches against the King," said Watzdorf.

"Then return from whence you came," said Cosel, leaving the room.

The Count stopped her.

"Think of what you are doing; you are forcing the King to be severe with you. He can use force! You cannot hide the paper so that it cannot be taken from you."

"Let him try, then," said the Countess.

"It would be a very sad extremity," rejoined Watzdorf, "and we would like to avoid it. If you oblige us to use force, you cannot expect anything else."

Cosel did not let him finish, but said to him,—

"You wish me, then, to sell my honour? I assure you that there is not money enough in the King's treasury to pay for the honour of such a woman as I am. I shall not return that document for anything! I wish to let the world know how I have been deceived."

Tears rolled down her cheeks.

"No!" she exclaimed suddenly, "you lie; it cannot be the King's will; you blacken the King, wishing to defend him. I have not yet doubted his noble heart, although I believe he is occasionally thoughtless. The King cannot ask for it."

The messenger silently took from his pocket the King's letter and handed it to the Countess.

She glanced at it contemptuously.

"If that which he signed for me has no value now," she said, "what weight can I give this letter? Tomorrow the King may ask you to return that to him."

Watzdorf, in confusion, replaced the letter in his pocket and said,—

"Countess, I pity you—you may believe me or not, but I am sincere. For God's sake, think of what you expose yourself to! remember the lot of many people. It is dangerous to oppose the King."

"I know him better than you," she answered.

"I beseech you!"

"Spare yourself the time and trouble," said Cosel quietly. "It is in vain; you can do less with me by threatening than by persuasion."

She threw a contemptuous glance at him and left the room.

Hardly had the carriage in which Count Watzdorf had come disappeared than Cosel called Zaklika to her. Being afraid of spies in her own house, Cosel told him to follow her into the courtyard, and there she tried to speak to him as if she were giving him some instructions concerning the house.

Zaklika had guessed her thoughts.

"We are watched here, are we not?" said Cosel.

"Yes," answered the faithful servant.

"Can we deceive them?"

"The principal spy is Gottlieb, but he is stupid."

"Gottlieb!" exclaimed the Countess.

"Yes; the man that talks so much of his fidelity to you."

"In the city everybody knows you, I suppose?"

"Many of them have forgotten me," answered Zaklika.

"Could you bring some news?"

"If I must, I will."

"It is dangerous for me to remain here," continued Cosel. "I must escape. I have confidence in you alone; you must advise me how it can be done."

Zaklika was silent and thoughtful.

"It is difficult, but if we must—"

"Then," said Cosel, "I must take my jewels and money with me."

Zaklika did not say a word; he pulled his moustache and lowered his eyes.

"Could you assure me that we shall be able to cross the frontier before our escape is noticed?"

"I will do my best."

His face was covered with perspiration; it was evident that he doubted the success of the enterprise, but he did not wish to show it.

"We should have done it a long time ago," said he.

He snapped his fingers and frowned. Cosel looked at him with fear and curiosity. This silent, energetic man was so different from the others, on whom she could not count; he astonished, but at the same time rejoiced her. She felt that he was a man.

"I have a boat," said he, "hidden in the bushes. During the night I will go into the town and learn everything I can; then I will think how we could escape. You must not call me—they will think I am shut up in my room, as has happened often before."

At that moment Cosel perceived Gottlieb stealing towards them, and not wishing that he should guess anything, she nodded to him. The German swiftly approached.

"Gottlieb," said she, "I would like some flowers planted, for I think I shall stay here a long while. If you go into town you must try and get me a gardener, for the Pole says he does not know anybody."

Gottlieb looked at them both as if trying to guess whether she was speaking the truth, and began to assure the Countess that he would do anything to please his beloved mistress.

Cosel entered the house, and Gottlieb tried to learn something from Zaklika, but it was in vain.

Towards the evening the Pole, as they called him, disappeared. This aroused the suspicions of the spies; they tried to open the door of his room, but found it locked. The room was on the ground floor, so they looked into it through the window, opposite to which was the bed. A man was lying there. This quieted the spies, and they let him sleep.

In the meantime Zaklika unmoored his boat, and, jumping into it, allowed it to be carried down by the stream, which bore it swiftly towards Dresden. In a couple of hours he perceived the lights of the capital. He already knew where to go for news.

In the Dresden Court, where every one squandered money, the bankers were very important people, and among them was Lehman. He came from Poland, he was a laborious and honest man, shrewd in money transactions, but scrupulously honest. Cosel had sent Zaklika several times for him, and they had had some important transactions.

The Jew, who had the best of opportunities for learning people's characters, had recognized in Cosel a noble soul; he had entire confidence in her, and respected her very much.

Zaklika knew that even after Cosel's downfall Lehman had given her proofs that he remained faithful to her, and he thought he could trust him and ask him for advice.

Having left his boat near the hostelry of a Wend, as in those days there were still many of them in Dresden, he drew his hat over his eyes and went into the town.

When he had passed the gates, although it was late, he recognized by the movement in the streets that there was an entertainment in the castle. Zwinger and the garden of Hesperides were illuminated. The King was giving a torchlight masquerade to the Countess Denhoff.

Zaklika did not go near the castle, but went directly to Judenhause, situated in Pirna Street, in which Lehman had a modest house. Zaklika was sure that he would find the banker alone at this hour, and he was anxious for nobody to see him. An old servant opened the door to him, and showed him into a room at the rear of the house.

Lehman, a quiet man, with steady black eyes, shook hands with him, and, in reply to Zaklika's inquiring look round, said,—

"You are safe here; no one can spy on you in my house. What is your news?"

"Bad news," answered Zaklika; "it couldn't be worse. They hunted us from the Palace, from the house in Dresden, and now they wish to drive us from Pillnitz—or perhaps something worse. We must help that unfortunate woman—persecuted as she is by these cowardly villains."

"Yes," said Lehman; "but we must be careful, and not hurt ourselves in the attempt."

"Cosel must escape," added Zaklika.

"To where?" asked the Jew. "She would be safe only beyond the seas."

"I hope the King will not ask his neighbours for our extradition."

Lehman moved his head.

"The Countess," went on the faithful servant, "must take what she can with her, for anything she leaves, the rapacious people will seize, as they did that which she left in the Palace."

The banker nodded.

"But it would not be safe to carry the money with us in our flight, for we might be caught and deprived of everything. You must help the Countess to save the rest of her fortune."

"Believe me," said the banker, "I am willing to help the Countess. I knew her well; she was the only pearl amid all that mud; but you must understand that it would not be right for me to endanger myself and my family for her sake."

"God alone will know of your good deed, and you know that neither I nor the Countess would betray you."

"Well, I consent," said the Jew; "but you must be careful that nobody sees you going out, for I, too, am watched by spies."

"I will be careful," said Zaklika.

"Everything you give me I will send you whenever it best suits you," added the Israelite.

Lehman took from a sideboard a bottle of wine and two glasses.

"No, thank you," said Zaklika. "I must hasten, for I want to learn some news to take to my mistress."

"It is always the same old story," said Lehman, gloomily; "those who drink with the King they are in favour; they enjoy themselves from morning till evening, and they send to Königstein those who are in the way of their amusement. You must not ask for pity or heart, for the least sensitive people are those who are lascivious. The King uses all of them, bestows favours upon them when he needs them, and he despises them."

"What about the Countess Denhoff?"

"She gathers money, that's all; and it seems the King already thinks of marrying her to somebody."

Lehman shrugged his shoulders.

"You wish to learn something," continued he. "Here the people are changed, but not the things."

They talked a little while longer; then Lehman led Zaklika to the gate at the rear of the garden, and gave him a key for it. Zaklika, wrapped in his mantle, went on further. He did not think it would be dangerous to mix with the crowd, to approach Zwinger, and see what was going on there.

He was already in the street leading to the castle thronged with nobles vénitiens, when somebody slapped him on the shoulder.

He turned, surprised—the fool Fröhlich smiled at him.

"How did you recognize me?" asked Zaklika.

"Besides the King, nobody here has such broad shoulders as you have," whispered Fröhlich. "What are you doing here? I heard that you were with Cosel."

"I left her," answered Zaklika, "There was nothing to do after her downfall."

"You are right," said the fool; "one must always take care of one's neck. Then you returned to the King's service—or perhaps you are with Denhoff?"

"Not yet," answered Zaklika. "But tell me, what do you think of her?"

"She is like those little black animals that jump and bite, but which it is difficult to catch," said the fool, laughing.

They were still talking when a passing Spaniard, with a mask on his face, stopped, and began to look attentively at them. Zaklika wanted to go, when the masked man approached him, raised his hat, and seized him by the hand.

Fröhlich disappeared immediately.

The unknown asked Zaklika imperatively,—

"What are you doing here?"

"I am looking for a position," answered he.

"Do you no longer like the service in which you were formerly?"

"They do not need my services there now."

"What kind of position are you seeking?"

"I am a nobleman," answered Zaklika.

The Spaniard muttered something, then he said,—

"Where is Cosel?"

"Probably in Pillnitz—I am not sure."

"Come with me."

"Where?"

"Don't ask; you are not afraid, I hope."

Zaklika went, and he soon noticed that the stranger led him to Flemming, who was at home, drinking with some friends. Masked men went to and fro; those who preferred the wine remained. Flemming expected the King. There was a great noise in the house.

The Spaniard entered, and whispered something to Flemming, who then came to Zaklika, and conducted him to a separate room. The Spaniard followed them.

"When did you leave Cosel?" asked he.

"A few days ago."

"What was she doing then?"

"She was settling in Pillnitz."

"Does she intend to stay there?"

"I think so."

"Why did you part from her?"

Zaklika understood that he must win their confidence, and he answered,—

"She dismissed me, for now she does not need many servants."

"Do you know Pillnitz well—the people and the roads?"

"Very well indeed!"

"Would you accept another service?"

"Why not?"

"Even were you obliged to act against your former mistress?"

"The King is my only master," said Zaklika, "for I am a nobleman."

Flemming laughed.

"Come to me in two days," said he.

"Very well."

Flemming wanted to give him some money; but Zaklika refused to accept it, and withdrew.

Thus he was sure he had two days in which to save his beloved lady.

He wrapped himself in his mantle, and visited some friends in the suburbs; then he took his boat and went towards Pillnitz, sculling hard against the current of the river.

Among other items of news that Zaklika gathered was this—that the next day another masquerade was going to be given in the old market square. There was not a day without either concert, opera or ballet, or some kind of entertainment. Musicians brought from Italy, singers, and composers, were so well selected that Dresden Theatre was the first in Europe. Lotti was the musical composer; Tartini gave concerts; Santa Stella was prima donna, Durastanti was called the princess of opera singers; Senesino and Berselli were famous tenors; Aldrovandini painted scenery; Bach was musical director.

Distractions were not lacking. The King himself, very often masked and disguised, took part in these entertainments, for he was fond of incident, and willingly bore the unpleasantness of such amusements. The King sent round numerous orders, for he wanted to see the square crowded. The preparations had commenced on the preceding night.

Zaklika arrived at Pillnitz at dawn, and found everybody sleeping; he entered his room unperceived, and waited there until his mistress should get up.

As soon as he noticed the windows of her chamber were open he began to walk under them until the Countess had seen him, and went out to talk with him.

Zaklika reported everything to her exactly, especially his conversation with Lehman. He suggested that the best way would be to carry the money and jewels to Dresden during the day, so as not to arouse any suspicions. The heavy boxes would have required two or three men to carry them; but Zaklika, being of extraordinary strength, could manage them alone.

The Countess consented to everything. Horses hired by Zaklika were to wait for them at dusk in the forest on the shore of the Elbe. He hoped her departure would not be noticed before he reached Dresden, and that they would be in Prussia before the pursuit commenced. Once on foreign soil, Zaklika expected they would not be molested. Zaklika was hopeful of accomplishing their escape, and he rejoiced at the thought, but when Cosel told him that she would stop in Dresden and glance at the masquerade, he turned pale.

"It cannot be," said he. "You would throw yourself into the lion's jaws! They would recognize you, and then—"

Cosel shook her head.

"I want to, and it must be done," said she. "I must see him—it is not a fancy, but a need, a medicine. I must look at them in order to shake off the longing from me, and learn to despise the man whom I loved."

"But you expose yourself—"

"I know it," interrupted Cosel. "They could seize me and shut me in Königstein or some other castle; they could kill me, but I must be there. To defend my life I shall carry a weapon—the rest you must leave to me."

Zaklika wrung his hands, but, knowing Cosel, said not a word more.

The Countess entered the house in order to pack what she wanted to give him; Zaklika went to Gottlieb to tell him to have a carriage ready to take different things to the Countess's children to Dresden. Happily the German did not suspect anything. Zaklika chose a groom who was stupid and not acquainted with Dresden. He himself put the boxes in the van, covered them carefully, and they went on.

On the road, for further safety, he made the groom drunk, so that when they came to the capital, he did not know by which streets they went. At Lehman's house he opened the gate with the key the Jew had given him, took down the boxes, and carried them into the banker's room. Not a soul noticed him. When he returned to the van, the groom was asleep; therefore he seized the reins and returned to Pillnitz.

In the meantime, Cosel was taking leave of Pillnitz, gathering her things, writing her letters, and everything she was obliged to do in such a way that none of the servants might see her doing it and betray her before the time. Dinner was served at the usual hour, when at that moment the Counts Friesen and Lagnasco came from Dresden, to make sure of what she was doing.

Cosel had so much strength that she received them with almost a merry mien and without betraying her secret. She pretended to be resigned to her fate, to be occupied with her garden and house, and perfectly indifferent to all that was going on in Dresden.

She played her rôle so well, that the two gentlemen were perfectly deceived. Count Friesen asked her to lend him quite a sum of money. Cosel, smiling, said to him,—

"My dear Count, I am poorer than you would imagine. It is the King's custom to take away that which he has given; at any moment I may lose everything I possess. I am sorry, but I cannot help you."

Friesen accepted the excuse without being angry.

The guests, chatting about Court, amusements, the King, remained till evening. Happily they were obliged to return for the masquerade, for the King would not forgive them their absence, and they took their leave and departed.

Dusk was beginning to fall, and the Countess, complaining of headache, announced to the servants that she would retire very early. Zaklika gave orders that everything should be quiet, and Cosel locked herself in her chamber.

When darkness had completely fallen on the earth, Zaklika, armed with pistols, rapped at the door leading into the garden. A figure dressed in black slipped out and seized Zaklika's arm. They went towards the Elbe, where they entered a boat together, and were soon flying down the stream. In about a quarter of an hour they landed, and found a carriage and four. In those adventurous times, no one was astonished at a woman escaping at night.

Zaklika, having put Cosel into the carriage, sat beside the driver, and they drove to Dresden, alighting at a certain hostelry where another carriage was ready for them. Zaklika tried once more to persuade the Countess to give up her plan of visiting the masquerade in the market place; but she did not want to listen. He was obliged to put on a mask and a domino and accompany her.

That day the streets were a scene of still greater animation. The houses in the street leading to the castle were ornamented with flags and tapestry and lighted with lanterns. The street was so crowded with people, carriages, and litters that it was difficult to move about.

When they came to the market square, they found it thronged with people. Music was playing in the galleries. Round the square stood booths, in which ladies dressed in oriental costumes were selling toys, drinks and dainties. Thousands of lamps threw their light on a kaleidoscopic crowd of masks and dominoes. Singing, music, bells, laughter, shouting—all contributed their quota to the general hubbub. In the windows of the houses one could see overdressed women, and here and there sombre figures of poor people, who were obliged to look on from their miserable dwellings at this luxury and listen to the wild outbursts of laughter.

At the end of the street, Cosel stopped—she had not strength to advance further. Zaklika seized the opportunity and begged her to return. Instead of answering, she moved forward, looking keenly around her.

A few steps in front of her stood a *noble vénitien*.

He wore a black hat with feathers, a black velvet dress, a small mask and a golden chain. Around him swarmed many masques.

Cosel recognized Augustus—Hercules and Apollo that he was, there was no mistaking him. She hesitated for a moment—then went up to him.

Although her dark domino disguised her well, it could not entirely conceal her identity from any one who knew her well. The King glanced at her and shivered, but did not wish to believe his own eyes.

Cosel passed him casually several times. Augustus drew towards her and made as if he would speak to her, but fear held him back. She challenged him with a look, and he went up to her.

The conversation began in French; the Countess changed her voice, which was trembling. Augustus did not take that trouble, and began to look at her attentively.

"Upon my honour," said he, "beautiful mask, I flatter myself that I know every one of you here, but—"

"You do not know me."

"And do you know who I am?"

"Yes, I know you."

"Who, then, am I?"

Her voice trembled, then the words flew straight to his ear,—

"An executioner."

The King drew himself up haughtily.

"A bad joke," said he.

"No, an honest truth!"

"If you know who I am," said he, "but dare to speak that way to me, then I would say that I too know who you are; but it cannot be."

"No, you do not know me," said Cosel, laughing.

"That is what I think. You cannot be the one whom I take you for, for that one would not dare to come here without my permission."

"A woman would not dare to come here?" said Cosel. "A woman would ask your permission?"

And she laughed.

The King shivered, as if he recognized the laugh; he seized her hand, but she withdrew it quickly.

"Beautiful mask," said Augustus, "you perplex me, and you pretend to know me."

"No, I do not know you," answered Cosel. "Some time ago I knew somebody who resembled you; but that one had a noble heart and the soul of a hero, while you—"

The King became angry.

"Mask," cried he, "this surpasses the limits of carnival freedom."

"The freedom is boundless."

"Then go on," said the King, "and I?"

"You?"

Cosel's voice failed her for a moment, then she proceeded,—

"If you are not an executioner, then you are a plaything in the hands of your executioners."

"Cosel!" cried Augustus, seizing her hand.

"No, no!" she cried, pulling away her hand and laughing ironically behind the mask. "How could she be here and suffer to look at her funeral banquet? I have seen the woman whose name you have pronounced. There is nothing in common between her and me. Cosel is killed and buried by her wicked enemies, while I am alive."

The King listened gloomily. Suddenly Cosel drew near to him and whispered a few words into his ear, and, before Augustus could overcome his surprise, she had disappeared.

The King wanted to follow her, but she, protected by Zaklika, vanished in the crowd and hurried behind the booths. Here she turned her black mantle, which was lined with red, and then went back into the square from another side. She went straight to where she expected to meet the Countess Denhoff.

There were three booths opposite the town hall. In one of them, ornamented in the Neapolitan aqua-fresca style, was sitting the Countess Pociej; beside her stood Count Friesen with a guitar, the Countess Bielinska, disguised as a Venetian lady, and the Countess Denhoff in a Neapolitan costume, glittering with precious stones. She was a little woman, with a withered face and painted cheeks. Her booth was surrounded by young men, among whom the most conspicuous was the French ambassador, Besenval, who was making her laugh with his witticisms.

Cosel succeeded in getting a good view of her. The Countess Denhoff, under the influence of her intent look, shivered. Cosel stretched out her beautiful hand for a glass of the lemonade which Denhoff was selling.

"Beautiful lady," said Cosel, "have pity on me, I am thirsty—I do not ask for alms, for I know that you ask to be paid well for everything."

She showed a gold piece of money.

Denhoff, as if she guessed a threat, handed her a glass of lemonade with trembling hand.

"One word more," said Cosel, drawing near. "Look at me!"

Having said this, she took off her mask in such a way that only Denhoff could see her.

"Look at me, and remember my face; it is the face of a foe whose curses will follow the inconstant coquette to the grave. Look at me; I am the same of whom you were afraid, whom you wanted to imprison, whom you robbed of the King's heart, who will curse you day and night. Remember that you shall meet a worse lot than I. I go away pure, innocent, betrayed; you will go from here soiled, without honour, an outcast of the outcasts. I wanted to see you and tell you that I know the blackness of your character."

Denhoff was frightened, and began to faint. There was a great disturbance round the booth; the King rushed to it; but Cosel escaped adroitly and disappeared with Zaklika up a side street.

They heard behind them a tumult of voices, the wave of crowding people shouting and soldiers calling. Zaklika had his pistols ready. Cosel walked swiftly in front of him. The noise grew fainter. Knowing the streets well, Zaklika was able to conduct Cosel safely to the gate of the city. Unhappily, before they reached it, there came an order to close it and not let any woman pass.

Having learned this, Zaklika led Cosel to Lehman's house. They found the banker at home, sitting quietly with his family. Both entered quietly, and Zaklika asked for men's clothes for Cosel. Lehman gave him a black mantle and an old hat, and, shivering with fear, he let them out by the back door. In the street they met a detachment of soldiers. The officers were dismounted, and walking in the street. Zaklika took the Countess's arm and led her along the middle of the street. Cosel dropped her head, and covered her face with the brim of her hat.

When they came near the soldiers, some of them looked at them attentively, but did not stop them. They overheard the conversation of the officers, who said,—

"Has somebody stolen the most precious jewel?"

"Ha! ha! ha! They seek Cosel, who avenged herself on the King."

"Cosel! but she does not exist now."

"They are still afraid of her."

"When Teschen fell into disgrace, nobody thought of her any more, but Cosel still rules, for they shiver at the mere mention of her name."

The others laughed.

An hour later a carriage rolled towards the Prussian frontier. Cosel was thinking of her last adventures, while Zaklika, sitting beside the driver, listened to hear if they were being pursued; but they were looking for Cosel in Dresden and Pillnitz.

At the beginning of the eighteenth century Berlin was a small city. It had only been recently built, and its principal characteristic was cloister-like order and tranquility. It was full of soldiers. Everything was prescribed, the business transactions as well as the pleasures. No other city could be more melancholy, after gay Dresden, than was Berlin. In the larger streets there were rows of houses, built there by order. The city was quiet and empty, although it already had five districts and large poor suburbs. Here and there stood palaces built in a pretentious but tasteless style. In Spandau shone the Queen's Montbijou; in Stralause, the King's Belvidere.

Here everything was new, like the state itself: the oldest buildings were thirty years old. A few statues were erected in this desert; a couple of large squares were waiting for animation.

One bridge had been built across the Spree—it was called "New Bridge," and instead of Henry IV., they put on it the Elector Friedrich Wilhelm. They began to build the King's castle, and its architect, Schluter, ornamented it with so many garlands, that its walls could not be seen beneath them.

Berlin had then the beginnings of a great city; it wanted only life and people. A theatre, library, and museum were hurriedly built, and filled as they could with what they could. In the meantime they did not spend their gold in manufacturing porcelain; they purchased soldiers instead, paying their weight in gold for them. And, in fact, the most interesting thing in Berlin was the army—drilled like a machine, regular as a watch, moving like one man.

Here one could see the battalion of the biggest and tallest grenadiers— the most famous in the world—composed of men of every nationality, and an example of the perfection that the mechanics of militarism can reach. Those big grenadiers were well paid, although the strictest economy was applied to other things.

Berlin, after Dresden, looked like a monastery after a theatre. When Cosel's carriage entered the streets of the capital, and the beautiful Countess glanced at those dusty and empty thoroughfares, her heart was ready to break; but she expected to find peace here: here she wanted to wait for the change of her lot.

A servant sent ahead had already rented a house, which, after the palaces she was used to, appeared poor to her, although it was only cold and uninhabited.

The next day Zaklika arranged it as comfortably as he could, while Cosel sat in a corner and dreamed of her brilliant past.

But in Berlin nobody could remain incognito. The third day Zaklika announced to her the visit of Marshal Wartesleben, the governor of Berlin; and another marshal, Natymer, commandant of the gendarmes, often passed through the street and looked at the house.

It was known in high circles that the dweller in that house was the Countess Cosel, and her arrival was agreeable, for they knew also that a considerable amount of money came for her to the banker Liebmann. Notwithstanding the good relations existing between Dresden and Berlin, Cosel would not expect still to be persecuted here. Only here, in that silent solitude, amid the city that slept at dusk, did her misfortune appear in its full size.

Her heart was filled with bitterness. She spent the days sitting motionless, looking at the wall and thinking about her past.

She was asking herself whether it was possible that one could forget true love, and pay for happy moments with ingratitude. The King's character seemed to her to be a monstrous conundrum. She recollected his tenderness, the proofs of his attachment to her, his oaths—and she could not understand how he could change.

She had doubts about the man, who seemed to her to be a wild animal. She could not understand how he could go back on the past, and contradict his former conduct towards her. She asked herself whether she had done anything so bad that she might look upon her present downfall as a penance for her sins.

A few days later Zaklika entered her room, although she had not called him. Cosel looked at his sad face, and asked,—

"Some bad news?"

"It seems that there is no good news for you in this world," answered he. "Spies already surround the house, and I wanted to tell you to be careful.

If I am not mistaken, sooner or later somebody will come and offer you his friendship; you must be careful what you say."

The Countess frowned.

"You ought to know me by this time, I cannot lie even by silence. I had the courage to tell him the truth to his face; I shall have it now, and shall tell the truth to any one who is willing to listen."

"What benefit will it be to you to make them angry?" said he sadly.

The stubborn woman said not a word more, and Zaklika left the room.

Three days after this an elegant young man asked to be announced to the Countess.

It was the Baron von Sinen.

The Countess knew him well in Dresden, and she told the servant to show him in.

He said he was very much surprised, while visiting Berlin, to hear the Countess was there.

Cosel looked ironically into his eyes and asked,—

"And where were you when I was leaving Saxony?"

"I was in Dresden the very evening that you made that poor thing Denhoff faint; but then I could not inquire what had become of you."

"I am glad you could forget me," said Cosel, "as I do not wish for anything but to be forgotten."

"I think," said Von Sinen, "that they would be glad also to be certain that you have forgotten the wrongs they did to you."

There was silence for a moment, then Von Sinen whispered,—

"I could tell you much interesting news."

It seemed that he wanted to gain Cosel's confidence.

"I am not curious," said Cosel, smiling sadly. "I have no interest in anything now."

"We enjoy ourselves immensely," continued Von Sinen, as if he had heard nothing. "It is nothing new to you, who participated in so many splendid feasts; but—" Evidently he wanted to make her speak. Cosel was silent.

"The place is very well known to you," continued the Baron, "for in Laubegast—"

"I lived there happily," whispered Cosel.

"Flemming gave a great feast to the King and Denhoff—on the plain near Laubegast, opposite Pillnitz."

"Ah!" exclaimed Cosel.

"In the first place six regiments went there," continued the visitor. "On the hills they placed cannon, and disposed the army in such a way that the Court might see the imitation of a battle. Everything succeeded admirably. The regiments advanced firing, and although, with the exception of a few who were trampled on, nobody was killed, one could have sworn the battle was a real one. The King was looking at the spectacle, Denhoff was beside him, he was surrounded by a splendid Court."

Cosel smiled ironically.

"Not far off they put up magnificent tents. Under one of them the King dined with the Countess Denhoff, Pociej, Bielinska, and the cream of the Court."

"Were you there?" asked Cosel sneeringly.

The Baron blushed.

"No, I was in another tent," replied he; "but I saw everything very well. Several bands of music played during the dinner, and every toast was announced by a salvo of cannon."

"How charming!" interrupted Cosel. "And that is the end of it?"

"No, it is only the beginning. When the dinner was over they did not clear the tables, as Flemming wanted to give the rest to the soldiers; but as there was not enough bread for them, he ordered a silver thaler to be put in every small piece of bread. Then they sounded the bugle for the attack. The soldiers marched in military order towards the tables, but the first ranks were broken by the following, the second by the third, and so on. The tables were upset, heaps of soldiers were sprawling on the ground. The spectacle was magnificent; we split our sides with laughter. Then the retreat was sounded.

"When evening came, dancing began, and lasted till seven o'clock in the morning. During the whole time Flemming was going from guest to guest with a bumper, praying them to drink. He himself was drunk first, and when the King started to go, he threw his arms round his neck and exclaimed, 'Brother, dear brother, if you leave me now, our friendship is gone,' and to our great surprise the King was not offended at such familiarity."

"For he did not want to spoil his amusement," said Cosel, laughing sarcastically. "But when he is tired of a man he only nods, the man disappears and the comedy is over."

She began to walk to and fro. The Baron said,—

"I do not wonder at your bitterness."

"Yes," she broke in, "if I had no heart—if I did not feel the wrong, but tried to make a bargain of it, I could talk differently. But I did not profit by the example left for me by Haugwitz, Aurora, Esterle and Teschen, who went hand in hand at Leipzig fair."

She laughed spasmodically.

"No, I am different. I thought there were hearts, souls, consciences; that love was not lechery, that promises ought to be kept, that the King's words were holy. All that was only my illusion. Consequently, while the other women are happy, I am dying of humiliation, longing, and shame."

The Baron von Sinen was moved and confused by the complaints of that still beautiful woman. Cosel noticed it.

"Listen," said she, "I know that you came here neither from curiosity nor in sympathy, but by order."

"Madam!" exclaimed he.

"Do not interrupt me, but listen! I forgive you, for every one of you cares more for a career than to be men. Repeat to them what you have heard from me; let them know what I think of them; and if you wish to be well rewarded, tell the King that you have heard from Anna Cosel's own lips that she will do as she told him, she will shoot him for his treachery and unfaithfulness. In one, two, ten years, the first time I meet Augustus, I shall fire at him. I always have a pistol with me, and shall not discard it until I have accomplished my vengeance."

The Baron was mortally pale.

"Countess," he exclaimed, "you force an honest man to be a traitor. I am a nobleman, and I am in the King's service. I shall be obliged to repeat what I have heard from you. It is my duty!"

"That is what I wanted you to do," said Cosel.

"But it would give to your numerous foes a new weapon."

"One less or more does not amount to anything. They use lies, calumny, treachery. The villains feel in me a being that cannot suffer their villainies; my honesty is a continual reproach to them. How can they forgive a woman who did not wish to be as soiled as they are?"

She laughed bitterly, while the Baron felt very uneasy. During that conversation her eyes were in turn wet with tears and burning with fire. Cosel possessed all the characteristics of Medea—everything that an ideal turns into reality. When she became silent, the chamberlain still stared at her as if he were mesmerized.

"I am very sorry indeed," said he at last, "that you force me to contribute to your misfortune." And he was sincere there.

"No one can make my misfortune greater," said she. "You are mistaken if you think that I regret the loss of palaces and luxury. No! I suffer because I have lost my faith in a human heart. Give me back his heart, and I will give up for it the crown of the world. I loved him! My whole life was bound up in him—he was my hero; he was my god; but the hero turned clown, his godhead is smirched."

The Baron tried to tranquilize her, but she cried,—

"O my golden dreams, where are you?"

Von Sinen could hold no longer. Pity was stronger within him than any other consideration.

"I implore you," said he, "to go away from here! I can say no more."

"What!" said Cosel. "Is it possible that even here I am threatened? Would the King of Prussia surrender a woman as Augustus surrendered Patkul?"

Von Sinen stood silent; it was evident he could not say any more.

"Where is there to go?" she murmured to herself. "I could not live too far from him; my heart still longs for him. Let them do with me what they please. I am disgusted with life. They have taken away my children—they have left me only bitterness."

The chamberlain had seized his hat.

"I pity you," said he; "but as long as you do not change your sentiments your friends can do nothing for you."

"My friends?" said she, ironically.

"You have more than you think," said the visitor. "I am the first."

"What! You my friend! I could find three or four such as you are. They are willing to console the widow and share her riches!"

Von Sinen was so confused that he could not answer. He bowed distantly, and, pursued by Cosel's scornful looks, left the room.

Cosel's enemies tried every means to excite the King against her. He did not wish to mention her, but it was no use. The deadly grudges were taking various disguises, mostly fear for the King's safety. They tried to represent the unfortunate woman as being very dangerous: she was free and still very rich; she might become very threatening.

Flemming, Löwendahl, Watzdorf, Lagnasco, without asking the King's permission, sent spies, and planned how they could seize her riches as they did those of Beichling.

Some of them acted under the influence of vengeance, others of cupidity. Cosel had not wronged any of them during her influence, and many of them were beholden to her for their freedom and elevation.

When Von Sinen returned from Berlin he did not appear immediately at court, for he was still under the spell of pity for the unfortunate woman, but Löwendahl spied him out and went to see him.

"How did you find Cosel?" asked he. "Does she still speak about the promise of marriage? Does she still threaten?"

Von Sinen answered sadly,—

"The fact is that she is very unhappy."

"Unhappy! It's her own fault! But speak precisely—tell me what you have seen and heard," pressed Löwendahl.

"Frankly speaking, my heart bleeds at the thought of what I have seen and heard. She is still angry, and never will forgive. But in her misfortune she arouses respect. She is marvellous and grand."

"Consequently dangerous!" said Löwendahl; "but she must have lost much of her beauty?"

"She is more beautiful than ever—she is beaming with beauty."

"So much the worse!" said Löwendahl. "The King might see her, and, being tired of Denhoff's withered face, she would capture him again."

"There is no doubt about that," said Von Sinen.

Little by little Löwendahl learned what he wanted to know in order to repeat it to the Countess Denhoff. The very same day he went to pay her a visit, and during the conversation he mentioned that there was news from Cosel.

"Where is she?" asked the Countess.

"She is in Berlin, and uses her liberty to blacken our King and his company," said Löwendahl. "But the worst thing is that she threatens to kill our lord."

Denhoff screamed and rushed from the sofa.

"But that is dreadful! We must warn the King," she said.

"Yes, we must try to deprive her of her freedom."

The Countess did not answer, for it entered her mind that the same fate might be hers too.

Löwendahl guessed her thoughts, for he added,—

"The King was never severe towards those whom he loved; the best proof of it is those ladies whom you have met here; but there are some cases—"

Here the Countess Bielinska, the mother, entered, and having learned what the question was, she became indignant.

"Truly, the King is too good for that mad woman! She challenges him! We must put an end to her daring!"

They agreed that Denhoff should warn the King; but, upon reflection, the mother said that she could do it better.

Löwendahl, having entrusted his vengeance to such hands, went out.

In the evening of the same day, there was an entertainment in the garden of the Hesperides, as they then called the garden surrounding Zwinger, now the famous picture gallery. The garden was laid out in accordance with the taste of those times; the flower-beds were surrounded by trimmed box trees; there were many fountains, grottoes and mythological statues. During the evening the lighted Japanese lanterns made it still prettier than it was during the day. On the balconies surrounding Zwinger, bands played lively melodies, which were carried afar on the sweet breezes. In the middle of the garden was an enormous tent, destined for dancing.

The King came dressed in blue, silver and white lace; he was looking quite young. The Countess Denhoff also wore a pale blue and white dress which was very becoming to her. Forcing herself to be merry, she greeted the King with some jests. Her sister, the Countess Pociej, helped her to entertain the King, who, as he grew older, was more difficult to amuse.

Augustus was gloomy and looked tired.

By a preconcerted arrangement, the Countess Pociej suggested that formerly he amused himself better with Cosel, and that perchance he regretted her.

The gallant King replied that in the presence of such charming ladies he did not remember and did not regret anything.

Countess Denhoff seized the opportunity of saying something about Cosel; but, as usual, she did it awkwardly, and her mother, waiting for the opportunity, came to her help. Then both began to lament on the theme of Cosel.

The King did not like that, for he was quite silent. At that moment both women were frightened, but at last the King said,—

"Dear Countess, pray be easy about me. I am watched by many guardians, some asked and some not asked; and nothing will happen to me. I do not like to talk about these matters. Better let us go and look at the dancing."

Thus the project of an attack was not carried out at that moment: but it was repeated in the evening by Flemming and Löwendahl, as they drank with the King. The King let them talk and he listened.

"Löwendahl, listen," said the King sneeringly, "it is a fact that you give me a great proof of your attachment to my person, warning me of the Countess, who is your relation, and to whom you should be thankful for all that I have done for you. I ought to reward you for it; but I cannot help telling you that it seems very strange to me."

Löwendahl became silent, and the intriguers understood that they must use some other means.

* * * * *

Although Cosel wanted to lead a quiet life in Berlin, her beauty, her wit, and her fame were too well known for her company not to be sought.

She knew many people in the court of Frederick since his visit to Dresden. The officers were so much bored by continual military reviews and quiet evenings in the palace of the Queen, that they were glad to have some other distraction. The King himself spent most of his time in Potsdam and Wurterhausen, rather than in the capital, but he never failed to be present at the change of guard at ten o'clock in the morning, to give audience to his ministers and to take a walk. About noon he took a modest meal with the Queen; in the afternoon he worked hard and did not appear until the evening. In the company of a few ladies and officers they played picquet, ombre and trictrac—they smoked, and thus passed the time until eleven o'clock; at that hour everything was officially ended.

This monotony of life was varied only by receptions given by some dignitaries. Life here was quite different from what it was in Dresden, at which they quietly laughed here, especially at Augustus' military amusements, which nobody took seriously in Berlin. The gorgeously dressed Saxon soldiers could not be compared with those of Prussia, clad in their modest blue uniforms. Instead of fanciful flags, here was used only a white one, with the proud motto, over a flying eagle, *Nec soli cedit*. In these times the motto seemed too bold; the future justified it.

There were no two characters more opposite than those of Frederick of Prussia and Frederick Augustus of Saxony. Since Fraulein von Pannevitz slapped the Prussian King's face for the kiss he tried to steal from her, he had not looked at any woman, and was the most faithful husband. He and the whole of his family led such a thrifty life, that they not only rose from his table sober, but even hungry.

The order in the country and the army was pedantic; the customs were Spartan. Before each repast prayer was recited; the cooking was bourgeois; no one thought about the court balls. They used to eat from earthenware, and only when there was a dinner in honour of somebody did they take out the heavy silver, which was locked up again the same evening.

The King had some fancies, but they were quiet—different from those of Augustus. When the Queen left the company after a meagre supper, the men gathered in the smoking-room, where the King treated them to pipes. During the smoking it was allowed to criticize some one. In the centre of the room there stood a simple table, round which sat ministers, generals, sometimes a guest. Every one received a Dutch pipe and a mug of beer. To make somebody drunk was a great point with the King. To sneer at savants, the aristocracy, officials, was the greatest pleasure. The jokes were sometimes interspersed with quarrels in which mugs were freely thrown about—many were hurt in these encounters, but nobody was ever killed.

At times a debate would be arranged—on the theme that savants were ignorant. Morgenstern would address the house; dressed in a long, blue robe trimmed with red and embroidered with hares; and wearing a red vest, a big wig and a fox's brush instead of a sword.

Such were the entertainments of the Prussian court. In Dresden they laughed at Berlin; in Berlin they laughed at Dresden, considering it the ante-chamber of hell, for Frederick Augustus of Saxony did not believe in anything, while Frederick of Prussia was pious after his own fashion.

Once when a new butler was reading a prayer before supper and came to the words, "May God bless thee," he thought it would be more decent to change it into, "May God bless your Majesty." The King did not like it and said, "You rascal, read it as it is written; for in God's face I am as good, rascal, as you are."

No wonder, then, that after meagre suppers, after entertainments in the smoking-room, there was a longing for different society, for better jests, for more elegant conversation. Cosel's acquaintances began to visit her; the wearied woman opened her door to a few of them, and a small circle of people gathered quietly in the evenings, for in Berlin no noise was permitted.

King Frederick, although he was well aware of this fact, for he knew well what was going on in his capital, said nothing at first. It encouraged a few officers and courtiers. They used to come towards seven o'clock, and as Cosel could not sleep, they usually chatted till midnight and after. They would bring gossip, and the Countess did not conceal her rancour towards Augustus. Many things said here were passed to the smoking-room, where they were repeated to the King. Then Frederick smiled, but he shook his head, and seemed to be surprised that Cosel was so daring.

One evening, as the usual young guests were gathered in Cosel's house, there came an old general, who was an habitué of the smoking-room. His presence made the young men careful in their conversation, but did not stop Cosel from bitterly criticizing Augustus.

The old general shook his head and listened; he seemed to wonder and not to believe his own ears. He remained until every one had left the house. Cosel was surprised.

The old man, who had spoken very little, said respectfully to her as he took his leave,—

"Countess, permit me to make a remark to you. Time flies pleasantly in your house; but although the doors and windows are shut, a great many things get out. Any breeze can carry gossip to the banks of Elbe; our neighbour may frown on our King, because such things are said here against our good neighbour and ally. The King would be very sorry—"

Cosel frowned.

"Then even in my own house," said she, "I cannot say what I please?"

"Yes, you can," said the General, "but one can also go where one does not wish to go."

"Even I?"

"Dear Countess," said the General, sighing, "it might happen even to you. A military order prevails in our country. I would advise you to play trictrac; it amuses, and is less dangerous."

Cosel dropped her head sadly.

"You may think," continued the General, "that I am grumbling, as old people do. Well, then, I will tell you that somebody advised me to warn you."

Having said this, he quietly left the room, and the Countess threw herself on the sofa and laughed bitterly.

But she did not listen to the warning, and when her guests gathered again, her words were many and loud, in utter defiance of the severity with which she was threatened.

One morning the Governor-general of Berlin came to Cosel's house. He saluted her civilly, smiled, twisted his moustache, and then asked her,—

"Is it true that you wish to change your residence and go to live in the quiet city of Halle?"

"I, in Halle?" exclaimed Cosel. "And what should I do there?"

"The air is very healthy there, the views are lovely, and it is quiet and secluded. There is no more agreeable place to live in than Halle."

At first Cosel did not know what to answer. Then she said,—

"But I never intended to go to Halle."

"It is rather strange," said the Governor-general, "somebody spoke about it to his Majesty, and the King ordered that every comfort should be assured you. The King's orders cannot be disobeyed; the best way, then, will be to go to Halle."

Cosel wrung her hands, and the tears began to flow down her cheeks.

"Then it is an order," she said, finally, "it is a new exile—why is it?"

"The King thinks you will be more comfortable there. You know that in Berlin every word echoes far. There in Halle, no one will hear anything. There is more freedom."

He had risen.

"You may go there tomorrow, in the morning," he added. "The weather is lovely; but as the roads are not always safe, His Majesty offers you a few men to escort you. It is great gallantry on his part; you should be thankful to him for that."

General Wartesleben bowed very elegantly and went out, leaving the Countess as one turned to stone.

The blow came from Dresden—there can be no doubt about that. They wanted to force her to be silent—to accept her fate. Her unbending spirit rose in indignation; every such blow made her more energetic.

She ordered her trunks to be packed and the horses to be hired, and the faithful but gloomy Zaklika worked hard without saying a word.

When Cosel was ready to enter the carriage, a small group of curious men gathered round the house; but seeing that woman clad in black going majestically to the carriage surrounded by dragoons, they were frightened and scattered, for they thought that a victim was being conducted to the scaffold.

In a narrow street in the city of Halle, in the first floor of a modest house, a strange woman had for some time attracted the attention of the peaceful passers-by.

There she sat all day long, looking out at the sky, with unseeing eyes, and her mien, her great beauty, and the intense sadness of her face attracted a curious crowd.

No one in Halle knew the lady, but from her sadness they guessed she was very unhappy.

She never looked at the human faces; her gaze was fixed on space. Only when many people gathered and began to whisper, with curious looks at her, she started and left the window.

The door of her house was always shut; nobody visited her; a servant obtained her meals from a restaurant. Only from time to time a young, elegantly dressed man knocked at the door. He went in and stayed for a few moments; then he returned, sad. The students called him the lover of the beautiful unknown, although he did not look like it.

The beautiful mysterious lady—for every one believed her to be a lady—was the sole topic of conversation in Halle at that time.

The landlord and his wife, questioned by their friends, even the bribed servant, would not give a word of information about her. When questioned, they threw a frightened look round, and muttered something about not knowing anything.

Besides the curious, from time to time a soldier walked past the house, looking in at the windows; then a man, whose mien indicated that he had been a soldier.

That beautiful unknown lady was the Countess Cosel, but how terribly changed!

The latest incident had broken the spirit of the woman, filled her soul with fear, and driven away all hope. She was now sad and in despair, and continually crying. The vengeance that persecuted her was so implacable, that now she expected everything—even death.

In Berlin she was free—she could escape; in Halle she was a prisoner.

Zaklika, who had accompanied her here, told her the next day that all the doors of the house were watched. She was still free, but she could not take a step. She wanted to go to church on Sunday, but, seeing that she was watched, she stayed home. The landlord and his wife were very civil, but could not be trusted. The burgher had fox-like eyes, and his wife was pale and did not dare to speak a word.

Zaklika tried to make friends with them; they ran from him as from the pestilence.

A few days later the Chamberlain Von Sinen was announced. He came in sad, modest, and confused, as if he did not know what to say.

"With what do you come?" asked Cosel, "for I know that you do not come in sympathy, but by command."

"You are mistaken," answered Von Sinen. "It is both; I preferred to come myself rather than let any one else be sent here."

"Speak, then," said Cosel, "I am ready for anything."

"Were you only ready to have more resignation," said he, "everything could be repaired."

"What do they require from me?"

Von Sinen sighed.

"The King has sent me to ask you for the paper which he signed for you," said the Chamberlain.

"And he thinks that I shall surrender it, so that from a wife I shall become a mistress, whom he can dismiss whenever he likes." And she added, "If you have come only on that errand, then return and tell the King that Cosel will never sell her honour."

"Madam, for heaven's sake," said the Chamberlain, "do not be stubborn. If you return that paper, you can yet recover your freedom—everything."

"Augustus' heart is what I want," whispered Cosel. "But he has none in that breast glittering with diamonds; he is as cold as are the stones. I shall never get back that which is dearest to me—faith in mankind."

Von Sinen remained a couple of hours; but not being able to prevail upon her, he stayed in Halle several days, giving her plenty of time to think it over.

He visited her each day, trying to persuade her by all possible arguments; but she was persistent in her refusal.

"I shall not give back the paper," she repeated. "It contains the defence of my honour and my children's. I shall die, but he shall not have it."

The second day after Von Sinen's arrival, Cosel called Zaklika to her. He looked awful—pale, angry, and silent. When he looked at people, they shrank from that face full of hate, seeing in it a grief only looking for the opportunity to change into madness.

They could not talk long in the house, being surrounded by spies. Zaklika used to come and go as though he had business to do, carrying something out and then bringing it back. Only thus could they speak. Cosel said to him,—

"Do they watch you, too?"

"Not yet."

"You must leave me, and be entirely free."

Zaklika shivered and stared at her.

"I? Leave you? And what am I to do with myself? to what shall I devote my life? Then I can only die."

"No," said Cosel, "it is only the beginning of my imprisonment. You must be free in order to help me to get back my freedom."

Zaklika became thoughtful.

"Speak, then," said he after a while.

"You will know where I am. I trust you, you must think about means; you will try and free me. There are still a few thousands with Lehman; I will give you a word to him—you will take the money."

Zaklika was indignant that she should offer him money.

"It is not for you, but you must have it to free me."

She looked at him. He nodded obediently.

"In the first place, go and try to find out whether they will let you go; you may tell them that you do not wish to serve me any more. Do what you please. Carry in your breast my treasure that I entrusted to you. Do you understand me?"

She extended to him her trembling hand.

"Only you do I trust, for only in you is a human soul. Do not betray me, like the rest!"

"I?" exclaimed Zaklika, indignantly, and his eyes shone so fiercely that Cosel retreated. "I?" repeated he, trembling. "I can die, but not betray."

"Then you must be free, without arousing suspicion. Go!"

Zaklika went out, and he did not reappear until the next day towards evening, when he brought with him a new servant, and took his leave from his mistress.

Cosel had enough strength to play a scene of anger, for the landlord and his wife listened at the door.

He left the room, and went to an official complaining that Cosel did not want to let him go, to which he had right, for he was a Polish nobleman, therefore a free man.

The Prussian laughed, for he knew how many Polish noblemen had been caught by the Prussians, and obliged to serve in their army, but he did not say anything. Perhaps, had Zaklika not been so pale and looked so miserable, he would have forced him to accept service in the regiment of gigantic grenadiers, but Zaklika was looking wretched, and it would have cost much to feed him up.

Therefore they did not hesitate to let him go. He returned at once to Cosel, but, knowing that he had quarrelled, they did not listen to him again at the door.

"Go to Dresden," said Cosel, "and tell everybody that you have left me. Lehman will give you the money. Take it in gold. You will hear what becomes of me. If I am free, you will come to me; if not, help me to escape. If you arouse suspicion, and they would capture you, then destroy the paper I have entrusted to you, but do not give it to any one. Do not destroy it while you have any hope of escape; destroy it only at the last extremity, but they must know nothing about its destruction, so that they may be always in fear of its discovery."

She extended her hand to him. He kissed it and cried, but said not a word. Then Cosel wrung her hands, and exclaimed,—

"There are still some hearts!"

Zaklika went out as though intoxicated.

The next day, when Von Sinen came to see her, he found her more merry, more resigned and quieter. He thought that perchance she might return the paper, that she would have pity on herself, but he soon learned that he was mistaken. Cosel said to him when he entered,—

"I pity you. You will not gain the King's favours, my brave relation, Löwendahl will not care for you; Flemming will not make you drunk, and you will not get even a thousand thalers. I am so stubborn—mad! Is it not true?"

"Then all my efforts were in vain?"

"Yes," said she, taking a ring from her finger. "I pity you, my unsuccessful messenger, and I should like you to preserve a souvenir of my goodwill: accept this ring. It is no longer an agreeable souvenir for me, it makes me ache like a wound. Take it, pray!"

Von Sinen accepted the ring. He tried once more to persuade her, but Cosel laughed.

"Spare yourself the trouble and me the worry. I know your arguments, they will not persuade me."

Before leaving Halle, the Chamberlain came once again. He was sad, but did not say anything. Cosel was surprised at his return.

"I pity you so much," said he, "that I cannot refrain from telling you what you have to expect."

"I know that it is nothing pleasant," she interrupted, "but it would not change my determination. I shall not return the promise signed by the King. He was perfectly free to give it to me or not, but the King cannot ask for the return of his promise given to a woman, and thus cheat her. I cannot even suspect that it is the King's will. Such vile men as Flemming and Löwendahl might wish to get hold of it without the King's knowledge in order to make him pay for it. The King cannot ask it from me!"

She turned and left the room. The same day Von Sinen left Halle; he went away with a strange feeling. The first time he was sent to her, he fulfilled his duty with the cold blood of a diplomat; little by little the stability of this woman, her bravery, perseverance, character, made such a deep impression on him that he was ashamed of his rôle. He pitied her and felt humiliated.

He was going back more angry with those who sent him than with the unfortunate woman who had sent him away with such an unshaken bravery displayed in defence of her honour.

When he arrived at Dresden he had plenty of time for rest. The whole Court was making preparations for a great festival, which was going to be held at Moritzburg; they had not time to call him and ask him to report the result of his mission, and he did not hasten himself. He was glad that he could for at least a few days stay the decision of Cosel's lot, which he thought would be still worse.

Moritzburg was a hunting lodge, built not far from Dresden, in the woods. It was a charming little castle surrounded by old trees. The King invited the whole Court there, many foreigners, as well as his former favourites, the Princess Teschen, the Countess Königsmark, together with the Countess Denhoff and her sister Pociej.

The site of the entertainment was a plain where game was to be driven from the forest to be shot. Hard by was a lake on which boat races were to be held.

The crowd of guests was a great one; the entertainment succeeded perfectly, and as the guests did not retire to the tents prepared for them very sober, the next day they were obliged to hunt for wigs, shoes, and swords in the woods and bushes.

Von Sinen mixed with the crowd, and wandered here and there; all this amusement seemed to him wild. The King was in an excellent humour, and was very amiable to his dismissed favourites. The Countess Denhoff burned with jealousy when he talked with the Princess Teschen, Königsmark looked sneeringly at Denhoff when the King was chatting with her.

Augustus was entirely taken up with the illuminations and the magnificent feast, and when towards midnight everything was over, he sat down to drink with his friends.

Here they let their tongues go; Flemming, Vitzthum, and Frisen could talk as much as they wished, even about those ladies towards whom Augustus was respectful.

They passed in review all the gross and scandalous stories of the Court.

Löwendahl was sitting at the other end of the table.

"It seems to me," said the King to him, "that I have noticed Von Sinen."

"He has returned from Halle," answered the Marshal sourly, looking at the King.

"Von Sinen was sent to Cosel, what news has he brought?"

"The same as always," answered Löwendahl.

"You should have offered her anything she wished in exchange for that paper, even freedom."

"She said that she would not part with it."

Augustus frowned.

"One must have done with her once for all," added Löwendahl.

"Yes, tomorrow we will send a letter to the King of Prussia, asking for her extradition," said the King. "Then we will see what can be done."

"And where does your Majesty order her to be put in the meantime?"

"Let her be taken to Nossen Castle, perhaps she will think it over there. I cannot bear the daring war she has declared against me. I have had enough of it. Denhoff splits my head with her!"

Those words, spoken in a moment of anger and under the influence of wine, were seized upon and utilized the next day. Flemming reminded Augustus of them.

In the letter to the King of Prussia, asking for Countess's extradition, they gave as the reason daring speeches against Augustus, as well as a plot against his life. The public threat justified it. The letter was sent by a courier to Berlin.

King Frederick did not hesitate for a moment. Lieutenant Ducharmoi, of the regiment of the Prince of Anhalt-Dessau, was called by his order.

"You will go to Halle," said the King to him, "and there you will find the Countess Cosel. You will take her under escort, on your responsibility, and you will conduct her to the frontier of Saxony; there you will give her into the hands of a Saxon officer, who will give you a receipt."

Ducharmoi went immediately to Halle, where he found Cosel.

Although prepared for anything bad, she paled at the sight of an officer. Ducharmoi, after having saluted her, told her that he was commanded by the King to conduct her to the frontier of Saxony, where she would be delivered to the Saxon authorities.

She stood for a moment as if struck by a thunderbolt.

"What an injustice! What barbarity!" she exclaimed, and two streams of tears flowed down her cheeks.

From that moment she said not a word more.

They ordered her to pack her things, and put them in a hired carriage.

Ducharmoi offered her his arm, and she descended to her carriage without looking at anybody. The horses went off; the carriage being escorted by a detachment of Prussian cavalry. During the whole of the journey she gave no signs of life. At last the carriage stopped. Cosel shivered; through the window she saw the Saxon uniforms worn by a detachment of dragoons, who were to conduct her further. She called Lieutenant Ducharmoi, who approached her carriage. Then she emptied her pockets; she found a gold box and a beautiful watch, and handed them to the officer.

"Pray, take that as a souvenir from me."

Ducharmoi hesitated.

"I beseech you to accept," said she, "it must not become a prey to those horrid Saxons."

The money she gave to the Prussian soldiers. Then she drew the curtains again, without asking what they were going to do with her.

From the moment Cosel passed into the hands of the Saxon authorities imprisonment was likely at any time. She passed the night in Leipzig.

In the morning an official, wearing a little sword and a big wig, silently executing the orders he had received from his superiors, entered the room in which she had spent a sleepless night, crying. He brought the King's order, instructing him to examine all her things, and to take them away.

She looked at him contemptuously, and did not say a word. He sealed all her boxes, and took the papers and jewels; he searched in her trunks, but could not find that for which he was looking. This humiliating inquisition lasted a couple of hours.

Hardly had she been permitted to rest a moment after such moral torture, than she was ordered to again enter the carriage—not being told where they were going to conduct her.

A detachment of cavalry surrounded the carriage—they rode till the evening. Against the sky, burning with the setting sun, there appeared the walls and towers of a castle, and the carriage, passing through a narrow gateway, entered the courtyard.

The place was entirely unknown to her. The castle was empty and had been uninhabited for some time. A few men were standing at the door. They were obliged to conduct the weakened lady up the stairs leading to a room on the first floor. It was an old habitation, with small windows, enormous fireplaces, thick walls, without any comforts, and sparsely furnished with the barest necessities.

Cosel, thoroughly tired, threw herself on the bed.

She passed a sleepless night, tormented by horrid thoughts aroused by her imprisonment. The dawn was breaking, the sky was growing red-gold in the east, the servants still slept; only the guard pacing in the corridor broke the silence when Cosel rose and went to the window.

The view from it did not remind her of anything. In front of her there was a vast plain, stretching towards the blue of a far forest. Here and there rose clumps of trees; a few roofs could be seen, and from behind the green columns of smoke were rising.

The castle stood on an eminence, which descended sharply towards a village. On the right hand there was a highway bordered with willows. The road was deserted.

She did not know the country.

From the room she went softly to another, which was larger, in the middle of it stood an oak table, and against the walls a few benches and chairs. Over the fireplace there was a battered coat-of-arms, cut in the stone, of which there remained only the shield and helmet. Behind this room, and like it, vaulted, was a small round room in the tower, on the other side of the castle. From here one could see forests, hills, and villages, and here and there in the distance the towers of some knightly castle, built like an eagle's nest on a crag. Still the country was unknown to her.

In the room in the tower there was some furniture; an empty wardrobe stood against the wall, and on one of its shelves was an old Bible, worm-eaten and covered with dust. Cosel seized it, but the book slipped from her hands, and the yellow leaves scattered on the floor.

In that room there was an iron door, leading somewhere into the mysterious rooms of the castle, in which no living human voice was heard.

The day was breaking. The swallows flew round the windows. Cosel returned to her rooms. The women servants that accompanied her woke up and offered to serve her. She dismissed them. Having stayed her hunger with some warm milk, she went again to the window; she sat on the stone bench and began to look on God's world, although she had nobody in it. She turned her eyes on the road, where she noticed some vans, men, and herds—clouds of dust. But she soon tired of them and sat at a distance from the window.

The hours were long. At noon they brought her luncheon. One of the servants persuaded her to eat. Cosel went to the table, and, looking at the modest meal, began to cry. The luncheons at which she entertained the King were different!

Then again she went to the window and looked on to the road, not willing to avow to herself that she hoped to see some one there. She believed that Zaklika would seek her out.

But neither on that nor the following day did she see anything except shepherds, herds, and vans. No one looked at the castle. She wandered from window to window; but all round the country was quiet and deserted. Towards evening she perceived a small peasant boy picking flowers near the wall, and she threw him a piece of money that she found in her pocket, and, leaning out, she asked him the name of the castle. The boy muttered, "Nossen," and ran away frightened.

She did not know even the name, but she remembered to have heard it, and guessed she was in the vicinity of Meissen and Dresden. She again thought of Zaklika, but what could he do alone against walls, guards, and the King?

The third day she was looking on the road when towards noon she noticed a horseman. He was riding slowly from the direction of Dresden.

He dropped his reins and looked curiously round the country; he had raised his head towards the castle. He seemed to be looking for something. He wore a grey mantle, and she thought it was her faithful servant. She shivered, and began to wave her handkerchief.

The cavalier had also taken out his handkerchief, and, apparently wiping his forehead, made signs with it. It was indeed Zaklika. His mien and his movements were easily recognized, even from a distance. Her heart began to throb. He at least did not forget her; he could save her.

Riding slowly and looking at the castle, he disappeared behind the hill.

Zaklika had remained a few days in Halle and watched. He wanted to follow the Countess, but the Prussians ordered him to leave the country. He made his way to Dresden, where he went directly to Lehman.

The banker received him with evident fear; he locked the doors, and first asked him whether anybody had seen him. Being assured that Zaklika had not met any one in Dresden, Lehman breathed more easily. But he could not speak for quite a while, and when he began to speak, he seemed afraid of his own words.

"It is difficult to know," said he, "what was the cause of that, but now there will be no measure to her misfortune. The King is angry, and the King's anger is cold like ice. When some one offends him, he is inexorable. Cosel is lost."

Zaklika listened.

"Yes, she is lost!" continued Lehman. "When the King wrongs some one, he persecutes him, and will not let him appear in his presence. Cosel has refused to return to him that promise of marriage, and he will never forget that. They have confiscated her all. Löwendahl received orders to search for her money and jewels. Pillnitz is taken by the Treasury, and the other estate also."

Here Lehman approached Zaklika.

"They have taken everything from me too. The King sent for it. The books showed I had it; I could not refuse," he added.

"What! everything? But not that secret sum that the Countess told me to take from you?"

He took a paper that was sewn in his sleeve. The banker took it with trembling hands.

"And do you know," said he, "what would become of both of us if they seized that paper? They would send us to Königstein, and my children would become beggars. Flemming and Löwendahl would seize the pretext to look into my safe." And he trembled.

"Then you have given them that sum also?" said Zaklika, wringing his hands in despair.

Lehman looked at him for a long time; he seemed to be wrestling with himself.

"Listen," said he. "Swear to me upon that which you hold most sacred, that you will not betray me even should they threaten you with death—"

Here the Jew took from a drawer a diamond cross pawned by the Princess Teschen.

"Swear to me upon that," said he.

Zaklika took the cross, and, raising his hand, said quietly,—

"I swear!"

Then he added,—

"It was not necessary to ask me for an oath: my word as nobleman would be enough. Zaklika has never betrayed any one, and never will."

Lehman looked at him, and he was as white as a sheet.

"Suppose they should catch you and find money upon you?"

"In the first place the money might be mine; then the Countess may have made me a present of it."

"But they take everything that used to belong to her."

"They know that I never had anything, and they will not search me. You will give that money."

Lehman still hesitated.

"I may have misfortunes on account of you, but it must not be said that I did not help some one in misfortune."

He opened the safe, took out a bag, and began to count money on the table. Zaklika breathed again and wiped the perspiration from his forehead; then he sat thoughtful, leant on his elbows, and fell asleep from fatigue.

When Lehman had finished counting, he turned to him, and perceived that he had fallen asleep; only then did he understand what the silent man had suffered if at that moment he could sleep so soundly.

He went quietly to another room, and there he waited till Zaklika should awaken. He wished him to do so as soon as possible; for notwithstanding the pity he had for the man, he was afraid to have him in the house.

Zaklika, who had fallen asleep from fatigue, but in whom the soul was vigilant, woke up soon, and, almost frightened, jumped from his place. He rubbed his eyes; he was ashamed to appear so feeble.

He glanced at the money, put it in his money belt, and buckled it under his dress.

Lehman was waiting, and when Zaklika took his leave he came to him, and, placing his hand on his shoulder, said,—

"Only God knows whether we shall see one another again. I pity you, but I cannot stop you from an honest deed. You have noticed my hesitation, but you must remember that I live for my children. Now, listen to me. I had in my possession a great deal of money belonging to the Countess, and in our hands money increases rapidly. Our account is closed; I have paid everything; but in the case of such misfortune a man should reckon differently; therefore, take this with you, and may God lead you."

He took a bag, and, handing it to Zaklika, said,—

"From this moment you do not know me. I do not know you either."

"It is for her," said Zaklika, shaking hands with him.

"Go through the garden," said the Israelite.

Zaklika was too well known in the city to show himself. He had left his horse in a suburb, at the house of his friend, a Wend. During his wanderings he had been struck by the similarity of the language to his own, as he listened to these Slavs talking. Speaking a similar language, he soon struck up acquaintances among them. The name of the fisherman with whom Zaklika became acquainted was Hawlik. He had a piece of land reaching to the bank of the river, but as the soil was not very good, Hawlik was not a farmer, but gained his living by fishing. Year in year out he lived his life in poverty and sorrow.

Zaklika often used to visit him, and they both chatted of their misery. The Wend remembered better times. "All around us used to belong to our people," said he, "but the Germans squeezed us out by different tricks, and now it is dangerous even to speak our own tongue. They do not give us any chance in the cities; it is enough to be a Wend to be pushed out. Our number decreases, but there is no help for it. It seems to be God's will."

Every time that Zaklika wanted not to be seen in Dresden he went to Hawlik, where he put up his horse and slept in the attic, and where he was always welcome to partake of the modest repast. They were glad to see him now also. They never asked him any questions—what was he doing or what had he come for.

Zaklika went to them to spend that night, much troubled whether it would be safe for him to show himself in the city and get some news; he was afraid of being arrested. Early in the morning, having wrapped himself up carefully in his mantle, he went across the bridge to Narrenhaus. He expected to meet Fröhlich as he went to the castle, and learn something from him. In order to be sure of not missing him, he sat on the steps of the fool's house and waited. Fröhlich, dressed in his pointed hat and adorned with silver key, coming out of his house, noticed a man sitting, and, not recognizing Zaklika, exclaimed,—

"Hey! Do you take my house for a hostelry?"

Zaklika turned; the fool recognized him.

"What is the matter with you?" he exclaimed. "You look as if you were married."

"I have returned from a journey."

"You are a Catholic, then you must have been in purgatory?"

"I wandered through the world," answered Zaklika. "But tell me what is going on here?"

"You wish me to be a historiographer," laughed the fool. "You had better ask what is not going on."

"Do you know what has become of my former mistress?" asked Zaklika.

"I do not know who was your mistress."

"The Countess Cosel."

Fröhlich looked round and put his fingers on his lips.

"Who pronounces that name?" said he. "There is nothing to laugh at, and you know that I live by laughter."

"But you can tell me at least what has become of her?"

"Then you do not know? Where have you been?"

"Far."

"I think that even afar they talk about that. That woman in whose slavery our lord was, it seems, is now imprisoned by him, and her captivity will last longer than her domination."

"And where is she?" asked Zaklika.

"They say that she is in Nossen Castle, but to be sure they will build something finer for her," laughed the fool by habit, but sadly. "No! I would not like to be a woman. Speaking frankly, it is not much comfort to be a man either. If I had my choice, I would like to be a donkey. Nobody eats donkey's meat, his skin is thick, and when long-ears begins to sing, everybody runs away and leaves him alone. If one adds that he has always a good appetite, and that he can live on old broom, one sees that there is no happier being in the world."

"Nossen! Nossen!" repeated Zaklika thoughtfully, having forgotten about the fool.

"I am talking about an ass, and you about Nossen! Do not prattle about sad things, and goodbye!"

Fröhlich, having put the official smile on his lips, went away. Zaklika returned to Hawlik, from whom he learned where the castle was; and he started in its direction the same day.

He was very glad that Cosel had noticed him coming, for he knew that he would bring her some consolation.

He went to the inn in the village, where he assumed the rôle of a buyer of skins, and thus, while apparently going round on business, had plenty of time to learn all about the castle. The building was old, and Cosel's guard was composed of a few old men. They did not let any one in, but they did not watch her very strictly. The windows were very high, and nobody thought that an escape could be accomplished through them; consequently there were no sentries. The soldiers spent their time smoking pipes in the courtyard, and at Cosel's door.

In the rear of the castle one could approach the windows very easily.

In order to have a good pretext for longer sojourn at the inn, Zaklika simulated being unwell. The innkeeper was glad of it, for he had to feed the horse as well as take care of the man.

At supper he learned that they had brought to the castle the lady who attempted the King's life, as well as how many soldiers guarded her. Two women servants, a cook, and a boy composed the whole court of this lady who formerly was surrounded by a crowd of servants dressed in cloth of gold.

They were telling wonders about the prisoner.

Zaklika remained a couple of days without raising any suspicion, and as he gave a couple of thalers to the innkeeper on account of skins, he felt more assured, and one day he went out towards noon to look at the castle. He convinced himself that from one side, where was the forest, he could steal through the undergrowth near to the walls; but he could not find out whether there were any windows from Cosel's room on this side. He proposed to see that later.

Towards evening he returned to the inn, drank the bears'-fat recommended to him by the innkeeper, and went to bed, thinking how he could deceive the German and remain longer in the inn without exciting suspicion.

The next morning, as Zaklika was drinking warmed beer in the common room, there entered, with a great noise, three soldiers from the guard of the castle.

Zaklika immediately recognized them as soldiers whom he had seen in Dresden, and one of them began to look at him attentively.

"Well," said the soldier, leaning on the table, "I seem to know you."

"To be sure," answered Zaklika, "for I was a long time in service at the Court, till I took to business."

"Ah! you are the man who breaks horse-shoes!" exclaimed the soldier.

"Yes, I could even stop an ox by taking it by the horns; but now I don't know whether I could do the same even with a sheep."

The soldier saluted him smiling. Zaklika called for beer for him, and they became friends.

"We are now doing penance," said the soldier. "We are in Nossen watching a petticoat! It is frightfully dull there."

"They might at least have given a few pretty girls to the Countess," said another soldier.

"How long are you going to stay here?"

"Who knows? And it is so dreadful to have nothing to do."

"Why don't you play cards?" said Zaklika.

"With whom? And then we don't have much money."

He gaped, and drank the beer.

When they started to return to the castle, Zaklika accompanied them to the gate, then, still talking, he entered the courtyard and the corridor.

The other soldiers were not surprised at the newcomer; on the contrary, they were glad he came. They began to chat together. They found cards, and won from him two thalers. This pleased them very much. As he was going, he expressed a wish to see the castle, and nobody objected to it. The officer was in the town, playing the guitar to a butcher's daughter.

He was not able, however, to do anything more that day.

Zaklika stayed on, pretending that he was not well, purchased skins, and looked about for a way of stealing into the castle. They did not suspect him, but the difficulties were great from the position of the castle. The part of the castle in which the Countess was imprisoned adjoined the empty portion of it. There the old steward and his family were living. Through the soldiers, Zaklika became acquainted with him. He was avaricious, and had a large family. Treating him with beer, Zaklika learned from him which way the windows of the Countess's rooms looked out, and also that the iron door of the tower, of which the steward had the key, led to a large empty hall. Zaklika told him he was very fond of old buildings; but to this the steward made no answer. Another day they were talking about the Countess, and Zaklika tried to arouse pity for her in the steward. They looked at one another—the steward was silent again.

"The Countess," said Zaklika, "has still many friends at Court, and some of them think that she will return to the King's favour. I would not be surprised if some of them appeared here one day and offered you a handsome sum of money for a moment's conversation with her."

The steward muttered something.

"What would you do in that case?" asked Zaklika.

"It would be a devilish temptation," answered the steward. "I would do as Luther did, I would throw the inkstand at the devil!"

But he smiled.

"Suppose someone should offer you thirty thalers?" asked Zaklika.

"For thirty thalers they would hang me," laughed the steward.

"But it is not a crime to let the Countess talk for a few minutes with a friend. However," continued Zaklika, "we are talking just in fun; but I am sure just the same that someone would give you even fifty thalers."

The steward looked at him with wide-open eyes and stroked his beard. The thought of getting fifty thalers intoxicated him.

"If you know someone who would give me fifty thalers, then tell him to come and see me," answered the German.

"Here he is," answered Zaklika.

"I thought so."

"Conduct me to the empty hall when the women are not with the Countess; I shall not be long with her."

"Were it not for the women everything could be done very easily. Unfortunately, they are with the Countess by turns."

"Tell your wife to invite them."

"No, a woman should not know about anything."

"Yes," said Zaklika; "but she can invite them without knowing why."

The consultation lasted quite a while, and they agreed that at the next opportunity the steward should let Zaklika see the Countess.

One day, as she was in her chamber, she heard a knocking at the iron door of the tower. With throbbing heart she rushed there and knocked at it too. At that moment the door opened and Zaklika appeared.

"I have only time to tell you that I am in the vicinity, and that I will do anything to come to your rescue."

"Help me to escape!" said Cosel.

"It is impossible just now," said Zaklika; "at least it requires a great deal of time. You must rely upon me—I will do my best. Drop a cord from the window in the tower, and I will attach a paper with the news to it, for it will be impossible for us to see one another."

The steward began to grow impatient. Zaklika slipped into the Countess's hand a bag of money, and whispered,—

"You must bribe one of the servants. I am at the inn called 'The Golden Horse Shoe.'"

The door was shut, for the women might come at any moment, but the Countess grew hopeful.

Zaklika, that poor servant, on whom she hardly deigned to look from the height of her majesty, had not betrayed her.

The steward took the fifty thalers with unconcealed joy. He was glad of the opportunity of making some money, and from that time it was he that ran after Zaklika, who had already conceived a plan to free the Countess.

The next day the steward showed him the castle, and during this visit

Zaklika noticed that there was a door in the wall near the road; it was encumbered with stones, but they could easily be cleared out.

But it was not enough to leave the castle, it was necessary to have the means of gaining the frontier and finding a hiding-place that could not be easily discovered by Augustus' spies. Zaklika thought that if he could cross Silesia and reach Poland, they could hide there, for he knew that the Saxon, as they called Augustus in Poland, had many enemies.

To purchase horses and hire people for the flight was a difficult task in Saxony, where the King had many spies.

The next day Zaklika attached a paper to a string, telling the Countess that he was going away to make preparations for her escape. Before going away, he had a conversation with the steward, hinting to him that there might come an opportunity for him to earn not fifty, but a thousand thalers.

"With a thousand thalers you could go quietly into the Rhine provinces and live there with your family in your own house."

The old man did not say a word, only nodded.

Having drunk lots of beer with the soldiers in saying farewell, he told them he would come back for the skins, and that he was going to Dresden.

After his departure, Cosel was in a fever, waiting for news. Every day she rushed to the window and drew up the string. She did not think of difficulties; it seemed to her that the man ought to free her immediately when she had told him to do so. In the meantime, she decided to bribe one of the servants.

Both of them were gloomy and unfriendly, but the younger was more accessible. She would talk a few words at least with her every day. Cosel was in the habit of treating every one in a queenly manner and assuring them of her favour. She was always majestic, thinking that she was the King's wife. But little by little she assumed a more gentle manner with the young servant Madeleine. She could not, however, make her friendly till she began to complain of the older one. The money acted still better, but a month passed before she could count upon her.

Zaklika had not returned. He could not act quickly, for this reason, that he was known in Dresden, and the purchase by him of a carriage and horses would arouse suspicion. Therefore a great amount of cunning was necessary to purchase what he needed without attracting attention. Through the Wend he made some acquaintances in Budzishyne, and there he worked out his plans.

It took a good deal of time, however, and the autumn passed by and winter came, and it was the worst time of the year for flight. Zaklika went to Nossen in order to ask Cosel to be patient until the spring. The steward was paid to open the door, at which Madeleine kept watch, and they were able to talk freely and come to an agreement that they would try to fly in the spring. There was no doubt that the steward, tempted by the money, would give in.

The winter was long, and such kind of enterprises, when they drag, are apt to furnish a chance for repentance on the part of those who help to accomplish them. The steward, being tipsy on one occasion, said something about it to his wife; the rest she got out of him. The shrewd woman thought that when one betrays it is better to betray everybody, and take all possible benefit out of it. According to her opinion they should agree to take the money from Zaklika, and then communicate the plan to the authorities in order not to lose their position, and thus not be obliged to fly into another country.

The steward smiled at the shrewd idea of his cunning wife. They awaited the spring.

The Countess was so sure of Madeleine that she told her all about it, and asked her to go with her. The woman became frightened at the idea. She wrestled with herself. Under the pretext of seeing her family, she asked permission to go to Dresden. She had a sister in the service of Countess Denhoff—she went to see her. The women consulted each other and agreed that it would be best to tell the Countess's mother of the plans of Cosel, for which act they were sure to be well rewarded.

The fear of the women may be imagined when they learned that Cosel could escape. Löwendahl was called up at once. The first step was to arrest both women. The same day a double guard of soldiers went to Nossen to replace those that were there. They doubled the sentries, arrested the steward, and led him in chains to Dresden.

During the night sentries were placed under the windows. In the morning Cosel found in the anteroom an unknown officer, who, accompanied by an official, searched all her things and inspected the doors and locks.

She was angry, but did not dare to ask any questions, being afraid that Zaklika might be detected and arrested. Happily nobody here knew him by his name, for he had taken precautions to assume another.

They found no proofs of the proposed escape, for she had destroyed the paper written by Zaklika; but from that time life in Nossen became unbearable. New servants were sent, who treated the Countess with great severity. She defended herself only with pride and silence.

When the official had left the room, the young officer, having a more tender heart than the others, said to her,—

"I am sure the Countess does not remember a lad whom she has seen many times as the King's page. I am here on a sad duty, and I came here only to spare you some suffering if I can. You must try not to make your position worse."

Cosel looked at him proudly.

"If you wish to prove to me your sympathy," she said, "tell me then what they have discovered and how."

"I do not know the details," said the officer. "The orders were given by Marshal Löwendahl. They have changed the garrison and the servants; the steward of the castle is arrested."

"And who besides?"

"Nobody else, besides the servants, I believe," answered the officer. "I will come to see you every day. I shall be very severe in the presence of the servants, but I will do anything to please you."

He saluted and went off.

A few days passed by in fear and uncertainty. Zaklika, having learned in Dresden that the plan of escape was discovered, kept quiet, waiting to see if they would try to arrest him. He understood that he could not show himself near Nossen, and in the meantime he felt it would relieve the Countess if she knew he was still free and that she could count on him.

In consequence he dressed as a beggar and stole at nights to the castle.

During the day, lying in the thickets, he noticed that the string was not at the window, and that a sentry was beneath it. Communication with the Countess was therefore very difficult, and he racked his brains how he could do it. Wandering through the country, notwithstanding the snow and cold, he met a pedlar named Trene selling various wares for Christmas. He had a small van which he used to draw to an inn, to which the women came to make their purchases, while to the houses of the richer people he carried the goods himself.

Zaklika had known this pedlar in Dresden. He stopped him and reminded him that he used to make purchases from him at the Wend's house.

"In Nossen," said Zaklika, "you can do good business, for in the castle the Countess Cosel is imprisoned. I am sure she will purchase some presents for the servants."

The pedlar's eyes sparkled.

"Thank you for the advice," said he. "I never should have thought of it."

"When you are there," said Zaklika, "remember me to her, for I was in her service formerly."

"What shall I tell her?" asked the pedlar.

"Tell her that her servant who used to break horseshoes is free, and wanders throughout God's world. Where are you going from Nossen?" asked Zaklika.

"I think home, for Christmas is not far off, and I would like to spend it with my family."

"Then perhaps we shall meet on the road."

The pedlar, like all sellers when it is a question of gain, knew how to act. When he came to the town he went straight to the castle. The soldiers wanted to drive him away; but he raised such a din that the officer came out. He was more indulgent, and sent to the Countess, asking her whether she would admit a pedlar. For distraction's sake Cosel consented.

The modest wares of the poor pedlar did not satisfy her refined taste, and she was looking contemptuously at them, when Herr Trene whispered to her,—

"I was asked to tell you that your faithful servant, the horseshoe-breaker, is in good health, and wanders free through God's world."

"Who told you this?" asked Cosel.

"He himself," answered Trene. "I met him in the neighbourhood."

When the Countess had heard those words she purchased a lot from him, and the pedlar was surprised at his good luck. He left the castle happy. He also did good business in the inn, and was obliged to stay overnight. The next day he met Zaklika on the road to Dresden. He greeted him cordially.

"Did you tell her about me?" asked the Pole.

"Yes," answered Trene, "and evidently the Countess was pleased. I did good business. I thank you."

In the meantime the prisoners were questioned in Dresden. The steward was intelligent enough not to avow anything whatever, and they released him; but he lost his position. The women were released too, but not rewarded.

The King ordered that Cosel should be watched carefully. He knew her too well, and was aware that she could be dangerous. When he learned of the plan for escape, he ordered Stolpen Castle to be prepared for her. It was a stronghold, built on basalt rock; the same which Cosel had once visited with the King, and it was while riding there that she met the Slav woman, Mlawa, who foretold her future.

At once orders were sent to Stolpen to furnish the St. John's tower, in which the Bishop of Meissen used to imprison refractory priests. Augustus was offended and angry. The unconquered will of a woman mocked his might; a woman dared to ask him to keep his promise, and accuse him of breach of faith. It was unpardonable daring; and whoever drew the lord's anger upon himself, for him there was no mercy.

Two days before Christmas there was a great stir in Nossen Castle. There was sent from Dresden another detachment of soldiers and a carriage, with the King's order to transport Cosel to Stolpen.

The surprised officer did not dare to enter the Countess's room with the new order, which announced to her a still harder lot.

Cosel, hearing an unaccustomed noise, rushed to the door. She still hoped at times that Augustus, whom she had not ceased to love, would have pity on her, and she thought that as a Christmas present he had granted her freedom. She stood trembling when an official entered and bowed to her profoundly. The apparition of the scribbler was the worse message for her. He was holding a paper in one hand, spectacles in the other; he was trembling too.

"What do you wish?" asked Cosel.

"I have brought an order signed by His Majesty the King, who has kindly designated Countess Cosel Stolpen Castle as her place of abode."

The Countess rushed screaming towards the wall as though she would tear it down. The servants tried to hold her, but she pushed them away vigorously with cries and moans. The official stood by as if turned to stone.

They were obliged to conduct her by force to the carriage, in which she was taken to Stolpen, and lodged in St. John's and Donat's towers, on the 25th of December, 1716.

Old Stolpen Castle was then in a half-ruined condition. The summits of its towers had been destroyed by lightning, and the old building would hardly shelter a small garrison. The commandant of the castle, Johan Friederich von Wehlen, occupied one of those uncomfortable towers; the other, called Johannisturm, was destined for the unfortunate favourite of Augustus.

The former inhabitant of luxurious palaces was now obliged to be satisfied with two rooms, one of which was intended as the kitchen, the second for the Countess herself.

When she looked round this bare and dreary room, lighted by small windows, she gave way to despair, and continued to weep so bitterly that they were obliged to watch her continually. Her guards and servants, specially chosen that they could not be bribed, stood motionless at the sight of such an outburst of grief.

Wehlen, an old soldier, who never made war against women, lost his head and patience. It was a hard thing for him to be severe on this unfortunate, but still beautiful woman. The first day of Christmastide, celebrated with such solemnity throughout the world, was spoiled for him by the scene of despair. The sentries walking under the walls were afraid of the crying and screaming of that unfortunate lady.

She spent the whole night in this way, till finally she fell upon the bed, half-dead from exhaustion. The women whispered that she would die. The third day Cosel rushed from the bed and asked for some paper; she wanted to write to the King.

They had foreseen this wish, and the order was for all her letters to be sent to Löwendahl. Augustus had strictly forbidden any communication to be brought him from Cosel, and ordered her correspondence to be burned; but she was not forbidden to write and to have some hope. Cosel still believed in Augustus' heart.

When the first outburst of despair had passed, she looked around and recognized the walls which had frightened her so much when she visited them with the King. From the windows she could see the thick high walls surrounding the castle, and in the distance the blue mountains covered with woods, bare hills, and the country which looked as if it were uninhabited.

This made her the prey to solitude, reminiscences, watching the soldiers, harassing the servants who were at the same time her guards and executioners.

Wehlen had received the strictest orders to watch her carefully, a responsibility which in those days might cost him his own life. Those who wrote the instructions, it is true, had recommended politeness towards the woman; but the watchfulness must be so strict as to destroy all hope of flight. At first glance such a thing as flight seemed impossible. The castle was surrounded by high walls; the St. John's tower was strong, and it had been lighted by so many windows that the sentries walking beneath them could see what the prisoner was doing. Two courtyards had to be crossed before the tower could be reached.

At the gateway were sentries; the castle was on a high mount dominating the country, every one approaching it could be seen.

There was nobody except the commandant, two officers, a handful of soldiers, and the Countess's servants in the castle. Nobody could enter it without the commandant's special permission, and the gates were always shut.

Old Von Wehlen, who had never seen the Countess, and concluded that the King did not care for her because she was old, was amazed when he set eyes on her for the first time. Cosel was then thirty-six years of age, and God had granted her eternal beauty and strength. Her face bore no traces of suffering, and perhaps she was never more charming than then. The brightness of her eyes, the freshness of her complexion, her majestic figure, and statuesque shape, made those who looked at her wonder. In cynical disdain, and as if sneering at her present position, Cosel assumed the manners and speech of a queen. She gave her orders, and in her voice there was pride in proportion to her misfortune.

The days were long, weary and monotonous. Cosel filled them with memories and sometimes with hope. She cursed Augustus' cruelty, but she could not understand how the one who had loved her so tenderly could become such a terrible executioner.

The letters that she wrote became by habit a necessity. By the silence she knew that it was in vain, but at the same time she felt better when she had committed her thoughts to paper, which could be only scorn for other people.

When they had packed up her things in Nossen, some one had picked up the old Bible, and the Countess was constantly reading its pages, in which so many sorrows are expressed. Those stray leaves aroused in her the desire to read the whole book. She sent to the commandant to buy a Bible for her. He asked permission from Dresden; they ordered her desire to be gratified; and from that time the Bible was constantly on her table. In reading it she found, if not consolation, at least forgetfulness. From it she learned that for thousands of years life had been constant torture.

Thus she found the spring! The spring, which awakes everything to life, was only going to prolong her sufferings. The swallows came to the old nests to repair them again; the trees began to open their buds towards the sun. Over the earth there blew a warm air, mingled with the scent of flowers. Even around the castle some life appeared; the ploughmen went freely to the fields—she alone could not move. Cosel used to stay at the window for hours deep in thought, and did not notice that a soldier, astonished at her beauty, would often look at her, and ask himself what this angel-like woman could have done to merit imprisonment. Old Von Wehlen, smoking his pipe on the ramparts, looked also at her windows, and his thoughts were bitter; his heart heaved, for he felt that he loved his lord Friederich Augustus less.

He pitied her. The space in which she could walk consisted of a small room in the tower, which the sun could not warm.

At the foot of the St. John's tower there was a piece of land, surrounded by the wall of the fortress—enough space for a comfortable grave. In that corner there grew wormwood, wild thyme and wild pinks. Wehlen thought it could be turned into a little garden; but to make the garden, permission would be necessary, for it would make it pleasanter, and to show pity for the rebellious woman would mean to make her bolder. Consequently he made a garden for himself, thinking that the Countess would at least look on the flowers.

Cosel looked from the window, and noticing that they were digging, she withdrew, thinking that they were making a grave. Only when, after some time, she perceived some flowers there, she smiled at them.

It seemed to her that if, instead of sitting on the stones, she could rest on the earth, she would revive. The flowers could be her confidants and companions; but considering herself a queen, she could not ask for it—she preferred to suffer.

At last, considering that she could not escape from it, old Wehlen told the servant to tell the Countess that she could go there. And when one morning she went down to see her garden, the air seemed to intoxicate her; she was obliged to lean for a while against the wall.

From that time she used to spend whole days in the garden, taking care of the flowers, which she planted herself then.

Thus passed the spring and summer without any change or hope. There was no answer to her letters; nobody came to see her. Out of an immense fortune taken from her, they paid her about three thousand thalers, which she could use as she pleased; but the commandant controlled all her expenses, and she could not transact any business without his knowledge.

Since coming to Stolpen she had been waiting for Zaklika; but month after month passed, and there was no news from him. Once, however, a Jewish pedlar, who used to bring her different things, whispered to her that the one who used to break the horseshoes was still alive, and that she should see him. Those few words were sufficient to awaken in her a slumbering hope.

In the meantime Zaklika was working constantly. His plans of facilitating the escape of the Countess from Nossen being ruined, he was obliged to begin anew. He knew that Cosel was imprisoned in Stolpen.

This cruelty they tried to justify by spreading reports that Cosel, when in Berlin, had tried to plot against the King's life, that she had threatened to kill him, that she was mad, and called herself a queen. And they ended in whispers that Augustus was ashamed of the levity with which he had given her a promise of marriage although the Queen was living. That promise, notwithstanding all efforts, they could not find or get back. It was the first time that Augustus had acted with such cruelty, and it frightened even the Countess Denhoff, although she could not flatter herself that she was much loved by the King.

It was true that her court was quite brilliant, but her following had no political weight. Even those who had helped her to rise, in order to get rid of Cosel, kept away from her. Watzdorf alone, who thought through her to overthrow Flemming, was attached to her, and served her by asking the King for considerable sums of money, which she squandered lavishly, sometimes spending 10,000 thalers on a ball. She was then already not counting on the King's long-continued favours, and she looked after Bosenval and the young Lubomirski, who seemed to be fond of her.

Augustus' cold and sometimes cruel treatment of his best favourite warned the others to be armed against the caprices of their lord, who could take everything from them. Thus Hoym, the Countess Cosel's ex-husband, whom the King needed but did not like, remembering the fate of Beichling, Imhoff, and even his ex-wife, had sold his estate in Saxony, sent away the money, and, resigning from the Saxon service, had retired to Silesia.

With Denhoff the reign of omnipotent King's favourites was ended. The actors of those comedies and dramas grew old and died out. The King himself lost his taste for noisy amusements. Leipzig fair alone could distract and animate him for a while.

Zaklika had been for a long time thinking of the best means to help Cosel. He did not know Stolpen; he went to see it. He could stop safely in the town, for they paid no attention to travellers. Here he learned everything—who was the commandant of the castle, and that it was difficult to get in.

Zaklika racked his brains to find a way, and he returned to Dresden with the determination to act openly. He had plenty of acquaintances from former times, but no friends. In the meantime, however, there came some lords from Poland, through whose influence he might do something. Zaklika thought that the best way would be to try to enter the military service, and be sent to the garrison at Stolpen. The way was long and difficult, but Zaklika had an iron will and boundless self-sacrifice. With the Polish lords his old name was of itself a good recommendation.

When he appeared at the Court, they were quite surprised, for they knew he had been with Cosel; but no one asked him what he had been doing since her downfall. Zaklika told every one that he had been in Poland for some time. When the Bishop of Cracow, Sieniawski, came to Dresden, Zaklika decided to try through him to purchase a grade of captain in the Saxon army.

On the Bishop mentioning Zaklika's name to the King, Augustus frowned, but ordered him to be called. He had not seen him for several years, and found him greatly changed. He looked at him suspiciously, but finding him bold but quiet, and learning that he left the Countess of himself, he raised no objection to his entering the army. The only question was to purchase the commission, which he soon was able to do. Zaklika had saved some money; he soon concluded the bargain with the German, and once again he wore a uniform, still more magnificent than before.

Great disorder reigned in the Saxon army; sometimes officers did not see their regiments for years; they preferred to remain in the capital, and boast before the women about their marvellous bravery. They did not respect orders, and led a dissipated life. All that was the worst in the country served in the army; adventurers, gamblers, usurers, blacklegs. The generals lived on the soldiers, and the latter, being driven to despair, and following the example of their officers, lived as they could.

Such disorder was favourable to Zaklika for carrying out his plans with money, and it was not difficult, having become acquainted with comrades, to find the way to replace some one in the garrison of Stolpen, which was considered a horrid prison.

Old Wehlen being, as he learned, a quiet and a good man, continually playing draughts and smoking tobacco, would not be difficult to deceive.

Cosel was greatly astonished when, after several long months of waiting, the pedlar Jew announced to her that the horseshoe-breaker would appear again.

Another spring appeared, and for the second time the garden became green; then the same flowers raised their heads towards the sun. Cosel opened the window; the day was warm; the air quiet and mild.

While sitting in her little garden she could see the soldiers and officers passing through the courtyard, from which she was separated by a low wall. The proud lady did not like her fallen grandeur to be looked at, but, being weary, she was glad sometimes to see a human face, forgetting that she was queen. And sometimes a soldier stood looking at her with commiseration, and the younger officers lost their heads when they looked for long into her burning black eyes.

One of those who walked very often in the neighbourhood of the garden as a pretext for approaching the beautiful woman was young Wehlen, nephew of the commandant. The old man kept him for two reasons; to have a partner for his game of draughts, and to look after his military career.

Henry von Wehlen did not like the service, but his mother, wishing him to be made heir by the commandant, who was an old and rich bachelor, persuaded her son to obey him. This twenty-year old Wehlen found life terribly dull on the basalt rock of Stolpen, but could not escape from it.

What bliss, then, for the young man dreaming in solitude was the arrival of such a beautiful if unhappy prisoner! At the first sight of Anna, Henry lost his head. He could not understand how they could keep such an ideal of an earthly goddess between walls, and let her die little by little. With the ardour of first, pure, exalted, but concealed love, young Wehlen was attracted towards the beautiful woman. The old commandant did not notice these sentiments in his nephew. He was the most prosaic of men, and did not care for feminine beauty. Formerly he had a smile for them all, but now for none of them.

It was Henry who had carefully suggested to him to permit the Countess to enjoy the garden. Very often acting as lieutenant to his uncle, he was practically master of the castle, and Cosel knew well that she could count on him, although she seldom deigned to look at him. She preferred to wait for Zaklika.

How great was her surprise and pleasure one day, on going into the garden, to perceive Henry Wehlen and Zaklika in the courtyard, talking quite amicably. The latter she recognized by his voice, for the uniform altered his appearance very much. She could hear the loud conversation; Zaklika was telling him that he succeeded Captain Zitaner, who was in a great hurry to visit his family.

"Captain von Wehlen," said Captain von Zaklika, "it is not very cheerful staying here among ruins. Had I known it was such a horrid place—"

"It is a bad place," answered Henry von Wehlen, "for those who want merry-making; but those who are fond of beautiful nature can live here very happily."

Cosel listened, but she turned away in order not to betray the interest she was taking in the conversation.

"Captain von Wehlen," said Zaklika, "if it could be done, you should introduce me to the Countess."

"With great pleasure," said Wehlen, who was glad to have a pretext for approaching the Countess.

They both went towards the wall of the garden. Captain von Wehlen saluted the Countess.

"Permit me to introduce to you Captain von Zaklika, newly arrived."

Cosel turned, apparently with indifference, and bowed slightly to the new-comer, who stood pale, full of emotion, looking at that beautiful face, still alight with the same charm which first shone for him under the linden trees in Laubegast.

After a moment of silence the Countess said,—

"Are you here on a visit?"

"No, madam, I am on service, which I daresay will last quite a long time, for I doubt whether anybody would care to exchange with me."

"It is surely the worst prison any one could find," exclaimed the Countess. "In a dark room the world is unseen, and so forgotten; but here the whole vast horizon lies before one's eyes, separated only by a big wall."

The officers stood speechless.

"What have you done that they send you here?" added the Countess.

"It is the caprice of destiny."

Then they saluted and went off.

Wehlen took Zaklika's arm, and conducted him into the third courtyard of the castle, where he occupied a couple of rooms, and where he also wanted to lodge his new comrade.

"Captain von Zaklika," said he, "I am sure this is the first time you have seen the Countess Cosel. What do you say about her beauty? Is she not worthy of the throne?"

He said this with such enthusiasm that he betrayed his secret, which he did not perhaps intend to hide before Zaklika.

"I do not wonder at your enthusiasm," said the latter; "but from your enthusiasm one would imagine you were in love."

"We are both soldiers," answered Wehlen, "and honest folks; why should I deny it? I have lost my head looking at her. I am not ashamed either. There is not another woman like her in the world."

"But," said Zaklika, "you should remember that a woman who was the King's wife would not look upon another man. Then so many misfortunes have withered her heart; finally, she is a prisoner for ever!"

"For ever!" interrupted Wehlen. "What lasts for ever? She is so beautiful!"

Zaklika smiled.

"You are so young," he said.

"You are right; I am young; but who could resist the charm of her looks? You have seen my uncle, his grey hair, wrinkled face, quenched eyes. Well, he looks at her from afar and sighs, till a game of draughts makes him forget her. The soldiers look at her as at a picture; then how can a youth of twenty resist her beauty?"

The same day they went to look over the castle, and already Zaklika tried to form some plans of escape. He found there was only one way to get out of the castle, and this was a subterranean corridor from the tower to the chapel, from which there was a narrow passage to the outside. Seeing this, he already had a plan. The Countess, dressed in man's clothing, would go down and slip into the exterior courtyard, where no sentries were posted. From there one could reach the door in the passage during the night. It would not be a difficult matter to get a couple of horses in the town, and the frontier was not far away.

A few days later he found an opportunity of entering Cosel's room without arousing any suspicion. The Countess extended her hand to him.

"You have made me wait too long," said she.

"I could not do otherwise," answered Zaklika. "The one who uses the last means must be careful. The question was not one of my life, but of not failing to deliver you."

"Yes, you are right," said Cosel. "I must preserve you for a last resource, for you are most faithful. Young Wehlen may be used first."

"What for?" asked Zaklika.

"To deliver me from here. He is madly in love with me. He knows the castle well. Do not mix in anything; let him do it. Help him as you can without taking part openly; prefer not to see anything. I will try to escape with him."

"But he is a crazy boy," said Zaklika. "Only crazy people succeed in accomplishing crazy enterprises," said Cosel.

"But suppose he does not succeed?" asked Zaklika gloomily.

"No matter; they cannot do anything worse to me. I should only regret having exposed the young man. You will remain in reserve."

"But I don't think he will have courage to do it," said Zaklika.

"Leave that to me. I will manage the whole thing."

A noise on the stairs stopped further conversation. Zaklika changed the subject and then went out.

He was hurt at Cosel's rejection of his help, but always submitted to her, determined to obey her will.

Wehlen took him into his confidence and told him he was ready to give up his own life for the Countess.

"I am sure you would not betray me," said he.

"No," answered Zaklika; "you may be assured on that point; but do not betray yourself."

Soon Zaklika noticed that Wehlen began to visit the Countess quite often, to talk with her while she was in the garden. Zaklika was obliged to play draughts with the uncle and to chat with him. Henry was constantly rushing about, and by his redoubled energy and some preparations that he easily noticed, Zaklika guessed that the flight was soon to be attempted. Not being in the secret, he did not want to interfere, but once he whispered to the youth,—

"For Heaven's sake, have a care, captain. I do not know your thoughts and plans, but I am afraid that the others may notice, as I have, some unusual preparations."

Wehlen was a little bit frightened; he took hold of Zaklika's arm, led him to a remote corner, and asked,—

"What have you noticed, then?"

"Well, I have noticed that you are preparing some *salto mortale*."

"I do not understand what you mean," said Wehlen. "The whole thing is that I am madly in love."

"You must try not to show that love to others, and not let them see what I see."

The same day Zaklika went to the tower and found Cosel walking about feverishly, wearing a different dress than usual.

"Zaklika," she said, "do not interfere with anything—be blind. Play with the old commandant. In case of alarm, keep him as long as possible."

"If you succeed in escaping, what shall I do then?" asked Zaklika.

"Then come where I will tell you."

She did not wish to say a word more.

Zaklika left the room with a sad presentiment. Wehlen, whom he met in the courtyard, was feverish, looking every moment at the setting sun.

The old commandant called Zaklika to have a glass of beer and play the usual game of draughts. The sergeant who locked the doors and brought the key usually found them absorbed in the game, which lasted late into the night.

The evening was beautiful. Zaklika played absentmindedly, listening to the smallest noise in the castle, and the commandant, winning each time, laughed at him.

"What is the matter with you today?" he asked.

"I have a headache."

Having played a few games, they began to chat. Wehlen filled his pipe. The night was growing dark; they lighted candles. Henry was absent, and this was unusual.

"I am sure he went to town," said the commandant. "He is weary here, and I prefer him to go out rather than sigh at that proud lady, who imagines she is a queen and does not deign to look at anybody."

Zaklika did not answer.

Everything was quiet in the castle, and the time at which the old corporal used to bring the keys was near; there was a knock at the door.

The old soldier, looking like a highway robber—a mercenary who had seen military service in every country, entered. He was pale, and his face was strangely twisted. The expression of it struck Zaklika; he was horrified.

The commandant did not like him. His name was Wurm.

"I have to make a serious report," said Wurm.

"What is going on?" cried the commandant, rushing from his chair.

"At this moment your nephew is running away with the Countess Cosel!"

The commandant rushed to the door like a madman.

"It is no use to hasten," laughed Wurm savagely. "I knew it would come to that, and I watched them; I am sure of a good reward."

"It is an impudent lie!" cried the commandant.

"I have done my duty," said Wurm coolly. "At this moment the soldiers are keeping them in the passage behind the chapel, and Captain Henry, who is so fond of giving me slaps on the face, will be shot."

The corporal smiled with hellish delight. The commandant trembled, and knew not what to do. The fear of his beloved nephew made him almost crazy.

"Captain von Zaklika," cried he, "help me! save him!"

"It cannot be done," said the corporal. "Tomorrow the King and the whole Court will know about it. Too many people have seen it. I have fixed everything right. I have avenged myself, and if you like to be avenged on me, I am ready for anything."

At that moment there was a noise in the direction of the tower. The soldiers were conducting the prisoners. The Countess was pale, and Henry was staggering, for he had wounded himself with a pistol, and he would surely have killed himself had they not bound his hands.

Cosel was behaving like a mad woman; Henry stood quietly. The old commandant came to him wringing his hands. Zaklika was behind them; he pitied the poor boy who had fallen into the snare. Nobody looked at Wurm, who smiled triumphantly and cynically.

The uncle was obliged to put his nephew into prison and send a report to Dresden. He was unable to write it himself; the old soldier cried like a child. He called the secretary, and, sobbing and cursing, he accused his nephew, begging for mercy and giving as a reason his youth, and putting his own services in the balance. He did not spare his own blindness; but finally he accused the corporal, who, instead of preventing the misfortune, dishonestly waited for it in order to profit by it.

The sentries were doubled, and they passed the night in uneasiness.

The commandant put the corporal under arrest also. The report was sent by courier to Dresden. The rising sun shone on Stolpen Castle, which seemed gloomier than ever. Cosel was in convulsions. About noon General von Bodt and several officials came from Dresden. At first old Wehlen handed his sword without a word, but the General returned it to him; by the King's order only Captain Henry Wehlen and Corporal Wurm were to be court-martialled.

Before the sun set the sentence of death had been carried out. The old commandant's tears and prayers were in vain. Cosel heard the firing, and she shivered; she guessed that the man who loved her was at that moment paying for his love. Zaklika stood pale, like a corpse.

The same day Commandant von Wehlen left the service, after having written a bitter letter to the King. Corporal Wurm had been put in chains and sent to the Königstein fortress.

Such was Cosel's first attempt to recover her freedom. She cried over the poor young enthusiast who had given his life for her, but she wept also over her own lot. She told the servant to take all the flowers from the garden to Henry's grave. After that event, everything was changed in Stolpen. The command was given to Bierling, who was still more strict, but less intelligent; he was passionate, impetuous, arbitrary, and proud, possessing all the faults of old soldiers, and had been more successful than he deserved. He forbade the Countess to leave the tower; the guards were changed, and Zaklika was ordered to return to his regiment.

Taking advantage of the fact that the commandant was drunk every evening, Zaklika went to take leave of Cosel. He found her crying; she could hardly speak.

"Then you also abandon me! Are you afraid?" cried she, bitterly.

"They have ordered me to return to my regiment, and I must go in order to serve you better."

"And I—have I to weep here for ever?" said Cosel. "Have I to die here?"

"I will do anything you order," said Zaklika.

After a moment of reflection, she said,—

"Go, and think what can be done; you will know best. I have lost my common sense. God and man have abandoned me. But, remember, if you too betray me, I shall curse you!"

Then she told him that in Pillnitz she had buried a box of diamonds under a certain tree. Zaklika was to dig it up, sell the stones, and use the money in preparing for flight. The approach of a servant interrupted their conversation.

For several years following, the faithful servant could do nothing else but let her hear from him through the pedlar. They would not have been any more strict with her, but for another attempt to fly similar to the first, and which ended as unfortunately as the preceding one.

This time the Countess was sure of success. She ordered Zaklika, when he had found some pretext to visit her, to wait for her at a certain place on the frontier, and so have horses and money in readiness. The certain amount of freedom they granted her, she used in gaining over Lieutenant Helm, who, like Wehlen, fell madly in love with her.

This love was still more poetic, more passionate than the first one. It lasted two years, till the Countess, having tested the man, having learned of his plan, consented to try.

Lieutenant Helm was captivated not only by Cosel's beauty, but also by her intellect, eloquence, and poetry; for by this time the constant reading of her Bible had made of her an inspired divine. Her speech, dress, movement, and looks, marked an unusual state of mind, which was accompanied by such assurance, such a deep faith and unshaken dignity—that her attractiveness was increased not only in the eyes of this one man, but of all with whom she came in contact.

Zaklika was surprised at such a great change. She was beautiful, as before; but the expression of her face was more severe; misfortune had impressed its mark upon it, but had not lessened its charm. Her liveliness of movement was replaced by dignity; her words were uttered with an impressiveness that made them seem inspired by some mysterious source. She seemed to be some priestess—some sibyl. Zaklika found her reading the Bible with a pencil in her hand. She looked at him and extended her hand. The man's eyes moistened.

"Do you see?" said she. "I am still alive. God has permitted me to live, and He has not done so in vain. I know that I shall outlive my persecutors and forgive them. God granted me life to open my eyes to great truths. I must be free, for I have great things to accomplish."

"Are you not afraid," said Zaklika, "that—"

"I was never afraid of anything," interrupted Cosel. "That young man will do what I tell him, and now I possess the secret of seeing clearly ways and means. He will not betray me, neither will Fate!"

They agreed about the place and the day. He did not ask any questions about the plan, but he had fears for the lady; he had a presentiment that it would make her lot worse.

She dismissed him with a nod like a queen. Lieutenant Helm, whom he had seen only for a moment, seemed to him to be as enthusiastic as was the unfortunate Henry von Wehlen.

Zaklika, obedient to Cosel's order, obtained leave of absence, for he was still in the military service, which gave him a certain safety, and he went with his friend the Wend to wait on the frontier.

Cosel was coming there the same night. Zaklika waited with unspeakable uneasiness. The night passed in undisturbed quietude; then came day, and he waited in vain. The two following days and nights passed in the same manner: nobody came, there was no news. On the fourth day a merchant coming from Stolpen told in the inn how the Countess, imprisoned in the castle, after having escaped with an officer who helped her to fly, was captured.

That was all he could learn. He returned to Dresden in order to learn more, and so act according to the news he received.

The merchant's narrative was true. Zaklika went to Stolpen. He had no need to go to the castle: in the town nothing else was talked of. Helm had been working the whole year in digging a narrow passage under the walls, leading behind the fortress in the direction in which there were no sentries. The opening was adroitly hidden with stones. Drunken sentries and the absence of the commandant seemed to promise success. During the night the Countess, dressed in man's clothes, succeeded in leaving the tower unperceived. Helm was waiting for her in the third courtyard, from which they could escape to the outside by the passage he had made. He quietly removed the stones. The Countess passed first; Helm followed her. Notwithstanding the darkness, they succeeded in slipping down the basalt rocks to the foot of the mount. Not far off horses were waiting for them; but before they reached them the alarm was given in the castle.

A servant who entered Cosel's chamber to see whether the lady was quieter than she had been in the day, during which she was feverish, noticing that the window was open and the bed empty, began to scream, thinking that the Countess, in a fit of madness, had jumped on to the rocks. Everybody sprang to their feet.

While searching in the castle, they noticed the opening under the walls, and they set out in pursuit. The man who was waiting with the horses, hearing the alarm, returned with them to the town.

Cosel and Helm began to run across the fields to the bush, thinking to hide there; but the commandant, knowing that his life would be in danger if he failed to capture the fugitives, gathered as many people as he could in the town, ordered torches to be lit, sent men on horseback in all directions, and before dawn they were discovered. The Countess and Helm had pistols, and they wounded a soldier in self-defence, but the shot attracted the attention of others, and they were speedily captured.

The officer was court-martialled like von Wehlen. They took him to Dresden, where he was to be shot on the New Market square. His relations were very influential, and they did everything to save his life. About noon a detachment of soldiers conducted Helm to the place of execution. A large crowd gathered to look at the beautiful, golden-haired youth, who did not lose his courage in the hour of death.

He was placed against the wall, the soldiers aimed their rifles, the officer was ready to give the order to fire, when the King's aide-de-camp galloped up with a pardon.

Helm was led back to the barracks; but no one knew what was to be done with him. The crowd scattered.

At Stolpen Castle, except for new precautions and a change of commandant, nothing was altered. They did not touch Cosel, who enjoyed even the little liberty she was allowed before.

Cosel was mourning in her heart the death of another victim of her love, for the news of his pardon was slow in reaching her.

Zaklika returned to his quarters, and began preparations for that which he thought was his duty. But being more experienced than those who preceded him, he wanted to be certain that the last attempt to fly was certain of success. He was not discouraged at all because Wehlen had lost his life and Helm broken his career. The only question was, would it be better to quit the military service and go to live at Stolpen or not?

A few months passed. During this time Zaklika learned that a friend of his, Von Kaschau by name, a good but very dissipated fellow, was in the garrison of Stolpen. He went to see him, and when the old soldier perceived him, he was overwhelmed with joy. He asked the commandant to let Zaklika stay at the castle. The commandant, being unwell, and needing

Von Kaschau to do his duty for him, consented. The two friends went to Kaschau's rooms, drank beer and chatted, naturally about the prisoner.

"I do not like to judge others," said the old soldier, "especially His Majesty, our King, but I do not see any reason for his severity to that woman! What could she do? The most would be that some one would fall in love with her, like Helm, for she is still beautiful. Nothing has injured her charms—neither prison, nor grief, nor tears."

"Had you seen her in her full splendour, as I did when I was at the Court," said Zaklika, "then you would know how dangerous she was. The King was not afraid of her pistol, but of her eyes and the influence she had over him; for if she could speak for an hour with him, he would lie at her feet and pray for pardon."

Kaschau laughed.

"Yes, but then he would lie at the feet of Fraulein Dieskau or Osterhausen—the old wheedler!"

"I would like to see her," said Zaklika, "for it would be interesting to see such a woman again."

"No one stops you from doing so," said Kaschau. "During the day you cannot steal her away; you may go there and bow to the former goddess."

Zaklika went to the tower and knocked at Cosel's door. As there was no answer, he entered, and beheld Cosel standing thoughtfully over an open Bible which was lying on the book-covered table. She was robed in such an odd dress that he feared she had lost her reason. She wore a full black robe with long sleeves and a girdle with cabalistic signs on it. On her head was a red handkerchief, arranged in Oriental fashion, with a roll of parchment on which some Hebrew sentences were written.

She was beautiful indeed, but quite different from that Cosel who received the Danish King in a robe covered with diamonds.

She did not take her eyes from the book, but remained thinking.

After a while she looked up at him, and said in surprise,—

"Are you a spirit or a living being?"

"I am your faithful servant; I have come to ask your orders," said Zaklika.

"Then there are faithful servants; and I, a prisoner, can still give orders? To whom?"

"To me," answered Zaklika, "as long as I live."

"How did you come here?"

Zaklika pointed to his uniform.

"Now is my turn," said he. "I will try to be more intelligent, and perhaps I shall be more lucky."

Cosel smiled bitterly.

"Everything is written above, predestinated, unchangeable—no one can escape his fate."

"And why should it not be my fate to give you liberty?"

She shook her head.

"For this reason, that I shall be free in another way," said she. "Formerly I was blind, but now I see my destiny in this book. There is no favour in this world; there is only iron, unbreakable, unavoidable necessity. One must submit to it. In the Old Testament alone is wisdom."

Zaklika did not know what to say to that.

"Do you remain here?" asked Cosel.

"I do not know yet. Tell me what I have to do; I am ready for anything."

Cosel turned over several pages, and began to read:

"'And he said again, Be not afraid; strengthen yourself and be wise, for thus will the Lord do unto all them against whom ye fight.'"

Then she said,—

"You must await God's voice."

"But am I to quit the military service or not?" asked Zaklika.

"Throw down that horrid livery—that coat of slavery of the Amalekites," said Cosel with animation.

"It will take some time to sell the commission before I could come to Stolpen."

"Go, then, and return," said she. "You are the only man who serves me faithfully."

Zaklika left her. In the courtyard he met Kaschau.

"What have you been talking about with her?" asked he.

"I could not talk at all," answered Zaklika. "She was reading the Bible. I did not want to interrupt her. I must come again."

"I doubt you will have a better chance. Now the Countess seeks distraction in holy books. It is better."

They spent the day in walking on the ramparts and chatting till the moment of locking the gates. Then he took leave of his friend and returned to his quarters in Ochatz, where he sold his commission, gathered as much money as he could, and came to Stolpen, where he purchased a little house in which he settled.

Many changes took place at the Court in Dresden. Cosel was avenged without putting her hand to it. Her foes disappeared one after another.

Amid the ruins King Augustus the Strong was always standing magnificent, throwing away gold, seeking pleasures, but not being able to find them.

The Countess Marie Denhoff, being afraid that she might meet the fate of Cosel, thought it would be wise to marry, and the King did not oppose it. The King enjoyed himself the best in Leipzig fairs, and preferred short amours to those which would fetter him for a long time. The beautiful and statuesque Sophie Dieskau claimed him for a while; but the King found her cold as an icicle, and he married her to Herr von Loss. After that he was in love for a while with Henriette Osterhausen. These temporary love intrigues were followed by the reign of Anna Orzelska, the daughter of Henriette Duval.

The King seemed to become younger at his beautiful daughter's side, who, clad in a uniform embroidered with gold, accompanied him to military reviews, manoeuvres, and hunting.

The King was always eager for distractions, and the arrival of Anna Orzelska furnished him with an opportunity for the display of still greater splendour.

Amid different pleasures furnished by the King's fancy, there were moments when Augustus thought that he was a military genius, and wanted military parades.

In 1727 the King was spending the spring in Pillnitz, where the troops were camping. They tried new cannons which were able to break the rock on which Königstein was built.

"I know some rocks," said Count Wackerbarth to the King, "which would resist those cannons."

"Where?" asked Augustus.

Wackerbarth looked at the King, and it seemed as if he were sorry for what he had said.

"Where?" repeated the King.

"At Stolpen; the basalt rocks would resist."

"In Stolpen!" exclaimed Augustus, and he was gloomy.

There was a moment of silence. The King walked to and fro impatiently; it was evident that he was tormented by some fancy which he did not want to satisfy.

"In Stolpen!" repeated he. "One could try the cannon on those rocks."

The general looked timidly at the King, who, as if he were pricked by that look, exclaimed,—

"Why should we not try the balls on the basalt rocks? We cannot destroy the castle, and a few shots—"

Wackerbarth was silent, and waited for orders, still not believing that Augustus wanted to show that he was superior to the childish consideration.

"Send two cannons to Stolpen," said he, "and give orders for them to be trained on the rock. Tomorrow I will see the trial personally. Yes, tomorrow morning very early, for it is warm already towards noon."

He turned and went off.

Orders of the King were always executed, notwithstanding all difficulties. The cannons were sent to Stolpen during the night. Zaklika was sleeping in his solitary house, when, about midnight, he was awakened by a great noise and shouting of impertinent soldiers. He thought that Saxony was being invaded by the Prussians, but soon he recognized the Saxons by the exclamation, "Herr Jesus!" repeated continually. Then he went out and asked the officer what had happened—why such haste.

"The King," shouted the officer, "will be here this morning."

"The King! In Stolpen?"

"Yes, yes; he will try cannons against the basalt rocks."

"Where?" cried Zaklika, amazed.

"Here, at the rocks on which the castle stands," said the officer.

The conversation was interrupted. Zaklika could not believe his own ears. The King was going to fire at the castle in which he had imprisoned that unfortunate woman! The King in Stolpen! His hair stood on end to think what suffering it would cause the Countess. He wanted to rush and tell her, to give her courage to bear such a trial bravely.

"It cannot be!" repeated he to himself. "At the last moment the King will be ashamed, and will not come! It could not be!"

The dawn was breaking when Zaklika left his house and rushed to the castle, where everybody was awake. The news that the King was coming electrified the soldiers and officers. In the town and villages soldiers were urging the population to make the emplacements. Crying, shouting, and loud commands were heard all around.

One of the batteries they had already begun to build in the park near Röhrpforte, the other at Hanewald.

When Zaklika arrived at the castle he found the gates already open. They were sweeping and cleaning; the commandant was hoarse with shouting; the officers did not know what to do. Round the St. John's Tower the Countess's servants stood half-dressed, for they thought it was an alarm of fire. They asked each other questions as to what they should do. At the open window was Cosel. She was pale and trembling. Zaklika rushed up the stairs.

She met him at the door with the exclamation,—

"The King is coming to me!"

"Not to you," interrupted Zaklika, "he comes to try his cannon balls on the rocks."

Cosel laughed.

"You are a simpleton!" cried she. "I have dreamed of him for a week. My spirit hovered over him and attracted him. He was searching for a pretext; he wishes to see me. He knows that I love him, that I shall forgive him. He is free; he wishes to marry me as he promised. I wish to be beautiful! I want to remind him of that Anna before whom he used to kneel. The King!" exclaimed she in ecstasy, "my king! my lord!"

"Call the servants," added she. "Tell them to take out my dresses!"

Zaklika rushed out and called the servants, then sat on the stairs, silent, full of grief, half-dead, unable to move.

The day was bright. They counted minutes and seconds. Merciless soldiers slashed at the peasants, urging them to work; the batteries were rising before their eyes. It was a most charming May morning. The scented trees were sprinkled with dew; all nature, like a baby in the cradle, was awake smiling. Amid the quietude of nature, everything in the castle was noisy, moving, seething like a bee hive.

The soldiers dressed in their best uniforms; the officers in new armour. The commandant learned, to his great despair, that the King's provisions were not coming to Pillnitz, and it was necessary to receive the lord. What could they find worthy of His Majesty's palate? They killed a couple of deer in the park, they found a few bottles of wine; but how could the simplicity of the camp table agree with the King's accustomed luxury! In fact they had only one decent glass with the arms of Saxony worthy of lordly lips, but the plates and the other things were very poor. The priest lent a table cloth from the church; the innkeeper furnished a great many things.

The cannons were placed in the batteries. It was already four o'clock—at any moment they might expect the King, who said he would leave Pillnitz at daybreak. The commandant put a soldier on the tower, to let him know when he should perceive dust on the road. The artillerymen aimed the cannons so as to be sure the balls would strike the rock.

Everything was ready when the soldier on the tower gave the signal. At that moment the mayor of the town, with the councillors carrying a rusty key on a tray, went out on the road. In the church, ringers were ready to receive the lord with a peal of bells. The inhabitants of the town were dressed in their best clothes, and crowded the streets and market square.

The clouds of dust approached swiftly, and at last they perceived, galloping at the head on a magnificent steed, a good-looking, majestic man. He was followed by aides-de-camp and a small retinue of courtiers and guests.

At the gate the King hardly nodded; the mayor and his councillors bent to the ground; he went immediately in the direction of the castle. Here the garrison was drawn up at the gate; the drum was beaten and the commandant came out with a report. But the King seemed uneasy and in bad humour. He did not say a word to anybody. He turned his horse to the battery at Röhrpforts, looked for a while, and then hurried to Hannewalde. In front of that battery there rose a black mass of basalt rock. From here the St. John's tower and its windows, in one of which was a white figure, could be clearly distinguished. But the King did not raise his eyes.

At that moment General Wackerbarth arrived from Dresden, and stood behind the King in silence. Augustus was in a hurry: he nodded. The artillerymen put a light to the touch-hole of the cannon, and there was a loud report which was echoed in the surrounding mountains. A sharp ear could catch at the same moment a dreadful cry of despair and grief. The King, however, could neither see nor hear anything, his attention being absorbed by the cannon and the result of the firing.

The first shot directed at the wall built of basalt, made a hole in it, but the iron ball was broken into pieces. The commandant brought some pieces to the King, who deigned to look at them, and shrugged his shoulders. The other shot was directed at the rock itself; the ball was broken into pieces, but the rock withstood the blow.

The King, growing feverish, ordered a third and fourth shot to be fired; the result was the same—the rock could not be broken, except for a few splits where the ball struck.

From the first moment that Cosel heard of the King's coming, she was half-mad. At first she thought that Augustus was coming to see her; she dressed with feverish haste and the greatest care, looked long in the mirror and smiled to herself.

"I am sure," she whispered to herself, "he is coming to see me. It is the end of my captivity, and the beginning of my triumph."

She rushed from one window to another. From one of them she could see the road coming from Pillnitz. She noticed clouds of dust, and her heart throbbed—she cried. Then the pealing of bells and the beating of drums were heard—the King was entering the castle. Then silence. She pressed her heart with her hand, and waited. It seemed to her that she would hear him on the stairs—that she would see him at the door, full of pity and benevolence. The silence lasted too long, then the report of a gunshot resounded, shot and cry. Cosel fell on the floor. Suddenly she rose, mad, bewildered, and rushed to the wardrobe. Her hands trembled; she opened the drawer and took a pistol that was hidden among silk dresses. Then she went to the nearest window, looking round. From this side she could hear the noise of the broken rock and the bursting of the cannon balls on it. Cosel leaned out; her eyes were aflame; her bosom heaved. She waited.

At each shot she beat her head and pressed her heart. Wild laughter was on her lips and tears filled her eyes.

After the fourth shot, everything became quiet. Cosel did not move from her place, and held the pistol in her hand. Soon the sound of the tramp of horses resounded on the road. Cosel leaned out and looked.

It was he! Augustus, riding on a path near the walls!

She screamed. He raised his head, stopped his horse, and touched his hat with his hand; he was pale.

Cosel leaned out still more, as though she would jump through.

"Sire! my lord! Have pity on me!" cried she.

Augustus did not answer; and Cosel laughed bitterly.

"To expect pity from you, vile tyrant! From you who break your promises and then imprison those who ask you to fulfil them! What do you care for human life? What do you care for human heart? Cosel, a prisoner, despises you and curses you: yourself, your family and your country! Die, you villain!"

She aimed and fired at the King. The pistol shot resounded in the castle mingled with laughter. The King, hearing the whizz of the ball, came to his wits; he saluted smiling, and galloped off in the direction of Pillnitz. The commandant's efforts to offer the King a luncheon were wasted.

When Zaklika, alarmed by the pistol shot, entered Cosel's room, he found her lying on the floor senseless. Beside her was a pistol, still smoking. He guessed everything. The servants rushed to help the lady, who seemed to be dead.

Many people heard the shot, but Augustus never said a word about it to any one. Hence they came to the conclusion that they must not speak about it.

It took the Countess quite a long time before she assumed her former order of living. Now she was persuaded that she could not expect anything.

They did not, however, forbid visitors to see her, and later on she was allowed to go into the garden.

Zaklika remained in town, but did not arouse any suspicion as he kept quiet. Cosel used to ask him to do different errands for her, but she never spoke about flight.

Only the next year she was irritated by the news of the gorgeous festivities given in Dresden in honour of Frederick William of Prussia, who visited Augustus with his son Frederick, since called the Great.

Cosel listened to the description of the festivities, and was irritated at the thought that formerly such splendour was displayed for her. It again aroused in her the desire of escape, and of revenge upon the tyrant for her suffering and humiliation.

Several times she was ready to say to Zaklika, "Now is your turn." He expected it, and waited. He was ready to die for her sake, but did not wish to awaken the danger himself.

One day when the Jewish pedlar brought to Cosel, together with some goods, a newspaper describing the last entertainments given for the King of Prussia, and among the others the same carousal that was for the first time organized for her, she became indignant.

Zaklika came in at that moment. She was walking to and fro thoughtfully.

"Are you still ready to risk your life for me?" she asked.

"Yes!" answered Zaklika simply.

"Have you any means of freeing me?"

"I will find some."

"I pity you; you were the most faithful to me," said she; "but I must escape from here, I must."

Zaklika stood thoughtful.

"Do you need much time?"

"I cannot calculate," answered Zaklika. "I must act so as to be sure of success."

Cosel nodded, and Zaklika went out into the park, he needed solitude to think over the matter. For a long time he had several plans, but every one of them had some drawback.

All the former attempts were unsuccessful because the flights were discovered too soon; therefore it was necessary to make a plan which would not be discovered before Cosel should be beyond the Saxon boundaries.

Unhappily Zaklika had nobody who could help him. He could count on the faithfulness of his Slav brothers, Wends and Servs, but they were timid and not artful at all. He came to the conclusion that it would be best to fly during day-time.

At the gate there was no strict control over who came in and who went out; they let in pedlars to the Countess and to the commandant; the men did not attract special attention. Therefore he came to the conclusion that during some rainy day Cosel could pass the gates covered with his mantle. He would follow her, and conduct her beyond the park, where he would have saddled horses, on which they could cross the plains towards the woods and mountains.

Zaklika was thinking for several days, but was unable to find anything better, and he at last decided to tell her about the plan.

She thought it very good.

"The first rainy day," said she. "It is no use to wait; we must try our luck. I have decided to defend myself. I hope you will do the same."

"I hope it will not be necessary," said Zaklika.

For several days there was fine weather. Zaklika was coming in and going out continually. Thinking that he should not return again to Stolpen, he sold his house, and converted everything he could into ready money.

At last the sky was covered with clouds, and it seemed to promise rain for several days. Zaklika, covered with his long mantle, was continually coming in and going out of the castle, not answering the questions made to him by the sentries, as if telling them that he did not like to talk much. The trials were very successful. One Friday it rained hard from the early morning. When dusk began to fall everything was ready. Cosel gave the servant leave to go to the town.

Covered with a long, military mantle, with a cap pushed over her eyes, Cosel went first to the St. Donat's gate, and no one paid any attention to her; at the second gate the soldiers looked at her, but let her pass.

A few minutes later Zaklika, dressed in the same manner, passed the first gate quickly, in which he did not meet anybody. At the second gate the soldier muttered,—

"How many of you are there?"

Zaklika uncovered his face.

"Devil knows you," said the soldier. "I know only that there came in one, and two go out."

"What are you talking about?"

"I am not blind."

Zaklika paid no attention and moved on. The soldier stopped him.

"But they all know me here," said Zaklika.

"Go to the commandant and explain to him, otherwise I shall not let you out."

They began to quarrel. The corporal came. Zaklika complained to him, and they let him out, and he disappeared in the bushes beyond the park; but the soldier grumbled.

"Why are you angry with him?" asked the corporal.

"When I am at the gate, I must count how many people I let in, and how many out. There entered one clad in a long mantle, and two of them went out. The first looked as if he never was a soldier. Suppose it was the Countess?" added he, laughing.

"You talk nonsense!" said the corporal, with uneasiness. He stopped, thought for a while, and went to the St. John's tower. Here he learned that all the servants had been permitted to go to town.

He rushed up the first flight—the room was dark and empty; on the floor above—nobody either. The corporal hastened to the commandant, who rushed out and began to search with the soldiers in the castle. Time was passing by; dusk was already quite thick. There was no doubt that Cosel had escaped! They struck the alarm, and the commandant, dividing his soldiers into several groups, rushed out to chase the fugitive lady.

In the meantime Cosel ran to the horses, which were ready at a certain spot; in her great haste she lost her way. Zaklika reached them, and, not finding the Countess, rushed to seek her, but not daring to call, for the alarm was already given.

He lost much time, but he found her standing under a tree. He seized her by the hand, and conducted her to the horses. Cosel jumped on her horse, and Zaklika was ready too, when the soldiers arrived and surrounded them. Zaklika cried to Cosel to run, he barring the road to the soldiers.

A few shots sounded, and the faithful man, struck by a bullet in the forehead, fell to the ground moaning. At that moment a soldier seized the reins of the Countess's horse. She killed the aggressor on the spot; but there rushed forward another and a third, and she was obliged to surrender.

The commandant arrived when the two cold corpses were already on the bloody ground—the third was dying.

"Countess," said he, "look how many lives your fancies of escape cost!"

She answered nothing, but, jumping from her horse, came to the dead Zaklika. She put her pale lips on his forehead, covered with blood. The dead man's hand was lying on his breast, as though it would defend the King's promise of marriage to Cosel that had been entrusted to him. She took it with her.

She was led back to the castle, where she spent long days sitting and reading the Bible. Zaklika was buried at her expense.

"Nobody would care about my funeral," she said to herself. "Now I am alone in the world. My children do not know me."

* * * * *

In 1733 Augustus died, and the commandant of Stolpen came personally to announce to her the news.

For a long time she stood speechless; then she wrung her hands, and, throwing herself on the floor, began to cry.

Imprisonment, cruelty, wrongs, oblivion, could not take from her womanly heart the love which she had for him. From that moment he was again for her the dear Augustus.

Five days later there came an official from Dresden, sent by the Kurfürst, who was then Augustus III., King of Poland. He asked to be announced to the Countess.

"I am sent to your Excellency," said he, "by our most gracious lord, to announce to you that you are free, and that you may live where you please."

Cosel rubbed her forehead.

"I? Free?" said she. "What do I need freedom for now? The people have become strangers to me, and I am a stranger to them. Where can I go? I have nothing; they have robbed me of everything. You want to make me ridiculous; you wish that those who bowed down to me should now point the finger of scorn at me?"

The official was silent.

"No!" she added. "I do not want freedom; leave me here. I am accustomed to these walls, where I have shed all my tears; I could not live in another place."

So they let her stay in Stolpen, where she outlived Augustus III., and the Seven Years' War.

She died in 1765, being eighty-five years of age. To the end of her life she preserved traces of her great beauty, by which she became so famous.